UNDETERRED

PUBLIC RELATIONS BOOK 3

LIZA GAINES

Edited by
RHONDA MERWARTH
Cover Art by
CROCO DESIGNS

For all the women who did anything to be there

CHAPTER 1

MAC

"Wʜᴀᴛ ᴀʀᴇ ᴏᴜʀ ᴏᴘᴛɪᴏɴs?"

"You're asking me?" Alex's eyes widen and he leans forward in his chair, elbows on his knees and hands clasped between them. At least he's making eye contact with me, which is more than can be said for Gwen. Or Cece, for that matter, although I can't say I blame her. Seeing your boss's sex tape probably isn't many people's idea of a good time.

With the grainy parking garage video spreading across the internet like wildfire, we came straight to work from the airport and, out of habit, Cece and Gwen made a beeline for my office. I redirected everyone to Alex's instead. There's something to be said for neutral territory, and I'll take all the help I can get right now.

His office is a mirror image of mine, his desk in the center with a couch and two chairs arranged around a low glass coffee table to one side. Gwen and Cece claimed the couch, so Alex and I took the chairs, but now he's antsy, like he might get up and start pacing. I'm that way too sometimes, restless with pent-up energy I don't have another outlet for.

Not right now, though. I'm calm, relaxed even, because I already understand what needs to happen. *I have to eat a shit sandwich.* It's going to suck, no way around that, and I can be—will be—pissed off about it later. But before I can wallow in my own misery, I have to convince Gwen I'm right, and after our argument at the airport, that'll be more challenging than I anticipated.

If I hadn't been so impulsive on Super Tuesday, if I'd waited until we got back to my place, there wouldn't have been a sex tape for the tabloids to get their scummy paws on in the first place. And in addition to being personally embarrassing, the scandal could damage both of our careers and impact Kim's campaign. The security camera didn't get a clear shot of Gwen's face, though, and that means I can protect her from the fallout, if only she'll let me.

"Believe me, I'm as surprised as you are." I flash my brother one of those easy, charming smiles that puts people at ease. The kind that masks my real feelings. Judging by the agitated glance he darts at Gwen, he isn't buying it. "Look, I know for a fact you've fielded more than one sex tape scandal for our clients over the years."

"So have you."

I shrug and turn my hands over, palms up. "It's a little different when it's your own fat in the fire." It isn't really. Maybe I've been in PR too long, but this shit—assessing the angles of a situation, evaluating the possible ways to manage it and the consequences spinning out from those choices—is second nature. Like breathing or jerking off in the shower. I know how the press and the public will react but Gwen needs to hear it from someone else.

"Well..." Alex drops his gaze to stare at his perfectly polished oxblood wing tips. I can see the wheels in his head turning as he works through the problem, just like he would if I was any other client instead of his fuck-up of an older brother. "It depends on your goals. I mean, half the time, our clients release the damn things themselves."

"We aren't washed-up celebrities trying to keep our names in the gossip rags, man. This is bad for the campaign and it's bad for Gwen. We need to do everything we can to minimize that."

"It isn't great for you, either," Cece points out, breaking her uncharacteristic silence. Her hazel eyes are pinched with worry and she's sitting close to Gwen, one arm slung over her shoulders in a comforting half embrace.

"That's true, but he does have the least to lose," Alex replies smoothly.

Yes. Thank you. I knew he'd see this my way.

Cece isn't convinced and she scrunches up her nose. "How do you figure?"

"He isn't running for office, for one thing." Alex raises one hand, counting the reasons off on his fingers. "For another, he's financially secure enough to lay low for a year. Take some time off, keep his name out of the press, and this'll be old news by next summer. No one would care. I think we all know people aren't so quick to forgive women."

"Don't you think you're forgetting something?" Gwen's voice is low and dispassionate, and Alex gives her a blank look in answer. Her gaze slides to mine, her blue eyes sparking with all the emotions—embarrassment, hurt, fury—absent from her mechanical tone. "Someday our kids will search for you online. What's their opinion of you worth?"

Everything. My gut clenches with the force of that realization, proof of both the depth of my feelings for Tristan and the twins and my inexperience. Among all the other public and professional dramas unspooling in my mind, that particular problem had yet to occur to me, and the possibility that my kids might find out about this and feel about me the way I feel about my dad? Unacceptable. But there are ways to mitigate that, things my dad never bothered himself with. When they're older, we can talk about it. I'll be honest with them and explain the situation, and they'll understand. *Won't they?*

Gwen doesn't give me the opportunity to respond, instead shifting her attention back to Alex. "I'd also like to point out that it's embarrassing to have a sex tape out there." Forcing Cece to press herself into the back of the couch, out of the way, Gwen flings one arm, indicating the world beyond this office. Like she's flung her calm away with it, her voice gathers steam as she takes her anger at me out on my brother. "But as bad as that is, it'd be way more humiliating to be pregnant and have people think the father is running around on me. I will not be pitied for something that isn't even true. So, if you have any stupid ideas like the one he suggested earlier—" she jabs her finger in my direction, "—you can forget about it right now."

Based on her description, it isn't hard to figure out what I proposed, or something close to it, and from the way they're gaping at me, Alex and Cece are appalled. I don't blame them. Not really. The problem isn't that I can't see her point. Of course I can. She's probably even right in the short term. But in the long run, my plan is better. If she acknowledges that grainy security camera footage is her, it'll follow her for the rest of her life. Why should she have to deal with that if I can prevent it?

"Well," Alex starts, his anxious brown gaze flicking between us before settling on her again. "I don't know exactly what he suggested, but I think you need to release a joint statement and then both resign from the campaign. That's going to be the best way to protect Kim, and honestly, yourselves too. Leaving the campaign gets you out of the spotlight. This'll all die down a lot faster that way."

Gwen gives him a curt nod, like that makes perfect sense to her, and my simmering frustration boils over. She must sense it, because she raises one hand to silence me, her gaze still fixed on Alex. "Can you help us draft the statement? I'm not sure what to say."

"Of course." He glances at me and shifts in his seat. "Although, I'm not certain you really need my help."

"We don't agree, so we need a neutral third party." With the steadiness of Gwen's voice and the determined set of her chin, it's impossible not to be bowled over by her unshakeable strength. Even in the midst of a humiliating scandal and her incredible anger with me, she's dug deep to focus on solutions. It's impressive as hell, and the knot of discomfort in my stomach tightens. *I have to let her do this her way.*

The realization almost knocks the breath out of me. I've been so worried about protecting her at all costs that I've dismissed what she actually wants. She's a tough, intelligent woman. Resilient as all hell too. I have to give her the space to make her own choices, whether I like them or not. "Draft a statement for Gwen's approval. I'll agree to whatever she thinks is best."

Eyes still averted, she doesn't say anything, but her shoulders relax a little. It'll take more than following her lead now to repair the damage I've done by insisting we do this my way back at the airport. Assuming it can be repaired.

"Sure." Alex leans forward to snatch a legal pad and pencil off the table, and if he's surprised by my acquiescence, he doesn't show it. Balancing it on his knee, he starts making notes. "I don't think it needs to be that long. A sincere but brief apology for your inappropriate behavior, wrapped up in a nice pretty package. Something about how in love you are and how that led you to get a little carried away."

"Oh, that's good. People love a romance," Cece agrees, brushing her chestnut hair over her shoulders and leaning toward him to peek at his notes.

"No." Gwen's shaking her head again, her voice even firmer than before. "Nothing about love."

Right. She's convinced I don't love her, and it seems there isn't a damn thing I can do about it. I don't believe in fate, but it's starting to feel like maybe we keep getting thrown together for the sole purpose of hurting one another. It's a mind fuck, because whatever is between us might be great if we could get our shit together. There are these fleeting moments with Gwen and Tris, like the night she decided to move in with me, where everything seems *right*. But it never lasts. We always end up right back here, stepping on each other's feelings and lashing out like wounded animals, and I suppose that's proof enough that outside of being parents, whatever we have can't last.

But Alex is right too. We need to give the public a reason to forgive us, or at least, not to hold our behavior against Kim. Convincing them we're the stars of our own fairytale is the fastest, easiest way to do that. After all, who hasn't done something stupid for love? But I get

Gwen's reservations. I'm not thrilled with telling the world I'm desperately in love with a woman who doesn't want me, even if they'd never know that part, so I offer a compromise instead. "Be vague. Something about how we have very strong feelings for each other." It has the benefit of being true, even if Gwen's feelings aren't of the warm and fuzzy variety, and most people will assume it means love, which is good enough. Shifting my gaze to her, I ask, "That work for you?"

Gwen nods stiffly, and Alex scribbles something on his notepad. He's still studying the paper in his lap, tapping his pencil against it, when he asks, "What do you want to say about the campaign?"

If we're going this route, we should both resign our positions. I can reassign Gwen to one of the other account managers, where she could work on other more low-profile projects, and I could come back to the office and throw myself into other work too. Even without this scandal, that's not an altogether bad outcome. Between Gwen's doctors' appointments, the campaign travel, squeezing in time for Tristan and her sisters, and the constant worry over a high-risk pregnancy, being here in D.C. for the foreseeable future, or at least until after the twins are born, wouldn't be terrible. Still, I've poured a lot of effort into Kim's campaign, and letting go now, four short months before the election, will be difficult.

Kim won't like it, either. Her loyalty has always been one of the things I admire most about her, but in this case, it's an enormous risk. The campaign is too important, there's too much at stake, and that means Gwen and I should go.

I'm about to say as much when Dad strolls into Alex's office without bothering to knock. Evidently, he's also been sent back to D.C. to cool his heels, but to be honest, it feels like his hot-mic gaffe was a lot more than twenty-four hours ago, and with my own fresh scandal I'd forgotten all about it. He hasn't, though, because he gives me a slick smile and says, "I guess we're both in the doghouse now, Junior."

GWEN

"I KNOW you're the one who leaked the footage."

Mac's accusation hangs heavy in the air, and Alex shifts in his seat, his voice lacking its earlier confidence as he attempts to smooth over the brewing confrontation. "How would Dad have even known it existed? It was probably someone who works at the hotel. They saw the opportunity to make a quick buck and they took it, that's all."

Senior shrugs and offers Alex an ambiguous smile. It's such a slippery gesture, designed to simultaneously soothe Alex and keep Mac on the defensive, wondering if his dad really is the culprit. William wasn't even in the same city that night; he couldn't have known what we'd done or that there was incriminating video. Nonetheless, I can't shake the suspicion curling in my stomach and prickling the fine hairs on the back of my neck. Judging by the narrow-eyed look Mac is giving his dad, I'm not the only one. Why can't Alex see it too?

"Why are you here?" Mac's voice is tight, abrasive, and every muscle is tensed in anticipation of an argument.

"As I'm sure you're about to experience for yourself, I'm persona non grata with the campaign at the moment." Shoving both hands in his pockets, William comes closer to stand in front of the coffee table. With a heavy sigh, he focuses on me and says, "Is there anything I can do to help?"

His familiar brown eyes are crinkled at the corners and they appear warmer than I've ever seen them before. Sympathetic, even. His gaze is so similar to both his sons, and Tristan's too, for that matter, that it's unsettling. How can this awful man be Tristan's and the twins' grandfather? He's a horrible person and his one redeeming quality, as far as I can tell, is that he managed to produce two fine sons who've both grown into good, if imperfect, men. No matter what I do, my kids will always have that connection to him, even if it's only biological. Of course, my own mother was pretty terrible too. Our kids got the short end of the stick when it comes to grandparents, that's for sure, but at least they have Mac's mother, Joan.

Whether or not Senior is responsible for our current predicament, he's enjoying it. I can feel it, crackling in the open space between us. This show of concern is for Alex's benefit, to keep him on Senior's side and fortify the barriers between the brothers. No matter what my issues with Mac are, I'm not going to help his dad hurt him. Maintaining eye contact with Senior, I keep my voice frosty. "There's nothing you can do to help us."

"No?" William glances at Mac, a slow smile spreading across his face. "He's never been shy about asking. Remember the time I bailed you out of jail? Even got the charges dropped, as I recall."

Everything about his expression and tone is meant to give the impression of good-natured reminiscence. A father happily recalling a time when he was able to lend his son a hand in one of those upsetting-at-the-time-but-hilarious-in-hindsight situations. But whatever he's referencing, it's a story I've never heard, and Alex seems to be in the dark too. His gaze darts between his father and brother. "What? When did Mac get arrested?"

I'm pretty damn interested in the answer to that question myself, but Mac isn't going to satisfy our curiosity. Not now, anyway. Rising from his chair, he ignores his dad, instead directing his attention on Alex. "Get started on the statement, and we'll let you know how to finish it once we've talked to Kim."

He doesn't wait for a response, doesn't check to make sure I follow, and definitely doesn't acknowledge his dad's existence before striding out of the room. Cece squeezes my hand before releasing it so I can go after him.

I have to pass Senior to get to the door and I give him a wide berth. It isn't enough, and he stops me with one hand on my arm. Although it's a gentle touch, I flinch away from the contact, my other hand rising in protective instinct to rest on my baby bump.

He gives me a startled look. "My apologies. I wanted to congratulate you. This is the first I've seen you since you announced I'm going to be a grandfather again."

I'd be more convinced of his sincerity if he showed even the least bit of interest in the grandson he already has, and I suspect this too is for Alex's benefit, another part of maintaining the façade that Senior is the aggrieved party in his ongoing war with Mac. But antagonizing him won't improve the situation. With a strained thank you, I make my exit, already thinking about the conversation to come. Mac and I are both still so raw, and dread makes my heart pound in my chest.

By the time I catch up to Mac, he's already in his office, standing in front of the windows behind his desk. I close the door, and he greets me with a halfhearted smile that's nothing like the flashy, overconfident looks he was throwing at his brother a few minutes ago. No, this is a part of him only I get to see. The strain and worry and hurt he tries so hard to hide. It's disconcerting to simultaneously feel so angry with and yet connected to him, like I'm the only one he shares his most vulnerable self with. How can he be so willing to throw *this* away?

His voice is low, husky with tension and the weight of responsibility, when he leans forward, planting both hands on his desk. "You know we both have to resign from the campaign, right?"

Swallowing hard, I nod. It's fitting, I guess, that my short-lived time with Kim's campaign is ending as it began—across this very same desk from Mac, amid a swirl of conflicting emotions. Things didn't have to be this way though, and that's making an already bitter pill even more difficult to swallow.

If I'd behaved like a responsible adult that night instead of like a lovestruck teenager with more hormones than sense, there wouldn't be a sex tape in the first place. And if I'd gone along with Mac's plan, I could've kept my job, which is so much more than just a job to me. But I can't allow him to suffer the consequences alone, especially not at the expense of our fragile little family. And if that means giving up the job of a lifetime…well, I'm going to have to suck it up.

"We'll find another role for you. I've been out of the loop lately, but I'll talk to HR and see what might be available. I know Emika is looking for an assistant. She does a lot of work with charitable organizations, planning fundraisers and that sort of thing, if that's something that would interest you." Emika Okada is a senior account manager but judging by the vague hand wave that follows his description, Mac isn't clear on the specific needs of her client list.

"You don't have to do this, Mac. I was hired specifically for the campaign."

"I know, and we can talk about it more later, but we need to call Kim. She's waiting on us. I just wanted to be sure you know leaving the campaign doesn't mean you're being fired too."

I'm still so fucking angry about the way he tried to steamroll me earlier, but his earnest sincerity makes it harder to remember that now. And since we do need to call Kim, I collapse none too gracefully into one of the guest chairs across from him, ignoring the twinge of discomfort in my already overburdened lower back, and wave one hand at the phone on his desk. There are a lot of things we need to talk about later. What's one more?

After dialing Kim and setting his phone to speaker, he deposits it on his desk and slides it toward me. Then, instead of sitting behind his desk as he did on the day of my interview, Mac rounds it to take the other guest chair next to me.

"Hey, how are you two holding up?" Kim's warm voice filters through the phone, and Mac extends one hand toward me, palm up. I don't hesitate in taking it. Whatever else this disaster means for us and our non-relationship relationship, I'm grateful for the contact. Resigning from my dream job seems a tiny bit easier with his strong fingers twined with mine.

"We've been better," Mac admits with a gentle squeeze of my hand. "But the important thing right now is—"

"I don't need you to tell me what's important, Mac."

It's the harshest I've ever heard her speak to him, and I give him a sidelong look, checking for his reaction. His cheeks are flushed and he sounds…genuinely chastised when he says, "Of course. I'm sorry."

A moment of silence follows his apology, and it stretches on so long I lean forward to peek at the screen, to verify the call hasn't dropped. It hasn't. Is she so angry with us that she's speechless? If this goes on much longer, I'm going to start talking. I don't know what I'll say, but I won't be able to help myself. I'll babble to fill the quiet and that wouldn't be helpful. *Say something, Kim.*

As if she's heard my unspoken demand, a deep sigh gusts through the phone. "I know what you think needs to be done, Mac, and you may very well be right, but we aren't going to be making any rash decisions today. Brian and the communications team have prepared a statement for me. Brief and to the point—you're both very good at your jobs and as long as that continues to be the case, I'm not concerned with your personal lives. Then you two are going to stay put in D.C. for a while. Keep a low profile." Her tone still stern, she picks up an almost imperceptible hint of amusement to add, "No sex on the National Mall if you can possibly restrain yourselves."

He winces, his grip on my fingers tightening. "Yes, ma'am."

"Good. I still expect your presence at the interviews for my V.P. picks and at internal planning sessions, but you'll both stay away from public events with me for now. We'll see how things are going in a few days. Before this broke, I was up in the polls by a lot. Granted, the republicans are splitting their votes between the incumbent and Whitaker, and that's helping me, but the two of them leave so much scandal and corruption in their wake, this may end up being little more than a blip on the radar."

Mac's jaw is clenched and it's so obvious he wants to argue with her but, having been chastised once, he's holding his tongue now. Since I tend to agree with him anyway, I give it a go. "But don't you think—"

"I'm not arguing with you, either. This isn't up for discussion and, who knows, maybe this'll end up being for the best. Lord knows you both could use a few days off to rest. You especially, Gwen. And you can make good use of this downtime. If you end up having to quit, Alex will take over for Mac, but we'll need someone to fill your role. And if you don't quit, you need a backup anyway in case the twins arrive before Election Day, so start interviewing now."

"Okay." Since she's unwilling to hear our thoughts on the matter, there's nothing else to say.

"Mac?"

"Yeah, fine." He's definitely not fine with this but, like me, must realize there's no point in arguing. Her mind is made up.

"Good." Her voice softens, becoming less commanding and warmer. More maternal. "I'm sorry you two are going through this. Is there anything I can do?"

It was easier when she was being stern. Unable to speak and with tears prickling the corners of my eyes, I shake my head, even though she can't see me. The fallout of our irresponsible actions could cost her an election, and she's asking what she can do for us? After she's already refused to accept our resignations? It's humbling, and I sure hope she knows what the hell she's doing, because I'm not convinced I'm worth the risk.

"I think we're all right," Mac answers, his own voice gruff.

"Well, let me know if you need anything, and take care of each other. I'll see you both in a few days." It's like a verbal hug, and I bite my lower lip to keep from making a sound until Mac's disconnected the call.

"You okay?"

"Fine. Just...you know."

Mac nods and rubs his lower lip, considering that. "Do you need a few minutes? We have a few other things to talk about and I'm afraid we can't put it off for long, but I can step out for a bit if you need some privacy."

Other things, like that we have movers scheduled for tomorrow to move me, Tris, and Olivia into his townhouse. "No, let's get it over with."

"Well." He takes a deep breath, followed by a quiet, bitter laugh. "That sounds ominous."

I hadn't meant it to, but I'm feeling pretty grim about our future, so I guess it isn't any wonder that's how it came out. With talking to Kim out of the way and Alex working on our statement, the practicalities have been handled, and all that's left is facing the messy reality of our personal relationship. Delaying the moment won't help. Drawing a deep breath, I square my shoulders and begin.

CHAPTER 2

MAC

"I'm angry with you."

When she doesn't continue, I give her a sidelong look, trying to read her expression, but it's no use. She's got it locked up tight, and all I can do is try to ignore the way my heart is thudding in my chest and hope she isn't about to tell me to go to hell.

It's strange, really. Until a few minutes ago, I was ready to end things because I thought that'd be best for her. But now, sitting here waiting for her to say the same thing—and there isn't a doubt in my mind that'll be her judgment—is a lot harder to accept. Maybe because I've had time to think about it, to consider what my life will be like without Gwen in it. What it used to be like.

She won't keep the kids from me, I'm certain of that much. But there won't be any more nights that end with the three of us sharing scrambled eggs in bed, either. A future without that seems pretty bleak from where I'm sitting now. That would've been impossible to imagine six months ago but...well, here we are. Swallowing hard, I give her hand a gentle squeeze and say, "I know you are, and you have every right to be. It's no excuse, but I had good intentions. I was trying to protect you."

"That doesn't make it better, Mac. It's the exact same thing you always do. Like with Jess and Amy. You're so willing to martyr yourself, to take everything on your shoulders, to make things easier for the people around you, but you can't see how you're hurting them in a different way."

She's right, I didn't understand that before, but I do now.

As a young man, learning that my dad had an affair with Jess and, worse, got her pregnant, gutted me, and I always thought it'd be so much worse for Alex. His relationship with Dad has never been great, but it's always been better than mine, and he was hungry for Dad's attention and approval. The truth would've crushed him.

Then Amy was born, and everyone assumed she was mine and... honestly, that didn't seem so bad. No one expected anything of me— no one even bothered to ask me or Jess about it, and as long as they believed I was her father, Dad's terrible secret couldn't hurt anyone.

Except it did. The choices I made in the past hurt Alex. He made that pretty fucking clear last night, and I've spent a lot of the last twenty-four hours mulling that over. Right up until he rushed up on me at the airport and shoved his phone in my face to show me the now-public security camera footage of Gwen and me having sex in a parking garage. And I reverted to old habits, because it's all I fucking know. But it doesn't have to be this way, does it?

Untangling her fingers from mine, she stands up, gently arching her back, stretching it. Without thinking, because I've done this for her a thousand times in the past few weeks, I lean forward in my seat and put my hands on her hips, turning her away from me so I can plant the heel of one hand in the small of her back. She lets out a loud sigh and glances over her shoulder at me before turning away again, but she doesn't object.

Gwen stares out the windows behind my desk while I knead the tired muscles in her lower back. For as emotionally bruised as we both are, this quiet bit of familiar intimacy feels like an anchor. If we could hang on to it, if we could stay in this moment forever, we could ignore everything else and just be us. Together. With our kids and a future and none of the baggage that's liable to tear us apart.

She pulls away, and I clench my hands in my lap to keep from reaching after her. Turning to face me, she leans against my desk, her fingers curling around its edge on either side of her hips. "Last night you said this wouldn't last forever, and then today you said you loved me and got upset I didn't believe you. And I don't. Because you've always got one foot out the door. I mean for fuck's sake, Mac, you said you loved me at the exact same time you were dumping me. For my own good. Which you decided without even talking to me. And now you're sitting here giving me sad puppy eyes like in those ASPCA commercials because I've got the nerve to call you on your bullshit. Do you really not see how fucked up this is?"

It's true, and every single word is like a razor blade, carving me up in a series of precise, penetrating slashes. But it isn't the whole truth, and I think it's time we both put all our cards on the table. "Yeah, I see it, but I'm not the only one ready to bail at a moment's notice."

"What's that supposed to mean?" Defensive, she narrows her eyes and crosses her arms over her chest.

"You use money like a shield to keep me at a distance, when all it should be about is Tristan and the twins. And yes, I've noticed you're making an effort to do better and I appreciate that. I really do. But you know, I'd like to understand why it requires so much effort in the first place, because for the life of me, I can't see how me paying child support is somehow a threat to you." I sound angrier than I intended, and my hands are clenched on the arms of my chair. This has been festering for a long time.

"Because someday you're going to leave." She shouts so loudly I'm certain if Cece has returned to her desk outside my office she can hear every word. Gwen must realize it too, because she lowers her voice when she continues. "Or I'm going to leave again. Or some other awful thing will happen. I can't afford to be dependent on you, Mac. I've already had to drag myself up from nothing once, and I'll be damned if I'm going to do it again."

Christ, I'm an idiot. It's so obvious. How did I miss that? As far as

I'm concerned, making sure Gwen and our kids are secure is the most important thing. It's the entire reason I was willing to sacrifice our relationship for the sake of damage control. But she's already been abandoned by the one person everyone should be able to count on. After being left to fend for herself and her sisters by her own mother, it's no wonder she's so determined to do everything on her own.

Why would I be any more reliable than the woman who gave birth to her? Especially when I've been so unwilling to commit to a future with her. I've kept her dangling in uncertainty because of my own issues and in the process exacerbated hers. It's like we're primed to hurt each other, all our individual flaws perfectly aligned to poke and prod at the other person's corresponding weaknesses, and we've made a damn mess of everything. Worse, I don't know how to fix it.

There've been a lot of situations like this since her return, where I don't know what to say. Too many. I'd like to think with experience I've gotten better at handling them, but given the way my stomach is roiling and my mind is stunningly, frustratingly blank, that's clearly not the case. So I do the only thing I can—start talking and hope for the best. "I love you. I've loved you for most of my adult life, and the only reason I took so long to tell you was because I was afraid. Terrified you'd reject me or realize you deserve so much better than me, and believe me, you really, really do. Or you'd give me a chance and I'd blow it, like I did today. All I want is for you to have everything you want. For you and our kids to be safe and happy. Which is why I did what I did this morning, but I didn't want to, and I couldn't make myself do it without telling you the truth first. I wanted you to know that you matter to me and that I'd give up anything—even you—if that's what you need."

She smooths one hand over her rounded stomach and opens her mouth, preparing to interrupt, but I'm afraid if I stop I won't be able to start again, so I keep right on talking. "I get what you're saying. We're both pretty fucked up in ways that rub each other all wrong, and neither of us seems to be very good at talking about this shit, but when things are good they're..." Struggling to find the right word, I remember something my best friend Jake said to me when I called him after her job interview back in January. That asshole was right, and I finally fucking get it. "When things are good it's like hollandaise sauce."

"What?"

She sounds as confused as I probably did that night on the phone, and despite myself, I smile. "Never mind. It's not important. I'm trying to say that I think what we have is worth fighting for. It'll be hard and it might suck sometimes, but it might be worth it. Our family is worth it."

"You…you sound like you're talking about a real relationship."

"I am. I think. Honestly, I don't know. God knows my family sucks and I've never done this before. Hell, if you ask my dad, he'd tell you I'm incapable of it. That I'm just like him and I'm gonna screw you over. I have no fucking clue how normal people deal with this shit. Maybe I'm fucking up already, but what we've been doing isn't working. Sometimes it feels like it is, but then something like this happens, and we both lose our shit and do all the wrong things. We can't keep that up—it isn't good for any of us, and we both know it, even if we don't want to admit it, but we can't give up without making an effort to do this right."

It's hard to guess what she might be thinking, but her cheeks are flushed and she's chewing the corner of her lip. I hope that means she's considering what I've said instead of trying to figure out the best way to tell me to fuck off. When she does speak, there's an almost imperceptible quiver in her voice. "That means being real partners. No more deciding what's best for me without asking me what I want first."

"Yeah." I nod to reinforce my agreement and ignore the almost giddy sense of relief and hope that's making my pulse race to give her a level stare. I know I have work to do, but she does too if we're doing this. "And it means sorting out the money situation once and for all in a way the works for both of us."

"Fine. You're paying for the movers tomorrow."

"I can do that." I'm definitely smiling now. The kind of smile that makes my face hurt. The movers were the most recent skirmish in our ongoing fiscal war and I'm glad to have won, but more importantly, she's still planning to move in.

"Stop gloating."

"I'm not, I swear." I might be, but only a little. "I'm just relieved you aren't kicking me to the curb."

"Not yet, but you're on thin ice." There isn't a doubt in my mind that's true, but she's smiling now too. And when she speaks, she sounds a lot like she did all those years ago back in Ann Arbor, before her mother and a decade of struggle crushed her hope. "Do you really think we can do this?"

Standing up, I take a step toward her and grab the back of her neck, pulling her toward me and resting my forehead against hers. It feels good to touch her, her body heat radiating next to mine, and my voice rasps when I say, "I hope so. I want to."

She tips her head to the side and peeks up at me through the long strands of blond hair that have fallen over her face. "Me too."

She appears so vulnerable, like admitting those two little words out loud was the hardest thing she's ever done. Part of me wishes I was better with words so I could convince her I'm sincere. It's sort of ironic for a guy who's made a career of using pretty words to sway public opinion in whatever direction I choose that I can't do a better job of it with her. But the reality is words would never be good enough anyway. After everything that's happened between us, the only way to prove myself is by following through on the things I've already said. With a little luck, I won't screw up too badly and maybe someday, when I tell her I love her, she'll believe me. In the meantime, I'll have to keep saying it until she does.

GWEN

I never dreamed Mac and I would be able to have a conversation like this one. That we'd both be on the same page with the same goals when it comes to our relationship. But now that we've talked about it, now that we agree we both want to work toward a shared future, I… well, I'm not sure how I feel.

Relieved, definitely. And happy too. But there's a small piece of me that's even more scared than before. I can't pretend that I'm indifferent, that I won't be crushed if this doesn't work. I've admitted I want more, and there's no going back from that. It's terrifying. The only consolation is he seems a bit shook up too.

That's probably why we stand there, me leaning against his chest, him with his arms locked around my back, until a brisk knock disrupts the quiet. Mac releases me and turns toward the door in time for Alex to poke his head through.

"I've got the first draft if you guys want to take a peek." Mac gestures him forward, and Alex glances at me before coming closer, offering the single sheet of paper in his hand to his brother. "I wasn't sure what you'd want to say about the campaign, so I put in a generic paragraph about leaving to focus on your family. If you've already spoken to Kim, we can change that up."

Rubbing one thumb over his lip, Mac sighs and angles his wrist so I can skim the page with him. More or less what we discussed earlier, it seems fine to me, although the bit about the campaign will need to be revised. "You'll have to change that. She wouldn't let us quit. We're taking a break and we'll reevaluate in a few weeks."

Alex's eyes widen and he looks between us. I can't blame him for being surprised Kim managed to out-stubborn Mac, especially when it comes to work.

"She's right, but you don't have to change much. Instead of leaving, we're stepping back. And here—" Mac turns the sheet of paper back toward Alex and points to the word *family*, "—change it to growing family. It can't hurt to remind people she's pregnant."

An unexpected giggle escapes before I can suppress it. Maybe after everything that's happened in the last couple of days, I'm too on edge, but the idea that anyone would need to be reminded of my current state strikes me as hysterical. My belly is like the Capitol Dome—big, round, and visible from the other side of the Potomac. Okay, that might be a slight exaggeration, but it *feels* true, and talking about it like it's something people could easily overlook is absurd.

"What's funny?" It's Alex, but they're both staring at me with puzzled expressions.

"Nothing. Never mind."

Mac arches one brow and I'm certain he's going to press me, but Alex speaks first. "Okay. Maybe now would be a good time to announce you're having twins?"

"Absolutely not." The speed with which Mac shuts him down is impressive, and I assume he's anticipating my reaction. This is the kind of thing that would've gotten an immediate negative response from me before.

But I'm supposed to be working on my knee jerk reactions, right? And didn't we just promise to be partners and make decisions together that impact our family? "Should we talk about this?"

As if in slow motion, Mac turns toward me, his expression equal parts chagrin and confusion. It's almost enough to make me laugh again. "Do you want to tell the world you're having twins? Today? When we haven't even told Tris or your sisters? Or...anyone but my mom, Kim, Alex and Cece?"

Alex is apparently pleased to learn he's one of the few who know our secret, because he smiles and his chest puffs out a little. For a grown man in his thirties, it's sort of adorable.

"No," I admit. "I don't want to think of this awful day every time I remember making the announcement. Although..." I trail off, pressing my lips together to suppress the laughter once more threatening to bubble out of me. At this rate, they're going to think I've lost my mind. Then again, maybe I have.

Mac sighs and peers up at the ceiling. "What?"

"It's just that, I mean, the twins were probably conceived that night."

His exasperation evaporates and his eyes widen, his lips quirking up in a surprised smile. "Really?"

Uninterested in walking through the timeline with us, Alex groans. "Look, it's clear you both have boundary issues or we wouldn't be here today, but could you do me a personal favor and save this conversation for another time?"

"Sure thing." Mac grins and passes the paper back to Alex. "Make the changes we talked about and run with it."

"Got it, thanks." Alex starts for the door then stops, hesitating for a moment before he turns to face us again. "What was Dad talking about when he said he'd bailed you out of jail?"

"A bar fight. It was no big deal." Mac shrugs with his usual confidence, but something's off. He's standing too still. Or maybe he's bracing himself for Alex's reaction. All the tension from last night—God, had that really only been yesterday?—seems to have returned. This is just another secret Mac has kept from his brother. True, a relatively harmless one, at least compared to the others, but Alex won't take it well.

"But Dad fixed it." He nods to himself, his brows drawn together in thought, but when he meets Mac's gaze again, his jaw is set. "He's an asshole—I get it, even if I don't know everything you do. But he does care, and it was wrong of you to accuse him of doing this." He waves the press release in the air. "He couldn't have done it. He wouldn't have."

"I don't know if he did it or not," Mac admits, his voice far more even than I expect. "But there's no question he's capable of it."

Alex is already shaking his head in denial, and my heart sinks. I guess I was foolish to be optimistic that they might work out their differences after their talk yesterday. That they might at least find some kind of tentative peace. Maybe it's too soon, maybe they need more time to work through their issues, but I don't think so. Their dad will always be between them.

"No." It's a flat, firm denial, and Alex's jaw is clenched, his hands fisted at his sides. "I'm tired of this bullshit. I'm tired of you two always going at each other. If you'd sit down and talk—"

"There's nothing to talk about. You were right last night—it isn't fair of me to expect you to take my side when you don't know what's going on. That's fine. Don't. But I'm not going to stand here and listen to you fucking defend him either."

"Jesus Christ, you're just like him, you know that? You're both so fucking selfish, you care more about your bullshit feud than you do about how it effects the rest of the family." He can't know what a direct hit he's landed, but I flinch, my stomach cramping in miserable sympathy for Mac. Comparing him to his father is the worst thing anyone could say to him, but Alex doesn't stick around to see the fallout. Instead, he stalks from the room, slamming the door so hard the frame rattles behind him.

Still staring at the closed door with a helpless, confused expression, Mac's voice is quiet. "It was that same Thanksgiving. After you left and Dad told me about Jess. I went out and got fucked up and got in trouble. He *did* get me out and make it go away, but only so he could try to use it as leverage."

Leverage against his own son, to force Mac to bully Jess into having an abortion. The depths William MacKenzie Sr. will sink to know no bottom. I've been angry and resentful of my own mom for all of my adult life, but in some ways, she did me a favor. Getting by without her was hard, but at least I haven't had to deal with her ongoing bullshit every day like Mac does with his dad, and right this minute, that's almost enough to make me thankful she took off.

CHAPTER 3

GWEN

MOVING DAY WAS A HEADACHE, but on the bright side, we had lots of help. My sister Willa and her girlfriend Diane, along with Cece, chipped in with the last-minute packing, directing the movers, and unpacking the essentials we'd need right away as the boxes were unloaded at Mac's place. But there were downsides too. More people available to follow me around and yell at me every time I so much as glanced at a box was annoying, and their boisterous presence made Alex's absence that much more obvious.

Like the others, Alex had volunteered to help us move, but that was before his argument with Mac yesterday. Early this morning he'd texted me to say he wouldn't be able to make it. He apologized and said something came up. It wasn't lost on me or Mac that I was the one he'd chosen to contact, and we both knew exactly why he'd decided not to come. Mac shrugged and acted like it didn't bother him, but after the hopeful progress they' made in recent weeks toward building a better relationship, it's disappointing.

No one else has mentioned his absence, but now that we're all exhausted and have accomplished as much as we can for one day, we're moving on to the pizza and beverages portion of the agenda, and Tristan acknowledges the elephant in the room. Or at least one of them. "I thought Uncle Alex was coming today?"

"He's working." Busy picking a few stray pieces of mushroom off a slice of pizza, Mac doesn't look up from his plate, but his shoulders are bunched with tension.

"It's awfully convenient that he's got something else to do when there are boxes and furniture to haul across town. It would've been handy to have him around today. The man is built like an ox," Willa jokes.

"Dumb as one too," Cece mutters. Mac shoots her a quelling frown, but she sticks her chin out, undaunted and a little defensive, like she might argue it's true. She has plenty of reason to think so, given her longstanding unrequited crush on Alex and his stubborn refusal to acknowledge it.

But Olivia, always curious and interested in the campaign, redirects the conversation, this time alluding to the other topic we've all been avoiding. "It must be weird being disconnected from things now."

With all the packing last night and moving today, we've been buried in boxes and there wasn't a lot of time for my sisters to scold me—or make fun of me—about the sex tape. But if I know them, the tide's about to turn.

"Haven't had a lot of time to think about it, what with carting your shit around all day." Mac takes a swig of beer and gives Olivia a sarcastic smile before adding, "Thanks for reminding me, though. I really appreciate that."

Unfazed by his surly response, she shrugs and grins. "Hey, I'm not the one who—"

With a glare and a subtle gesture toward Tris, I shake my head. "Not now."

Although it might not seem like it, she means well. She's accepted Mac and is teasing him like little sisters do. But I'm not sure he's in a place to recognize that—or appreciate it. Not when it appears what little relationship he has with his own brother is crumbling. What we need is a complete change of subject. "This is probably a good time to talk about new house rules."

Willa's kept our old apartment, and I suspect she'll be moving in with Diane when the lease expires, but now that the rest of us are living with Mac, he should have a say in things too. Especially since it's his house. So it isn't just a handy distraction. It's necessary.

"I only have one." Olivia leans back in her chair, both palms flat on the table on either side of her plate, smirking at the rest of us.

"It's cute she thinks she gets to make the rules," Diane murmurs next to Willie, who covers her mouth in a poor attempt to hide her laughter.

"Pierce family rules have always been collaborative," Olivia points out, and that's mostly true, especially once the girls were old enough to drive.

I haven't ever had the energy or interest to micromanage their lives, maybe because that's what our mom did to me. But it's possible I've swung too far the other way and am lucky it's turned out okay so far. Tipping my head toward Mac, I remind her, "Yeah, but it isn't just us Pierce's anymore. His house, his rules."

"Oh, God." Apparently this has only just occurred to her, and Olivia's eyes widen in horror. "You aren't going to give me a curfew, are you?"

"She doesn't have a curfew?" Mac gives me a sidelong look, and judging by Diane's equally mystified expression, it seems I've been laxer than most.

I shake my head. "I have to know where she is and who she's with, and she has to call or text if she'll be later than midnight. She's never abused it, so I didn't see any reason to be stricter than that."

Mac thinks it over, slowly chewing his pizza. Once he's swallowed, he shrugs and says, "She's an adult now. That's reasonable." He scowls at her and adds with a gruff voice, "But you keep us both updated on your plans."

I know what he's hiding with that stern tone and my insides go soft and squishy. Olivia knows it too, and she blinks at him in surprise, the corners of her mouth quirking up with delight. "Would you worry about me?"

"Yes," Mac confesses, no less grumbly. It's hard to guess if he's irritated that he cares or that he's had to admit it. "And I'm not as nice as your sister, so don't try me."

"Pfft, you're a big old softie." Olivia waves one hand in dismissal.

The furrow in his brow deepens, but Tristan doesn't give his dad the opportunity to deny what we all know is true anyway. "I shouldn't have a bedtime, either."

Unfortunately for Tristan, Mac isn't quite that gullible. "Nice try, tiger, but I've already been around too many times when you haven't had enough sleep to know better than that."

"What about pork rinds?"

The mention of one of Tristan's favorite snacks makes my stomach turn, and I nudge my plate away. "No."

But even as I'm denying him, Mac is hedging. "Well…"

"What?"

Mac and Tris share a secretive, conspiratorial look. "I let him have them once in a while when you aren't around on the condition that he doesn't puke." He pauses in thought, tapping the edge of the table with one hand. "You know, I never really appreciated how much of parenting is trying to keep them from throwing up all the time."

"Yeah, as far as I can tell, that's, like, ninety percent of it," Willa agrees. "Be glad you weren't around when I was his age. I was a nervous puker."

Despite the unappetizing subject, contentment and happiness fizzle through me like sparklers on the Fourth of July. Gathered around a dinner table, sharing greasy food and affectionate ribbing with your family, is a banal, everyday event that probably wouldn't even ping on most people's radar. But for me it feels special, one of those weighty moments that'll stick with me forever. Even though I've had thousands of dinners like this one with my sisters and Tris, it's different tonight. Diane and Cece and Mac—especially Mac—make it different. *These are my people.*

I suppose in this one way I ought to be grateful for that stupid video. I mean, yes, it's the most humiliating thing that's ever happened to me, and I'll never forgive myself if there's negative blow back on Kim and her campaign. But it forced Mac and me to have a conversation we should've had ages ago. If there's one good thing to come out of the last forty-eight hours, I'm hopeful that's it.

~

MAC

"I'LL GET IT!" Olivia jumps up from the table and heads for the stairs before I've even fully registered that someone rang the doorbell.

It's a little insulting that even after a full day of moving, she and Tris are still bouncing with unspent energy. The rest of us aren't so unaffected. I'm not going to complain, though, if it means for once I'm not the one hauling ass downstairs to get the door.

A moment later, Olivia returns with two teenage girls trailing behind her. Swiping an untouched pizza box off the table, she heads for the living room explaining as she goes, "This is Harper and Abby." She waves the pizza box at the tall redhead with a knit cap inexplicably pulled down over her ears—Harper, apparently—and then at the much shorter Black girl whose friendly, if a little shy, smile is instantly endearing. "They came over to help me set up my room. Is that okay?"

Olivia's sunny temperament couldn't be more different from my own, but sometimes she reminds me a little of myself, especially when I was her age. *It's easier to ask for forgiveness than beg for permission.* That's what I used to say to Jake when we were kids. He was—is—a terminal rule follower, and that didn't work for me. Olivia either, apparently, and I sort of have to respect that.

Gwen shifts in her chair, her expression apologetic. "Sorry. I guess we should've had the rules talk a little earlier."

"It's fine. She lives here now, right? She should be able to have friends over." It's unclear if Gwen can hear me over the clamor of teenage laughter coming from the living room. The girls have settled on the floor around the coffee table, the box of pizza open between them, but I assume they'll go upstairs once they've eaten.

"You say that now, but you have no idea what you're in for living with a teenager," Cece says, and it'd sound ominous if she weren't also giggling.

"It's just a couple of months until she leaves for college," I remind her. And anyway, it won't be long until Tristan will be a teenager. These few weeks with Olivia around will be good practice.

Willa snorts and glances toward the living room. "Liv can make a week seem like a year."

Olivia *is* kind of overwhelming and Willa ought to know, being her older sister, but even so, I feel a little defensive on her behalf. At least I do until Harper speaks, loud enough to be heard over the placid conversation in the dining room. "He's hotter than he looks on TV."

"Omigod," Cece gasps before dissolving into a fit of giggles that Willa and Diane soon join.

Gwen's cheeks have turned an outrageous shade of red and I feel like I've missed something. Before I can ask who they're talking about, Olivia responds to her friend. "I guess he's all right, but you should see his brother. Alex is a beast."

A beast? I don't even know what the fuck that means and I'm pretty sure I don't want to, but at least now it's clear Harper was talking about me in the first place. How am I supposed to react to that? I mean...just...*what the fuck?*

"Okay, but is he hotter than Sean Hennessey?" Abby asks in a more moderate volume. She's definitely the most subdued of the threesome, which isn't saying a lot.

Olivia's demeanor undergoes a speedy transformation and she tries to hush her friends, but Harper brushes her off with a meaningful grin. "All I'm saying is, I think I'm going to be hanging out here a lot until we leave for school."

I don't have a lot of experience with teenage girls. Sure, Jess and I have always been close, but we never lived together, and I'm not sure I've ever heard a bunch of girls talk among themselves like this—and definitely not when I'm one of the subjects of their conversation. It's awkward and uncomfortable. Like I've been sucked through the looking glass, because none of it makes sense.

I lean back in my chair for a clearer line of sight into the living room. "You know I can hear you, right?"

"See? Grumpy." Ignoring me, Olivia circles her face with one hand. "It kind of overshadows the pretty face."

"I'm not grumpy!" My attempt at self-defense comes out a little, well…grumpy and I cringe.

Willa grins, her voice low enough it won't carry to the living room. "They're doing it on purpose. They're messing with you."

One glance at Gwen, who seems more embarrassed than amused, confirms Willa's explanation, and I mutter, "Those little shits."

Tristan glares toward the living room. "I hate when she has friends over."

"Yeah, but at least now there's someone else for her to pick on," Gwen points out before turning to me, her forehead creased with worry. "You aren't upset, are you? They're just having fun."

I shake my head and tell her it's fine, and it is…mostly. But I spend the rest of the evening wondering about one thing in particular that Olivia said. And by the time everyone else has gone and Tristan's been tucked into bed, I'm still thinking about it.

Gwen comes out of the master bathroom, wearing a plain black sleep shirt. Her golden hair is brushed until it's glossy and as she settles into bed next to me, I can't resist touching it.

"Do you think I'm grumpy?"

She's lying on her side, her back to my chest, the perfect position to enjoy the coconut scent of her shampoo, but she pulls away, peeking over her shoulder at me with wide eyes. "What?" And then, with a small smile, she settles back against her pillow again, sounding amused when she adds, "You need to grow a thicker skin and be thankful no one saw fit to give us a hard time about the sex tape."

Christ, I hadn't even thought of that. "Do you think they've seen it?"

Gwen snorts and reaches behind her to grab my wrist, pulling my arm over her. "For sure."

Well, that adds a whole new level of embarrassment to the situation, and I feel stupid for failing to consider the possibility on my own. Splaying my hand over the swell of her abdomen, I press my lips to the soft patch of skin below her ear. "I'm sorry."

"It's okay." Gwen shrugs. "If it weren't that, they'd find something else to give me a hard time about."

"Like being grumpy?"

"Silver lining. They also think you're hot."

"Yeah, but that's just objectively true."

Gwen's answering laugh is such a light, carefree trill it takes me by surprise. Ever since she came back into my life, it's been a never-ending parade of complications, and the near-constant stress and worry is often reflected in her voice. I need more of her like this, relaxed and happy, and my voice is gruff when I pull away from her. "Prop yourself up on your pillows."

"Why?" Even as she asks, she's obeying.

"Because it's been a long, exhausting day, and you deserve to feel good for a few minutes before you go to sleep."

Gwen grabs my pillow and stuffs that behind her back too. "Oh, I like the sound of that."

"I thought you might." I wait for her to spread her thighs then kneel between them, tugging the hem of her night shirt up. "This is going to have to go. I want to see your tits while I lick your pussy."

A blush spreads over her cheeks and down her throat, but she lifts her hips and leans forward enough to pull the shirt over her head. Tossing it aside, I help her find a comfortable position again and stretch out on my stomach between her legs. Sliding one hand up the inside of her thigh, I gently part her folds.

"Mac."

The way she says my name—soft and breathy with a husky note of need—makes my skin prickle with awareness. *So fucking sexy.* I lean closer so she'll feel my breath on her already wet pussy. "Do you want my fingers first, baby?"

A small feminine growl accompanies the weight of her hand landing on the top of my head, tugging on my hair, and I let her guide my mouth. *Both, then.* Latching on to her clit, I tease it with the tip of my tongue and press one finger against her opening.

She moans. It's a long, low sound, and I can't decide if I like that or the achingly familiar taste of her more. One thing is certain—my dick likes all of it. All of her. But it's the way her scent, warm and a little spicy, blends with the earthy taste of her, enhancing and amplifying it, that makes me groan and thrust against the mattress to relieve the unrelenting throb of arousal.

Gwen gasps and tugs harder on my hair. Hard enough it stings my scalp, and I nip gently at the swollen nub at the apex of her pussy. She takes the hint and eases her grip a little, but it's enough. Her other hand finds my wrist, urging me to give her more, so I ease my finger inside her slick channel. Her impatient moan makes me grin. I fucking love how hungry she is for this—for me —and I apply more pressure to her clit. Giving her a second finger, I pump my hand, relishing the way her hips rock in rhythm with my fingers and my tongue, both of her hands tangled in my hair.

Her soft cries of pleasure are so sweet and sensual, my balls draw tight and I grind against the mattress harder. There's a real risk I might come in the sheets before I've made her come, which would be embarrassing as fuck but nonetheless worth it. This is about her plea- sure. About giving her a few minutes where she doesn't have to think or worry, where she can just feel. It's about showing her I meant the things I said yesterday.

Lashing the flat of my tongue over her clit, I curl my fingers and press them against the sensitive spot at the front. She rewards me with a shuddering moan and the lift of her hips, her thighs clamping on my shoulders. She's so close, and I'm torn between wanting to draw this out, to make it last as long as she can possibly stand and needing her climax right away.

Propped against the pillows, she's spread out before me. The swell of her stomach. Her perfect tits, full and firm with hard nipples that have begun to darken over the last few weeks. The line of her collar- bone on full display as she pushes her shoulders into the pillows, arching her back. The point of her chin, the line of her jaw. Her plump lips parted as she pants for breath. And her eyes.

Our gazes meet, and the jolt of desperate, needy desire that races down my spine is electric. She must feel it too, because she shivers and stares back at me, her fingers tightening in my hair. Except now I hardly notice. All that matters is making her come.

Just as aroused as she is, I groan against her pussy, and the vibration of sound is all it takes to tip her over the edge. Her inner muscles flutter around my fingers, clamping around them, and I tug her clit between my lips, savoring the way she trembles through her orgasm.

She's still out of breath, her chest heaving, when she relaxes into the pillows and whispers, "God, I needed that."

"Glad I could help." Withdrawing my fingers, I rest my forehead against the soft, silky skin of her inner thigh and breathe deep. The enticing smell of her floods my senses, which isn't really helping the painful erection situation I've got going on, but even so, I can't quite drag myself away. *I could spend the rest of my life right here.*

"Come here, and I'll—"

"No." I shift in an attempt to relieve some of the aching pressure in my groin but, twelve hundred thread count sheets or not, even that slight friction is too much, and I wince. "It's been a rough few days, and I know how exhausted you must be after moving today. I wanted to make you feel good. I just need a minute here."

"You did make me feel good." She strokes one hand through my hair and over the back of my neck to my shoulder. I smile against the smooth skin of her leg, laughter bubbling in my throat. She's petting me like a dog. *Good boy.* Her soothing gesture and my own juvenile sense of humor distract me from my raging hard-on until she adds, "But I want you inside me now."

Fuck. Trapped between my stomach and the mattress, my cock jerks with enthusiastic interest. Resisting the urge to thrust against the bed, I scrape together every ounce of self-control I can muster and move back up to lie next to her. Propping myself on one elbow, I lean over her and palm one of her ample breasts, flicking the hard nub of her nipple with my thumb. I've always appreciated her breasts, but they've grown fuller with pregnancy, her nipples enlarging. I can't keep my hands off them. Mouth either, for that matter, and I draw one taut nipple between my teeth.

She gasps, her fingernails digging into my shoulder while her other hand finds my cock. Taking it in a firm grip, she slides her fingers over the shaft and brushes her thumb over the tip, spreading the moisture already beading there. I'm so close...too fucking close... and I let her nipple slip from between my lips and squeeze my eyes closed, pressing my face to her chest. "Gwen, baby, don't..." It's too late, I can't finish the thought. She's stroking me faster, and all I can do is give myself over to the building pressure at the base of my spine and thrust into her hand. Once. Twice. And then...*oh, fuck, I'm coming.*

The pleasure burns through me, almost paralyzing me with its intensity. It's fast and sharp and so, so good but over too soon. With the last spasms of release fading, she's still fondling my suddenly over-sensitive dick and I raise my head from between her glorious tits. I gently grasp her wrist, urging her to stop. But I make the mistake of allowing my gaze to sweep over her naked body, and the sight of my semen splashed across her belly and dripping toward her hip makes my traitorous cock twitch. "On your side, baby."

Her eyelashes flutter against her cheeks, and she bites her lower lip, tugging it between her teeth as she rolls over. Cupping one breast, I grasp her hip with my other hand and press close behind her, my chest against her back and my mostly-hard dick nestled into the seam of her ass.

She rocks her hips, increasing the pressure on my dick until I groan. "I still want you inside me."

I don't know if it's her husky voice or the actual words, but it makes me shiver, and I shift behind her, grinding against her ass. "What did I tell you yesterday? I want you to have everything you want. But you've gotta give me a minute here."

She chuckles and catches my hand, her fingers tangling with mine. Is she thinking about the other things I said yesterday too? Or the things we both said? The promises we made? No more holding back or letting our past define our future. No more secrets or hastily built walls between us. Just the two of us, committed to our future and the family we're building together.

I let my hands wander, stroking and petting her soft curves while I nuzzle her neck and nip at the sensitive place where her pulse thrums wildly just beneath her skin. And when I can't bear to wait any longer, I adjust our position one more time, nudging her top leg forward with my knee so I can slowly penetrate her. The slick heat and tight grip of her pussy are almost too much. Combined with all the big, raw emotions fizzing through me, it *would* be too much if I hadn't already come once, and I still, letting several seconds and the sharp edge of my desire pass.

Gwen pulls her leg further forward, as far as she can, and the deeper angle rips a groan from somewhere deep in my chest. It feels like my heart went with it, because even if I wanted to, I can't stop myself from pressing my mouth to her ear and whispering, "I love you."

Writhing in my arms, she acknowledges that with a nod and a shuddering moan. I hope someday she'll say it back, but for now it's enough that she didn't try to invalidate or deny my feelings. That she knows and believes I love her. We're both all in now, and I trust that the rest will come with time.

CHAPTER 4

MAC

I'M GETTING out of the family business. Or at least the family firm. Not today, but soon. Kim's offer to appoint me Press Secretary if she wins the election would be a convenient, low-drama escape, at least as far as explaining things to my family goes. But after my own appearance in the tabloids over the last few days, it's off the table. Or should be, even if Kim's too stubborn to withdraw the offer.

To be honest, I'm not sure I want to be Press Secretary. A year ago, I'd have jumped at the chance. It would've seemed like the pinnacle of my career, and I would've done anything to make it happen. Things are different now. It's a high-pressure, high-stress job with long hours and a lot of travel. Haven't I already missed enough of Tristan's life? I don't want to miss any more of it or repeat those same mistakes with the twins. And it'd be worse this time, wouldn't it? I'd be missing their first words and their first steps because I chose to, and I don't think I can do it.

I'll have to figure something else out, though. Once I'm finished with the campaign—whether that's in a couple of weeks when this ridiculous cooling off-period is over or in a few months after the election—I'll be done with the MacKenzie Agency too.

It was stupid of me to ever think Dad, Alex, and I could work together. Granted, we've made it work for several years, but this moment was always coming; it was just a question of when. And now that it has, I have to go.

"Give that back!" Olivia's screech, followed by the sound of stampeding footsteps overhead, distracts me and I look up at the ceiling, half expecting little chunks of drywall to crumble to the ground.

It's been four days since Gwen, Tristan, and Olivia moved in, and it's going…well. It's been a bigger adjustment for me than I anticipated. For one thing, I wasn't prepared for all the bickering. And when Olivia and Tris aren't fighting, it's almost worse. Basically, no matter what they do, they do it loudly, and it's taking a little getting used to after living alone so long.

I'm not the only one having difficulty adapting to the new normal. Willa, who kept their old apartment and is as unaccustomed to the quiet as I am to the cacophony, has turned up at my place for dinner every night. She says it's because her girlfriend Diane is working nights at the hospital this week, and I'm sure that's at least partly true, but she isn't fooling anyone, except maybe herself. She misses them, and who could blame her? They've only been living with me a few days, and they've already worked their way into all the cracks and crevices of my life.

I'm the first one downstairs this morning and I've just finished pouring a glass of orange juice and buttering my toast when Olivia breezes into the room. She takes one glimpse at my plate, licks her lips, and says, "That looks good." Her hopeful expression suggests she's angling for me to make her breakfast.

Waving one hand in the general direction of the toaster and open loaf of bread still on the counter, I suggest she help herself. For the first time since the scandal and their move, Gwen and I are headed into the office today. That means Olivia is watching Tris, but he's pretty self-sufficient, at least when he wants to be, and in my limited experience I haven't gotten the impression that she's an early riser. "You're up early."

Olivia shrugs and drops two pieces of bread in the toaster. "I know this is probably weird, but can I ask you something?"

Suspicion prickles the back of my neck, and I narrow my eyes. If this were Tristan, I'd be bracing for an attempt to play me against his mom and undercut her rules, which he still hasn't quite accepted are now *our* rules. But that isn't Olivia's style, at least not so far as I can tell. "About what?"

"A guy."

"I think that's something you should talk to Gwen about. Or Willie." Or the mailman. Anyone but me, really.

She rolls her eyes and retrieves a glass from the cupboard. "I need a guy's perspective, and it's not like I have a dad to talk about these things with."

"I'm hardly the person to be giving anyone relationship advice and, not that it matters, but I'm not old enough to be your—" *Oh, shit.* I snap my mouth closed so fast my teeth hurt and I must appear as stunned as I feel, because she presses her lips together to stop herself from giggling. "Okay, sure, technically I'm old enough to be your old man, but I would've been younger than Gwen when Tris was born, so that barely counts."

Pouring a glass of juice doesn't require so much concentration that Olivia can't also throw a cocky grin in my direction. "Fine, but I mean, you're with my sister and you're the father of my nephew, so that makes you sort of like my brother, right? And you told me to talk to my sisters about this, so I don't see why we can't talk about it if we're basically siblings too."

The beep of the toaster saves me from having to answer. She's distracted, slathering her toast with an unholy amount of peanut butter, and she doesn't seem concerned with whatever I might say next. Probably because she's confident I can't refute her argument. She's wrong about that, but the thing is, I'm not so sure I want to.

This isn't at all how I envisioned my relationship with Olivia. Of course I hoped we'd be friendly, and she's already proven herself a better ally than my own brother when it comes to my dad, but she's Gwen's sister and Tristan's aunt and beyond that, I haven't thought of her as anything but a short-term roommate until she leaves for college at the end of August.

I'm not adverse to having a more personal relationship with her, but I'm out of my depth here. This is the part of sibling relationships that I don't get. Alex and I were never close enough to confide in each other. It's a strange but pleasant realization that I might be able to have that kind of relationship with Olivia. *If I don't fuck it up.*

I've taken a seat at the bar, and she carries her plate and juice over to join me. Once she's seated on the stool, her plate and glass of juice safe from spills on the counter in front of her, I bump her shoulder with mine. "All right, lay it on me, little sister."

She chews her lower lip and avoids making eye contact. "So, right, there's this guy."

She pauses again, so I give her a gentle nudge. "And?"

"I really like him. Like, really, really like him. Like, a lot."

It's difficult not to laugh at her egregious overuse of "like" and "really," but I manage. "So what's the problem?"

"Well, for one thing, he doesn't even know I exist."

"Why not? Oh, wait, are we talking about Harry Styles or something?"

"O. M. G." Her high pitch squeal is followed by a stinging slap to my upper arm. "This is someone real. I mean, not that Harry Styles isn't real, but you know what I mean. Someone I've met."

"Then you should tell him you're interested."

"I can't."

"Because?"

She gives me a sidelong look. "He's older than me and I'm leaving for school soon, so even if that didn't freak him out—and it'd definitely freak him out—it's not like we could be together or anything."

Uh-oh. I'm five years older than Gwen, and she was Olivia's age when we first met. At the time, it hadn't seemed like a big deal, and remembering it now, it still doesn't. Well, as long as I ignore that she ended up pregnant. But her sister seems so much younger than Gwen did back then. Maybe that's because I'm even older now and that's changed my perspective, but the idea of Olivia with some random asshole in his midtwenties isn't okay. I have to be cautious about how I approach this, though, or she'll dismiss me as a hypocrite—which, apparently, I very much am—so I force my voice to remain casual and ask, "How much older?"

"Older than you."

"You mean older than I was when Gwen and I met?" That isn't what she means. I'm not even sure she knows how old I was when Gwen and I met, but I'm grasping at straws, because the alternative…

She shakes her head. "Older than you now."

Bzzt. Wrong fucking answer. "It's a damn good thing he doesn't know you exist, sweetheart. Because whoever he is, I'll break his face if he even looks at you." Olivia's eyes widen and she's staring at me, mouth agape, so I dial it back, going for a lighter, teasing tone. "Hey, you're the one who wanted a big brother. Don't cry now if you're getting more than you bargained for."

"Oh, come on. I already said I know nothing can happen. He's not some creep like you're making him out to be. There's no way he'd go for it if I approached him. He'd tell me I'm just a kid, and I'd die of embarrassment."

Alex is a beast. That phrase from her conversation with her friends the other day lights up my brain like a neon sign, and foreboding settles in my stomach. But no, she can't be talking about him. Alex is younger than me, and she definitely knows that much.

Reassured by the math and more than a little relieved, I ask, "Then why are we even talking about him? You'll go to college in a few months and meet someone your own age and forget all about him." I'm not sure that's true—I didn't forget Gwen, did I?—but if we're all lucky, that's exactly what'll happen. Hell, I'm not sure I even care if she starts seeing some guy in his twenties now. Younger than me is a pretty low bar for her future boyfriends. I don't think I'm asking a lot here.

"I won't. I know I won't. He's the one, Mac. And after I finish school, I'm going to tell him how I feel. Which means I have a few years to…become…more. To figure out how to get him to see me as not just a *kid*." The emphasis she places on the last word—all frustration and a little disdain—is telling. I want to interrupt, to tell her there's nothing wrong with being a kid and she should enjoy it while she can, but somehow, I don't think she'd appreciate that observation, and she doesn't give me the chance anyway. "That's what I wanted to talk to you about. I thought maybe you could give me some advice on what I should be doing now so I have the best chance possible to…I don't know, win him over later, I guess." She frowns and leans forward in her seat, bracing her elbows on the counter. "It's just, I don't really know any men. I mean, not well. There are the boys at school, but that's not at all the same. I don't know what men want or what they care about."

There's zero chance I'm going to help her snag some man twice her age and, to be honest, I wouldn't know what to tell her anyway. But her whole plan rubs me the wrong way. Not because of who she's trying to attract—or, not only that—but how she's trying to do it. "You're looking at this all wrong, Liv. It doesn't matter who the guy is. If he's the right one, you won't have to make yourself into someone you aren't to get his attention. You're a bright, charming, pretty young woman. Find the one who thinks you're enough exactly as you are."

"Now you sound like Gwen."

"That means I'm right."

That coaxes a smile from her, but it's followed by a heavy sigh. "I really want it to work out."

"And if it's meant to, it will." *Over my dead body.* "But relationships are hard enough without trying to force it."

"Yeah, I guess." She slides off her stool and plants a kiss on my cheek before heading for the stairs. "I'm going to call Harper and see if she wants to come hang out with me and Tris today."

Like Willa, Olivia's best friend Harper has been over every day this week. She's headed to NYU in the fall, which as far as the girls are concerned might as well be a million miles from William and Mary, where Olivia is enrolled. I remember what that was like—the excitement of taking what felt like the first real steps into adulthood juxtaposed against the sadness of leaving behind many of your closest friends—and it's no surprise they're spending every spare moment together while they can. So it isn't Olivia's parting announcement that's left me frozen to my bar stool in a confused daze. It's that silly little kiss.

No, not just that, either. It's also that she confided in me in the first place. That she sought me out, that she valued my opinion, even when I didn't tell her what she wanted to hear. And that surge of protective instinct that shot through me when she confessed her interest in a much-older man. Where had that come from?

Jess. Thankfully, I'd been too off kilter throughout my conversation with Olivia to connect the dots until now, but yes, of course. A young woman's crush, fleeting and full of fantasy as it may be, is easy for an older man to exploit. I should've—

Gwen's quiet voice behind me finishes my thought for me. "You should've asked who he is."

I peer over my shoulder at her and arch one brow. "Eavesdropping? Really?"

She nods, her mouth turning up in an unrepentant smile. "Totally."

"How long?" I turn on my stool to face her, and she comes closer, stepping between my spread knees.

"The whole time. You did a great job."

"Yeah?"

"Yeah. Except—" she pauses to jab me in the chest with one finger, "—not finding out who he is."

"It's better that I don't know."

"Or you might break his face just to be on the safe side?"

"Mmm." Let her make of that what she will, but the answer is yes. Definitely yes.

Gwen shakes her head, her voice firm like when she's discipling Tristan. "You're not allowed to break faces unless they've done something to deserve it and..." She pokes my sternum again, her lips curling in a smile, "...you're always required to get the gossip in these situations."

"Noted, although I'm surprised your only interest in the creep is gossip. I'd have thought you'd be more concerned." Is it unfair calling some dude who, if Olivia's to be believed, doesn't even know about her crush a creep? Probably, but I don't give a damn.

"I'm a little worried." She holds up one hand, her thumb and forefinger pinched together until they're nearly touching. "But it's pretty normal. When I was in high school, I had an enormous crush on one of my teachers. Mr. Thornton. He taught calculus and he was kind of stern. He sort of reminded me of Daniel Craig, and I was convinced he was the only one for me. But then…" Her smile grows wider and she leans closer. Almost close enough to kiss. "I went to Ann Arbor and met a boy who liked me exactly the way I was, and I haven't thought about Mr. Thornton since."

How can I argue with that?

CHAPTER 5

GWEN

"Before we get started, I have something I'd like to say, if that's all right?" Sean Hennessey's bottle-green eyes scan the faces seated around the oval table—Kim's campaign manager Brian and her husband Arnie. Alex, her personal assistant Holly, and Mac. Me. Finally, his gaze settles on Kim, and he arches one brow in question.

The Democratic convention is only one week away, and we've all gathered at campaign headquarters in Arlington to settle once and for all who'll be the Vice Presidential candidate. This is the last meeting today and, if all goes well, the last in the process too.

Kim keeps her expression neutral, but she sounds amused when she answers. "I'll be honest with you, Sean. Unless you fuck this up, you're getting the job, so think long and hard about if you really want to go off script right now."

Soft titters of laughter follow from most of us, and one side of Sean's mouth hitches up in a crooked smile. "Well, it seems like I'd better, since I'm planning on talking you out of picking me."

"You don't want to be Vice President?" Brian asks, bewildered, and it's safe to say he's speaking for all of us.

My phone, face down on the table in front of me, vibrates. Next to it, Mac's does the same, but he's a better person than I am, because he ignores it, focusing on the conversation taking place around us while I turn mine over to read the text.

Stef: Please, please, please give me an interview. I can get you a segment in prime time.

Once Mac's booty call and now our mutual friend, Stef is a reporter above all else, so I'm not even a little bit surprised to receive this kind of text from her. Tilting my phone toward Mac, I nudge him under the table, but after reading it, his only response is to roll his eyes and turn back to Sean, who's answering Brian's question.

"Oh, I do. But this election is critical, and my image could hurt you."

Kim shrugs. "You walk a fine line, outrageous enough to be endearing without making people question your competence. It takes a special kind of charisma to pull that off. That's one of the biggest reasons some on my team like you for the ticket, and according to our internal polls, after being a woman, my biggest weakness is that voters think I'm boring."

"I'm not boring," Sean agrees. "But I'm a risk. At any given moment, the general public may decide I'm no longer a charming bad boy and instead a little too much like the sitting President for comfort. Putting me on your ticket undermines the argument that he's a dangerous loose cannon, and the math doesn't really change if Whitaker's convention coup is successful." It's looking more and more like Whitaker's—and Mac's father's—strategy will work and he'll come out on top after the Republicans hold their convention, but Sean's right, Whitaker's only marginally more disciplined than the President. "There's also the matter of that photo you received from my cousin. The polling won't be so hot if my bisexuality becomes a headline."

"Your cousin leaked the photo?" Holly blurts. As Kim's PA, her primary role today is note-taking, but I have to admit, I'm surprised by that revelation too and might've opened my big mouth if she hadn't beat me to it. *Better her than me.* And I'm equally surprised by the casualness with which Sean mentions his sexuality. It doesn't matter to anyone in this room, and it shouldn't matter to anyone outside of it. But it would and, in his shoes, I'm not sure I'd be so calm about it.

Sean shrugs and gives Mac and Alex a wry smile. "We all have *that* family member, don't we?"

Something the three of them have in common, which Mac acknowledges with a muttered, "Unfortunately." Alex is stone-faced though, as if this discussion has nothing at all to do with him. Since the argument in Mac's office the other day, they haven't spoken, and when they've been forced into each other's presence for work, it's been strained.

Kim is laser focused and won't be sidetracked. "You weren't my first choice." This announcement seems to surprise everyone but her husband. "I'd have taken the risk on an all-woman ticket if she would've accepted, and I'll take the risk on you. Those things shouldn't matter, and they won't matter if we make our best argument."

I knot my hands under the table to keep from fidgeting. I want so badly for Kim to be right about that. Under the current President, we have no foreign policy, the economy's in tatters, and life has gotten even more difficult for our most vulnerable citizens, and Kim's the only candidate who's outlined in-depth policies to right the ship. Her gender or her Vice President's sexuality don't have anything to do with fixing the festering problems caused by the current administration. But we could still lose because of them, and then what?

Sean laughs and shakes his head, voicing my own concerns more succinctly and with much less angst. "You're an idealist. It'll bite you someday."

"Maybe, but I'll take that chance. Are you in?"

Reluctantly, Sean nods. "I'm in."

His response is followed by a lot of handshakes and backslaps, but after several minutes, when the milling bodies start to file from the room, Kim stops Alex, Mac, and me from following. "Could I have a minute?"

The four of us resume our seats. She's probably noticed the ramped-up tension between Mac and Alex—it'd be pretty hard to miss—which doesn't really involve me. So why did she ask me to stay too?

The stupid sex tape. It's been a week and, honestly, the furor has died down a lot more than I thought it would by this point, but it hasn't gone away and I'd be lying if I said I'm not worried she's going to tell us we can't rejoin the campaign. Which is even stupider than the sex tape, because that's exactly what she should tell us. I was prepared for it the day the story broke. I didn't like it, but I recognized what needed to happen and I could accept it. But this stupid cooling-off period and some of the more favorable coverage have given me hope.

"What's going on with you two?" Kim gestures between the brothers.

"Nothing." Mac's denial is quick and decisive, not inviting further discussion.

"He thinks Dad leaked his sex tape." With his gaze fixed on Kim, as if Mac and I aren't even in the room, he adds, "Apparently worrying about that is easier than taking responsibility for the fact that it exists in the first place."

Shots. Fired. Mac leans forward in his seat, one elbow on the table and his finger pointed at Alex. Judging by the furious slant of his brows and the hard set of his jaw, whatever he's about to say is going to be ugly, but Kim doesn't give him the chance. Her voice is firm, and she looks between them when she says, "I'm not your babysitter anymore, and I will not referee your squabbling. Nor do I have the time to figure out who's to blame. Get your shit together or you'll both be off the campaign for good. Am I understood?" Their tempers are still simmering but they nod, and she gestures toward the door. "Alex, you can go."

Alex's chair scrapes across the floor, and he stalks out of the room. Watching him go, Kim shakes her head, but as soon as the door has closed behind him, she turns to us. "So, let's talk about your sudden popularity and that sex tape, Your Majesties."

It's impossible not to cringe. Yesterday, a popular celebrity gossip blog posted a long screed about how unfairly the media's treating us. Which, you know, I don't in general disagree with, but as part of the article, they drew all kinds of wild comparisons between us and various celebrities, including but not limited to British royalty. It was all meant to illustrate their point about "toxic media culture" which, again, I agree and definitely appreciate the defense, but it's all kind of ridiculous and embarrassing. It turned the tides, though, and there's no denying it, as evidenced by Stef's promise of prime time—I'd rather die—and some of the tweets I read this morning over breakfast.

"Dude is hot af. I'd meet him in a parking garage anytime."

"Say what you will about the sex tape, but she's adorable!"

"I'd do him."

"They're a cute couple. Bet that baby is going to be a sweetie pie too."

"Leave 'em alone. They're two kids in love! When we were young, my husband and I had sex at a Broadway play. Sometimes you can't wait!"

Sure, there were still tweets calling me a slut or commenting on how immoral and unprofessional we both are, but not as many as I expected. I guess the more vitriolic of our detractors have already gotten bored and moved on to someone or something else. But even with our improving coverage, Mac still thinks it'd be best for him, at least, to leave the campaign, so I'm expecting it when he says, "I'll admit I didn't see being equated to British Royalty coming." He gives her a self-deprecating smile before adding, "At this point, it's probably safe for Gwen to remain with the campaign. But you need to accept my resignation."

"Why?"

"For one thing, I don't know any other way to resolve the tension with Alex." It's painful to hear so much frustration and regret in Mac's voice. His bleak expression emphasizes his sorrow and it makes my heart heavy. But he straightens his shoulders and raises his chin, unwilling—or unable—to wallow in the grief he must feel for their fractured relationship. "For another, with Dad, Alex, and me all working on campaigns, the firm is stretched too thin. Our other clients are suffering." That's been one good thing to come out of our being home for the last week. The other account managers have really stepped up and are working hard to keep the firm running on all cylinders, but with all three principals out of the office most of the time, some things were falling through the cracks, and he's spent a large part of the last few days putting out fires.

"What about a reduced role to allow you more time for the firm's other clients?"

Mac sighs and scrubs one hand over his face. "My dad is a real problem, Kim. Maybe Alex is right and Dad doesn't have anything to do with our current problem, but I don't trust him. I'll never trust him. And if Whitaker comes out of the convention on top, I can't promise my dad won't try to use me against you."

Kim is quiet for a moment, considering that. Finally, she asks, "But he won't use Alex against me?"

"I don't think so." Mac rubs his lip, giving the question serious thought before continuing. "Even if he wanted to, there aren't any skeletons in Alex's closet. Attack ads about the one time his shoes weren't perfectly shined won't be very compelling and certainly wouldn't reflect on you."

"Your brother isn't perfect." The tone of her voice suggests maybe she knows something about Alex we—or at least I—don't, but Mac either misses it or chooses to ignore it.

"Yeah, I'm aware."

"But you think he could use you in some way that'd reflect on me? How?"

He goes still; I'm not even sure he's breathing, and for one long second time stops and I think he might tell her the truth. Mac reaches under the table, lacing his fingers with mine and giving my hand a gentle squeeze. I don't know if it's meant to reassure me or him, but it does help settle my twitching nerves a little. "It doesn't matter how, only that he might. I'm a liability."

Kim scoffs at that. "No, your father is a liability, and I'm not going to hold you responsible for him."

That's an admirable view and truth be told, I agree with her. Besides, it seems unlikely that Senior would out himself and ruin his own reputation by telling the world he's Amy's father. And even if he did, that doesn't reflect on Kim. Jess is her daughter and she was young at the time, but she was an adult and didn't even live at home. How could her affair with Mac's dad and Amy's subsequent birth be held against Kim or her campaign? It doesn't make a lot of sense to me.

"I think…" Mac trails off, his gaze fixed on the empty beige wall across the room. His tension and anxiety flows through our joined hands, and my knee bounces under the table in an utterly useless attempt to burn it off. He gives my hand another squeeze, this time so hard my knuckles ache a little, and turns back to Kim. His brown eyes are so dark and full of pain I think it's his tumultuous emotions, not my own, that form the knot in my throat. With a deep, steadying breath he says, "You're sure this is what you want?"

It isn't hard to guess what he's thinking. He believes in her and her campaign and wants to see it through, but he's also aware that sticking around might be counterproductive to achieving their ultimate goal— winning the election. He's a protector by nature and honestly, I expected that instinct to win out today, but maybe I shouldn't be surprised he's wavering. The current situation with Alex, not to mention our recent argument over how to address the sex tape, illustrate how his instinct to protect can backfire and, before she was anything else to him, Kim was his babysitter. A trusted adult, an authority figure he's admired and respected for as long as he can remember. Perhaps that makes it easier for him to cede to her judgment.

Sensing victory, Kim grins. "It is. Let's keep an eye on the press for another week and if things continue as they are, I want you two to rejoin us in Miami at the convention. I want you there the last night when I give my acceptance speech."

CHAPTER 6

MAC

"Gwen!"

"Ms. Pierce!"

"Gwen!"

"Mac!"

Being back on the campaign trail isn't as dissimilar to our home life as it once was. In either place, someone's always demanding our attention, and it's a mixed bag whether the reason they want it is good or bad. Tonight, it's all bad.

It's the last night of the Democratic convention, and Gwen and I have arrived at the convention center. We were meant to slip in unnoticed through a backdoor, but a collection of reporters from various outlets have found the rear entrance and gathered around it like a pack of starving dogs. No doubt they hoped to catch one of the A-list celebrities speaking tonight in a candid moment, and that's what motivated the paparazzi to stake out the rear entrance. But since our little sex tape scandal, Gwen and I have become unwilling celebrities in our own right. D-list at best, but even so, the vultures aren't going to pass up an opportunity since they're already here. I don't know how real celebrities live like this. It's disconcerting, and the animal part of my brain is on high alert, ready to make a split-second decision between fight or flight.

With one arm around her waist, I hold Gwen close against my side and guide her through the crowd. She's wide-eyed, her hand squeezing mine on her hip with her face turned toward me, like if she doesn't look directly at them, they aren't really there. This isn't the first time I've been in the middle of a situation like this, but in the past, the media's target was always a client. The worst was a floppy-haired kid from a boy band who hired us to scrub the tarnish off his image after he'd been arrested for going on a bender and demolishing his room in a swanky hotel in New York City. The crowd that ambushed us on the way into the studio for a television interview was enormous—easily ten, maybe even twenty times the size of this one—and restless. A teen idol had fucked up big and there was blood in the water, but as intimidating as that situation was, I never realized how much worse it is when it's your own name they're shouting. Your own life they're dissecting. Your own family they're threatening.

Adrenaline floods my system and my muscles are tense, ready to spring into action at a moment's notice, but two secret service agents flank the door about thirty yards ahead, giving me some measure of confidence we'll make it inside without a major incident. We just have to wade through this mess first, which shouldn't be a problem. Yes, the reporters are shouting our names and demanding our attention, but even the ones in front of us move with us, backing up so we're able to make slow but steady progress toward our destination. But rationally knowing that does little to convince my nervous system it's safe to settle down.

Until one doesn't. I recognize him instantly. Carl Weaver is a balding, white man in his fifties. Wearing a dilapidated suit and ragged sneakers that've probably seen more action running from his targets or their security details than from intentional exercise, he looks like exactly what he is—tabloid scum. He steps in front of Gwen and puts one hand on her arm, his beady eyes scanning her face. "What's it like, knowing the whole world has seen you having sex?"

Rage prickles the back of my neck, and I grab his wrist, removing his hand from her arm. "Don't touch her. Don't talk to her. And get the fuck out of our way."

Carl shakes his arm like I hurt him even though I know damn well I didn't, but he otherwise ignores me, his attention still focused on Gwen. "It must be so upsetting, especially in your condition." He glances down at her midsection, his lips pursed. "It'd be unfortunate if there were other scandals lurking in your past, waiting for the right moment to come to light."

I'm going to kill him. In front of all these other reporters and their cameras and the secret service, I'm going to kill the smarmy little shit. Except she doesn't give me a chance. Sensing my mood, she places one hand on my stomach in gentle restraint and smiles at Carl. "Who are you with?"

He seems pleased by her question, and I clench my fist at my side. Whether that's in preparation to deck him or to prevent myself from grabbing him by the throat is anyone's guess, but she shouldn't be engaging with him. It'll only encourage him. Besides, one of the secret service agents is shouldering through the crowd toward us, and Carl is far too big a coward to tangle with him. But he hasn't noticed the approaching federal agent yet and he takes a step closer to Gwen when he answers. "I'm with *Seek.*"

"Oh." Her eyes widen a little and she tilts her head, like she's surprised by this.

Started as a website and now available in print in grocery checkout lanes across the country, *Seek*—formerly *Seek the Truth*—is the trashiest of the tabloid trash. But the secret service agent has reached us, expertly stepping between Gwen and Carl and ushering us forward. Still, I can't resist the impulse to give him a piece of my mind as we go.

Lagging behind Gwen and the agent, I lean toward Carl, stabbing a finger in his face. Flash bulbs pop in my peripheral vision like a warning, but I don't give a fuck. "You leave my family alone, or I'll destroy you."

Carl smirks. "Threatening reporters now, MacKenzie?"

"That isn't a threat, it's a fucking promise."

He says something else to my back as I follow after Gwen, but I can't decipher it over all the echoing noise in the alley. Once I reach her side, she grabs my hand, her fingers tangling with mine, and we both follow the agent inside.

"I'm sorry about that. I got to you as soon as I could. They've been a little riled up ever since Madison Cunningham flipped them all off an hour ago," he explains, lingering in the still open door.

Madison is a pop superstar and one of our clients. Alex oversees her public relations needs, but I've met her a handful of times. She's the rare exception to most of the rules of PR because no matter how outrageous she behaves, no matter how outspoken she is, no matter who she tells to go fuck themselves, the public almost universally adores her. She's the un-smearable celebrity, and it drives the muck-rakers around the bend.

"It's okay." Gwen tightens her grip on my fingers, gently tugging.

Thanking the agent, I let her pull me down the long, empty corridor. She seems to be in a hurry, her low heels clicking on the cement floor, but I'm happy to follow along until we reach a junction and she ignores—or doesn't notice?—the sign taped to the wall, instead turning in the opposite direction. I hook one thumb over my shoulder in the direction we should've gone. "We were supposed to go that way. Are you okay?"

She casts a sidelong look in my general direction but keeps right on going, only slowing long enough to read the identifying name plates on each door. "I'm looking for a bathroom."

Oh. I've always had a general understanding that the whole human reproductive process is unfair to women, but in the last few months I've learned it's much worse than I ever realized. I mean, Gwen has to pee all the time. That's not an exaggeration, or not much of one, and it makes her life difficult sometimes. Like now. Whereas I'd have probably pissed back in that alley if I needed to, reporters be damned, that isn't an option for her, another injustice of human biology. Actually, now that I think about it, that's what I should've done. It would've served the weasels right. But she's tugging me into the bathroom behind her, so my fantasy of pissing on Carl Weaver's ratty sneakers will have to wait.

"Hey, what—" I don't get to finish my question. As soon as the door swings closed behind us, she launches herself at me, smashing our lips together in a hasty, hungry kiss that knocks the wind out of me.

She takes advantage of my momentarily stunned response, one hand on the back of my neck and the other fisting my tie, using it to pull me closer. She presses into me, her generous curves reminding me how much—and how fast—her body is changing these days. Every time I see her naked or hold her close, it seems I notice something new or different. It's like I get to rediscover her every time we touch, and it's fucking intoxicating.

But now isn't the time or place. Especially not after recent events. So, for possibly the first time in my spoiled, self-indulgent life, I ignore my aching dick and put my hands on her hips, gently moving her away from me. "I don't know what's gotten into you, and I'll be happy to fuck you until you pass out when we get back to the hotel later, but we can't do this here." I have to force the words out, because I don't want to be saying them. I'm not even sure how much I mean them. If she senses the frailty of my conviction and pushes back, it's going to be all over but the orgasms.

And she does push back. Of course she does. "There aren't any cameras in this bathroom, there wasn't anyone in the hallway, and we still have more than two hours before Kim's speech." She dips her chin and licks her lips, her eyes dropping to the front of my pants. Staring at the very obvious erection pressing against my zipper, she adds, "And I know it's probably kind of messed up and wrong, but it was pretty hot the way you told that jerk off, and I want to thank you." Another lick of her lips, but this time the tip of her tongue lingers, caressing the plump curve of her lower lip, and my dick throbs.

"You can thank me when we're back in our room?" It shouldn't have come out like a question, but it did, and I cringe—inwardly, I hope—at my own uncertainty. Why is it so fucking hard to tell this woman no? *Because I know what she can do with that tongue.*

Gwen steps into my space again, palming my cock through my pants. My vision blurs around the edges, and it takes every ounce of concentration I can muster to focus on what she's saying. "I want to do it now. Do you remember when we were kids, the time I blew you inside one of the floor-model tents at the sporting goods store?"

Oh, fuck yes. I was twenty-three. Calling me a kid is a bit of a stretch, but now isn't the time for quibbling over small details like that. We were going camping with some of my friends, and I took her with me to pick up supplies for the trip. It was a weekday and the store was deserted but for a handful of employees, and I was the one who dragged her into the tent in the first place. My plan involved a few kisses and some heavy petting, but Gwen took things even further.

"I remember." I clear my throat in an attempt to get rid of the weird croak in it. "But you're not getting on your knees in a public bathroom. You're five months pregnant, for fuck's sake."

Gwen hums, and it *almost* sounds like agreement. She turns away from me, heading for the door. But instead of opening it, she turns the latch, locking us in. The click of it sliding into place is loud, almost like a gun shot, and hell, it might as well be, because my ability to resist this moment, to resist her, is dead on arrival.

GWEN

THERE ARE certain things about my relationship with Mac that have been a constant across the years. The sun rises in the east, predators hunt prey, and brash, adventurous Mac becomes a prude when I turn the tables on him. It's basically one of the laws of nature.

And sure, I can admit that given recent events, going down on him in an out-of-the-way restroom in the remote bowels of a convention center packed with thousands of people was possibly stupid. It wasn't *that* dangerous, though—the door did have a lock, after all, and we got away with it. Even the embarrassment of having to ask for his help getting up again when I was finished couldn't dim the moment for me. Discovering that I'd managed to pull it off without getting a run in my nylons or a stain on my dress? Icing on the cake.

Stepping out into the hallway, Mac glances both ways before opening the door wider so I can follow. When I pass him, he catches my fingers in one hand and tugs until I turn my face up to his. His voice holds a note of censure, but that endearingly crooked smile of his outweighs it. "That was reckless and unprofessional. As your boss, I have no choice but to discipline you for such outrageous behavior at a work event."

"How will you punish me, Mr. MacKenzie?" I catch my lower lip with my teeth, chewing it to keep from laughing.

He lets go of the bathroom door and it slams closed with a loud thump that echoes in the deserted corridor. Starting down the hall, he says, "You'll have to wait and see when we get back to the hotel, won't you?"

"Whatever you think is appropriate, I'm sure I deserve it, but I'm not sorry." And why should I be? We didn't get caught, it chased away my nerves, and...well, I guess it's silly, but it almost feels like reclaiming a little bit of ourselves from the tabloids. This is who we are, who we've always been together, and I'm not going to let that creep from *Seek* and the others of his ilk take that from us. Okay, yeah, that's definitely stupid, but it doesn't change how I feel.

Still holding my hand, he turns us down another corridor, following a sign directing us toward the green room. "Oh, you shouldn't be. That was some of your best work."

I almost ask if he has a rating system for blow jobs. Like, does he keep a diary or Excel spreadsheet, complete with notes so he'll remember how they all compare? *Four stars. Good suction but too much teeth.* That thought makes me giggle, but we're getting closer to our destination now, so it's best not to ask. Having gotten away with furtive fellatio, the last thing we need is to be overheard talking about it.

The hall is getting more crowded, with some people standing in small groups chatting while others are coming and going, on their way to and from backstage and the front of the house. I can hear the crowd too, clapping for the current speaker, whose impassioned speech is blasting from the sound system. It's like a campaign trail rally on steroids, and a rush of excitement jolts through me.

Turning through a wide set of double doors propped open by garbage cans, we arrive in the green room, although in my limited experience, calling it that seems like a massive understatement. It's as large as a hotel ballroom, and with the buffet setup along one wall, it sort of looks like one in the midst of a wedding reception, assuming the bride really, really likes the color blue and minus a dance floor and DJ. That doesn't mean we're lacking for entertainment. A dozen TVs are mounted around the room, most tuned to a live feed from the stage, but the twenty-four-hour news channels and their endless, droning analysis are being broadcast too.

The size of the crowd is staggering. I expected it to be larger than usual, what with Kim's friends and family included and the leaders from all fifty of her state campaigns present. There are also several dozen very dedicated volunteers who are being rewarded for their hard work with behind-the-scenes access, any number of state, local, and national-level politicians, and celebrities of every stripe. Professional athletes, Hollywood stars, and musicians—some of whom are performing tonight—mingle with everyone else.

It's overwhelming and, honestly, intimidating, so I'm relieved when I recognize Brandon Bennett's familiar face among a small cluster of people near the bar. He's a tech tycoon, and we met last spring at a fundraiser in California. He was very kind, surprisingly down to earth, and complimented me on my work for the campaign. Making a mental note to say hello as soon as I have a chance, I scan the faces of his companions and... *Oh.* One of the men Brandon's talking with isn't just an A-list actor, he's *the* A-list actor—the one every director wants for their film, regardless if it's an artsy little indie or a summer blockbuster, and almost everyone, movie buff or not, would recognize his face, if not his name.

We're threading through the crowd, on our way to the front of the room, and I have to tug on Mac's hand to get his attention. "Is that…?"

He follows my gaze, his brow furrowing. "Yes, and he's an enormous asshole." Taking in the rest of their group, his eyes settle on Brandon and the crease in his forehead deepens. "They both are."

What the fuck? Except then I remember the way he acted the night I met Brandon. There'd been a lot going on that night and there were a lot of reasons for Mac to be upset, namely that I'd just told him about Tris. It hadn't occurred to me that he might be jealous too. "Are you…jealous?"

"Yes," he admits with a shameless grin. "But that isn't why he's an asshole. Trying to poach my girlfriend is understandable. Who wouldn't want her? She's amazing. But he told Kim he intends to offer you a job after the election. Trying to poach the best damn social media specialist I've got is, well, also understandable but unforgivable."

My chest swells with warm, fluttery pride. This isn't the first time he's complimented my work. He often tells me I've done a good job and asks for my input on campaign matters that cross over between more traditional media and social media. But the way he's framed it, like he's more secure in our personal relationship than our professional one and that offering me a job is a bigger offense than flirting with me? *Be still, my beating heart.* And he called me his girlfriend. It isn't the first time he's done that either since our come-to-Jesus meeting two weeks ago, but I'll never get tired of hearing it.

There's no sign of Kim, not that I expected to see her here. With the biggest speech of her life rapidly approaching, she's probably sequestered in her dressing room. And if I know her, she's still editing and refining her speech, wanting it—and this moment—to be perfect.

Other than a quick hello and congratulations, Cece is too busy for conversation too. This is a big night for her, the culmination of a lot of work and planning to pull off the biggest event of her career. At least so far. She's already begun the planning for election night, and if

Kim wins, I'm sure Cece will have her hand in organizing one of the inaugural balls.

But there's no shortage of people to talk to, and Mac, especially, is in high demand. Well, no, that isn't right. As we make our way through the throng, plenty of people speak to me too. It's just that where they talk to Mac about the campaign and upcoming election, the only thing people seem to care enough to ask me about is my pregnancy. *When are you due? How are you feeling? Do you know if it's a boy or a girl? What about names?*

It's exhausting and demoralizing. Haven't I been an integral part of this campaign? Shouldn't at least some of the congratulations being heaped on Mac's broad shoulders be directed my way too? To his credit he always mentions me and my contributions, as well as those of the rest of the team, but as soon as he does, whoever he's talking to blinks at me and then…congratulates me on my pregnancy. Even Mac is growing frustrated, his grip on my hand tightening as the evening progresses.

It's a difficult pill to swallow tonight of all nights. Kim is accepting a major party's nomination for President, only the second woman ever to do so, and we're surrounded by the party faithful who claim to be progressive. Yet when confronted with a woman who's both pregnant and an integral part of Kim's team, it isn't my work for the campaign they mention. It's depressing as hell and a good reminder that no matter how good tonight feels, there's still a lot of work to do.

We break away from the latest batch of self-important assholes—Mac deserves an Academy Award for the way he effortlessly charms them—and he snatches a glass of champagne from the tray of a passing waiter, downing it in a single gulp. He offers me the empty glass, and I take it with a confused frown. "What do you want me to do with this?"

"I just think when you inevitably start screaming 'I'm more than a baby-making machine' it'll be more impactful if you have something to throw."

That forces a laugh from me. "Cute, but I'm fine. And it's a good reminder, tonight is a step, not the final destination."

"You're brilliant and far more forgiving than these assholes deserve." He lets go of my hand to slide his arm around my waist, pulling me close to his side.

"Have you seen Alex?" He's pretty hard to miss in most crowds, what with his height and all, but I haven't seen him all night.

Mac gestures across the room with a lift of his chin, and I follow along, finding Alex, laughing in a group of people near the entrance. He seems to be enjoying himself, but as we resume our circuit of the room it becomes clear he's avoiding us. For every step Mac and I take in one direction, he takes two in the opposite, and even as the crowd begins to thin, most of the guests heading to the front of the house to find their seats for Kim's speech, he keeps his distance. Mac, who's most definitely noticed, is stoic about it, but I'm...well, pissed. Alex has good reason to be upset with his brother and God knows I've tried to convince Mac to come clean with him, but he has to know this is only going to make the rift between them worse and I'm far too protective of Mac to be fair about this.

Twenty minutes before she's scheduled to take the stage, Kim joins us. She's flanked by her husband Arnie and her daughter Jess, with her personal assistant Holly and her campaign manager Brian trialing behind, and she's almost immediately swarmed. As soon as Brian spots us, he makes a beeline in our direction, a sheet of paper in hand. Without greeting, he thrusts it at Mac and says, "Final-ish draft of her speech. She wants you to have the last look."

It's the perfect opportunity to have a word with Alex, and if Mac suspects what I'm up to when I excuse myself, he doesn't try and stop me. I'm still a good twenty, maybe thirty, yards away and Alex sees me coming, but he doesn't try to escape, confirming what I already know. It wasn't us he's avoiding, it's just Mac, and my pulse quickens, my face hot with irritation.

Giving me a smile that seems genuine, Alex waits until I'm in range then says, "You look great tonight, Gwen. I hope you're enjoying yourself."

"I am. It's a big night." The woman he was speaking with has already begun to turn away in search of a new conversation, but I wait a beat to make sure she isn't coming back before adding, "And because it's such a big night, you're going to grow the fuck up and stop avoiding your brother."

He raises both brows at my coarse language, but his smile doesn't falter. "I have no intentions of making a scene, if that's what you're worried about."

"The thought never crossed my mind." It really didn't. Alex is too dignified for that sort of thing, and besides, he took Kim's lecture to heart the other day. But he's apparently drawing the line at any interaction beyond what's required for their respective jobs. "You're hurting him, and it's pretty hard to watch."

His smile falters and his eyes don't meet mine. "You don't think he's hurt me too?"

Of course he has. I'm not so naive or addled by my affection for Mac that I can't recognize that and I know, too, there's no bridging the canyon their dad dug between them unless Mac is willing to share his secrets—and realistically, maybe not even then. But instead of crossing it, they could go around it, the way our circulatory system sometimes bypasses a blockage by building a network of collateral vessels. They have to talk to each other for that to happen, and that means Alex has to stop stonewalling his brother.

My initial approach was wrong. As defensive and protective of Mac as I feel, it was understandable, maybe, but still wrong if I want them to reconcile. Alex has to come to it on his own, to want a relationship with his brother despite their differences, and I can't strong-arm him into that, no matter how much I might wish I could. This requires a change in tactics. "I know he has and I'm sorry I snapped at you. It's just—"

I'm interrupted by Arnie's loud claps and an ear-splitting wolf whistle from Jess. It's time for Kim's speech, or for the winding walk through the maze of corridors to the stage, anyway. We're being herded into the hallway, and Alex glances down at me, his expression neutral.

"I appreciate what you're trying to do, Gwen. I really do and I know you mean well, but leave it alone. Please."

With no choice but to accept defeat, I fall back until I've rejoined Mac and Brian. "How's the speech?"

"A real barn-burner. You'll love it." Mac catches me around the waist, pulling me into his side and slowing his step to match mine. With a sidelong look, he adds, "How's Alex?"

Right, there was no way he was going to let that go without comment, and so there's no excuse for not having an answer ready. "Um, not ready to talk."

Having heard exactly what he expected, Mac nods and stares straight ahead.

CHAPTER 7

GWEN

A BLISTERING summer has receded into nothing short of a pleasant fall, at least as far as the weather's concerned. But even with the mounting anxieties of the rapidly approaching election—one week from today—it's hard not to enjoy such a beautiful morning.

To be honest, I feel a bit like an old-fashioned movie star, relaxing on a chaise lounge on the terrace in my butterfly sunglasses and over-sized hat while I scroll through social media. The glamour is tarnished a bit by the constant aches and pains of late pregnancy, but life could be a lot worse.

Brett Whitaker's attempted coup at the Republican convention failed, but it was close, and with Mac's dad egging him on, he decided to mount an independent campaign. He has enough support within the Republican Party that he's splitting the vote, excellent news for Kim's prospects, and she's led the polls ever since. The only downside is instead of one opponent slinging mud her way, there are two. If she wins, it'll be worth it.

Everything is still going well with the twins. I started having

Braxton-Hicks contractions in mid-August, the day we dropped Olivia off for college, so beginning the first week of September, Dr. Williams forbid me from travel for the remainder of my pregnancy. Fortunately, we'd taken Kim's advice and hired an assistant for me. There were several excellent candidates, but Tori Vázquez and I clicked in a way that, in my experience, is pretty rare. Fresh out of college, she's younger than I am, with blue hair and a passion for voter outreach and Mochi ice cream. She's definitely had her hands full since I quite traveling with the team, and she's risen to the challenge. She's also kind enough to humor me when I text her with ideas or suggestions.

It's been weird being off work. The campaign consumed so much of my life this year that sitting on the sidelines has been a huge adjustment, especially since Mac is still traveling with them. Between his frequent absences, Olivia leaving for college, and Tris's return to school, I have a lot of time on my hands. There's no shortage of things to do in a city like D.C. and there are all kinds of ways I might entertain myself if I weren't so obscenely pregnant. But I am, and my weekly outing for lunch and shopping with Mac's mom is about all I can manage.

Initially, boredom was a real problem. This is the first time since before my mom left that I've had so much time to myself—or any time to myself, really—and I didn't know what to do with it. In fact, that was what prompted me to finally spill the beans and tell everyone we were having twins. The predictable outpouring of shock and excitement was more entertaining than I'd expected. I also let Tris stay home from school one day so I'd have someone to talk to—I know, bad Mom—but now I've managed to adjust and learned something about myself in the process. After my maternity leave, I'm going back to work.

I didn't have a choice when Tris was born and it'd be easy to convince myself that I don't have one now. But I do, and Mac's been insistent that I acknowledge that. He's made it very clear that he'll support whatever decision I make, and it took me a while to accept that. Once I did, the answer became clear. I want to work, just not the way I did when I was twenty with three kids to support and no one else to help.

My phone vibrates in my hand, the buzzy ring of the doorbell camera notifying me someone's at the door. Mac installed it as a security measure long before I moved in, but I'm not going to lie, it comes in damn handy when you're up on the roof and don't want to make the trek down all those godforsaken stairs for a door-to-door salesman.

Opening the app, Stef's face resolves on the screen, and I activate the speaker with a smile. "Hey! Give me a minute and I'll be right down. I'm on the roof."

It'll take me long enough to get down three flights of stairs without having a conversation about it first, so I heave myself off the chaise lounge without waiting for her response. It's a pathetically arduous journey, and I'm hot-faced and wheezing by the time I swing the door open for her. "Hey."

I must look and sound as awful as I feel, because Stef's mouth draws down in a worried frown. "I'm so sorry, are you okay?"

"I'm fine. Just a little out of breath, you know?" I pat my stomach and roll my eyes to emphasize my point, but her strained expression doesn't ease, prompting me to ask, "Are you okay?"

"Is Mac here?"

The fine hairs on the back of my neck stand on end. It isn't like her to avoid a direct question, at least not without good reason. Her question strikes me as odd too. She must know if Mac were home, he would've spared me all those stairs and answered the door himself. "He's on a plane. On his way back from..." I can't remember and I wave one hand in frustration. "Wherever. What's going on?"

"Ohio. I flew back late last night myself." Stepping into the entry and closing the door behind her, she guides me toward the stairs as if I'm the guest. "You should probably sit down, and I'll get you a drink. This was his last trip with the campaign, wasn't it?"

Her conversational tone and warm smile aren't enough to mask the pinch of her eyes, and I haven't forgotten that she still hasn't told me what she's doing here. But if she's determined not to answer, she won't, so I concentrate on my breathing as we climb the one flight of stairs between us and the living room.

Once I'm settled in my favorite armchair—an enormous, over-stuffed thing that's as comfortable as it is impossible for me to get back out of on my own anymore—I answer her question. "Yeah. I have a doctor's appointment this afternoon. They're two a week now and he's still upset he couldn't make the one last Thursday, so he's taken himself off the road." He'll spend the next week doing what he can from home or the office and fielding more interviews on all the cable networks as a surrogate for Kim. Somehow the most embarrassing moment of our lives—that damn sex tape—ended up transforming the two of us into media darlings, and he's been in high demand ever since the convention. *Who'd have guessed?*

She hands me an ice-cold bottle of water she retrieved from the fridge and gives my belly a pointed look. "Well, and the twins could come any time now, right? He wouldn't want to miss it."

"Sure, I guess. But they aren't coming until after the election."

"Lord, but you're stubborn," Stef laughs and takes a seat on the end of the couch nearest me. She's dressed for work in charcoal slacks and a pale pink blouse, but that doesn't stop her from getting comfortable. Kicking off her fashionably high heels, she curls her legs under her and leans one elbow on the arm of the sofa.

"True, but they don't seem to be in any rush, either."

"How are you feeling?"

Why does everyone always ask that? My back aches and my hips are sore and I'd swear even my hair hurts. But no one wants to hear all that, so I plaster on a tired smile and say, "I'm hanging in there." She's pulled a throw pillow into her lap and is fidgeting with the fringe on its edge. Narrowing my eyes, I bluntly add, "Stef, why are you here?"

Her brows fly up in mock outrage. "What, I can't drop by to check on my very pregnant friend?"

If I stop and think about our unlikely friendship for too long, it feels a little weird. Mac and Stef were friends with benefits until my reunion with him. Awkward, right? But, unlikely as it might seem, Stef and I have forged a friendship of our own and have gotten to know each other pretty well after months on the campaign trail together. That's how I know this isn't just a social call. "You can. But you didn't. Or at least, that isn't the only reason you're here, so spill it."

She sighs but still isn't ready to give in. "I think maybe we should wait for Mac to get home. When does his plane land?"

If I were still capable of sudden movement, I'd probably lunge at her right about now and shake the answer out of her. Since I'm not, I check the clock on my phone. "About twenty minutes." If baggage claim and traffic both cooperate, he'll be home in an hour or so, and Stef surely realizes that. But even in my current state of limited physical mobility, I'm not without options for making her talk and in this case, I'm absolutely manipulative enough to use them. Frowning, I rub both hands over my stomach. "You're kind of stressing me out. Can't you tell me?"

"I'm sorry." She follows my movement for several seconds and then nods to herself and meets my eyes. "What do you know about Kim's daughter and granddaughter? Jess and Amelia?"

Dread surges, and I swallow hard against the bile in my throat. *She knows.* Maybe not the truth—almost certainly not the truth—but she knows something, and that means someone talked. Mac's dad. It has to be. Mac didn't and Jess wouldn't, and there are no other fucking options. Senior has gone to the press. It's the only possibility when reality damns him, and his one goal seems to be hurting his oldest son. If this impacts Kim's campaign, well, that's a bonus, but Mac's the real target. He always has been.

"You're the reporter, Stef. I think you'd better go first." The words come out colder—meaner—than I intend them, and her bright eyes cloud with hurt.

I feel bad because that wasn't what I meant. But my love for Mac is woven with too many years of heartbreak. Too many secrets we both kept for too long. Too many times I should've been there for him and wasn't. Should've protected him and didn't. Should've told him I love him and still haven't. Every instinct I possess is on high alert, screaming at me to protect, defend, guard. Even from Stef, who I'm confident would never intentionally harm either of us. She's a pawn in this, like the rest of us.

"I'm sorry. This is so awful. Awkward doesn't even begin to describe it." She puts her face in her hands, like she can't bear to look at me. "I don't even know if it's true, but if it is and you don't know—"

"I know." Her head flies up, startled, and I set aside the bottle of water she brought me. My palms are wet with condensation—or maybe sweat—and I wipe them on my dress before I continue. "I know what's true, so whatever you've heard, it's okay."

Stef takes a deep breath, followed by a long drink from her own bottle of water, but she still sounds agitated. "*Seek* will be publishing an expose on Mac in their Friday edition. They claim to have evidence that he's Amelia's father."

"Okay." I nod absently. A part of me always expected his dad to do this. Well, maybe not this exactly but somehow, he'd try and hurt Mac. It was a forgone conclusion, and I'm already calculating our next steps.

The situation could be a lost worse, to be honest. Jess is Kim's daughter, and Mac grew up with her. Even if they did secretly have a kid together—and they don't—that doesn't really reflect on Kim. Hell, these days, a lot of people won't even think it reflects on Mac or Jess. Still, it's salacious gossip so there'll be a lot of noise at first, but once the initial shock wears off, I bet everyone but the conspiracy theorists will move on pretty quickly. Besides, it's only Tuesday. Friday gives us time to try and get ahead of this. It's cutting it close to the election, but we should be able to mitigate the damage there, since this isn't relevant to Kim anyway. Mac will be furious, but we can figure this out. If he—

"That isn't all."

The wheels in my head come to a screeching, shuddering halt. "What?"

"I don't know where they've gotten any of this, but they're saying he's had a decades-long—and still ongoing—affair with both Kim and Jess. That's it's caused all kinds of drama in both families. I mean, they're making it out to be this huge thing, like it's some kind of reality TV show instead of real people's lives, and I know that part isn't true, Gwen. He would never cheat on you. Not ever."

"I know," I rush to reassure her, but I have to admit as much as I was expecting his dad to do something, this part has taken me by surprise. Maybe it shouldn't have. From his dad's perspective, if he's willing to lie about Amy's paternity, it isn't much of a stretch to fabricate more from thin air.

"And Amy? Is that true?" It isn't Stef Clark the reporter asking, it's Stef our friend, but even so, I can't tell her.

The truth will come out now. It has to. But it isn't my place. As angry as I was at Mac for trying to control the situation with the sex tape, I'd have to be a major asshole to turn around and do the same to him. *We have to deal with this together.* Which means it's my turn to start evading questions. "How did you find out about this?"

Stef scrunches up her face. "I have—had—a friend from college who works there. She doesn't know about…uh…our history, but she knows I've been covering Kim's campaign, so she called to see if I'd heard any rumors or know of anything concrete."

"What did you tell her?"

She arches one brow at me. "I played it cool. Acted surprised and said I hadn't heard anything remotely like that about any of them."

"Can you stop it? Would she can the story if you asked?"

"No." Stef shakes her head. "She says they have proof."

MAC

"WHAT KIND OF PROOF?"

Gwen and Stef were so absorbed in their conversation, neither of them noticed my arrival, and my question startles them. But instead of answering me, they both stare at me like I'm an alien making first contact instead of a dude coming home from a work trip to find his whole life imploding. *A-fucking-gain.*

"How much did you hear?" Gwen asks. She's struggling to heave herself out of her chair and failing pretty spectacularly. It'd be amusing if I didn't know how uncomfortable she is and, you know, if I hadn't heard their discussion. But I did, or enough of it.

Eager to be home and bothered by how miserable she'd sounded on the phone last night, I got an earlier flight this morning. I hoped an earlier than expected arrival might cheer her up a little, and it didn't even strike me as unusual when I let myself in and heard voices upstairs. Tristan's at school, of course, but it seems like everyone finds an excuse to check in on her while I'm gone, a fact that's eased a lot of my own anxiety about traveling. Except that's done now, and that's what I was thinking about—my relief and almost giddy happiness that I won't have to leave again before the twin's arrival—as I crested the stairs and recognized Stef's voice.

"Seek will be publishing an expose on Mac in their Friday edition. They claim to have evidence that he's Amelia's father."

I almost puked right there on the landing. Probably would've if Gwen's response hadn't been so strong and steady. So calm. She must've been upset, but she didn't make assumptions or jump to conclusions. She didn't get hysterical or freak out. She took a deep breath—one that I'll swear to my dying day I felt in my own chest— and asked for more information. I was momentarily awestruck by her strength.

Leaving my bags at the top of the stairs, I cross to Gwen's chair and squeeze her shoulder. "Don't get up. I heard enough." And then to Stef, "What proof do they think they have?"

Stef seems bolstered by my arrival. She was probably worried about upsetting Gwen, so it's understandable, and she slips into a more professional tone. Like we're two colleagues, working over a news story as we have a hundred times before. "The affair stuff is nonsense. Just a lot of pictures of you in what appear to be intimate situations with Kim or Jess or one of the others."

The emphasis she places on the word "others" isn't lost on me. In some ways, I've made this too easy for them. Before the hectic campaign schedule and Gwen and all the other changes she's brought to my life, I enjoyed the D.C. social scene. Maybe a little too much. There must be dozens of pictures of me taken over the years at various work events and charity fundraisers, and with few exceptions, I never took the same date twice. Hell, I even had a fucking sex tape scandal. Add it all up, and it gives an impression of me that makes the allegations about Kim and Jess easier for people to swallow.

I'm not tabloid gutter trash, but even I know how I'd do it if that's the story I wanted to tell. A few pictures of me with random women, a freeze frame from the parking garage video, and mixed among them photos of me with Kim or Jess. Hugs. Kisses on the cheek. My hand on Kim's back or Jess's arm around my waist. Woven with the other photos, those innocent moments of affection with women who are like family to me will seem like something else. But that isn't the worst of it, and I'm not sure I have the courage to ask about that.

My hand is still on Gwen's shoulder and she reaches up, resting her much-smaller hand on mine, her fingers gently squeezing. It's the push I need, except she saves me from that too. "And Amy? What's their evidence that he's her father?"

Stef drags in a deep breath, and I can tell she doesn't want to tell us or doesn't know how. But then she looks me square in the eye and says, "Your name is on her birth certificate."

What? No. How could that have even happened? Weak-kneed, I sit on the arm of Gwen's chair, and she leans into my side, her hand dropping to my leg. "They must've digitally altered it. Or they're lying. Have you seen it?"

The trust in her tone is almost as startling as Stef's revelation. How can she be so certain I didn't lie to her about Amy? Honestly, I wouldn't blame her for doubting me, and I'm not sure I could be so loyal if I were in her position right now. *I don't deserve her.*

"She emailed me a PDF," Stef explains. "It looks legit to me, but I don't know enough to be sure if it's been manipulated or not. We have a guy at the paper who's good at that. I could have him take a peek at it if you want?"

"No," I blurt. Right now, the last thing we need is more eyes on the evidence if we have any hope of controlling the story. Besides, I don't need an expert to tell me if the birth certificate is fake. I can go straight to the source. "I'll talk to Jess."

"Smart. She'll have the original." Gwen turns hopeful eyes on Stef. "If we can show it to them before they publish, they'll have to pull the story, won't they? They can't go ahead on fake evidence."

"Well…" Stef draws the word out, delaying the bad news. "Not really. They're a tabloid. They publish fake news all the time. They might leave the birth certificate out, but they'd still go ahead on nothing but innuendo. Or, they might take a gamble that Mac won't want to prolong the story by suing and use it anyway." She shrugs and shifts her gaze to me. "Assuming it's faked."

Always a reporter, Stef won't be one hundred percent certain until she's seen the evidence for herself. There isn't any point in trying to convince her, and to be honest, I'm not sure I care enough to try. It's her job to be cynical and demand corroboration. Being friends doesn't change that. Still, I say, "It's fake. It has to be. Unless immaculate conception really is possible, there's no way I'm Amy's dad."

"Finally." Stef's lips twitch, and she tips her head to one side, but her voice is a perfect deadpan. "Definitive proof you aren't in fact a god."

The grudging laugh that bubbles out of me feels strange and inappropriate, but it's a good reminder too. We'll get through this, and everything will be fine. There's no other option.

CHAPTER 8

MAC

HALF A DOZEN ATTEMPTED CALLS—ALL of which went straight to voicemail—and I'm left with no other option but to go to Jess's apartment and hope she's home. This isn't exactly a time when I can sit on my hands and wait, after all. But now I've been standing outside her door for almost five minutes because she isn't answering that, either. Strange, since her car is out front.

Just as I'm raising my fist to knock one last time, the door swings open, and Jess squints at me through watery eyes. She's pale, except for her alarmingly red nose, and her voice scratches. "Mac?"

"Are you all right?" *Has she been crying? Does she know?* No, how could she? Unless the same reporter who reached out to Stef called her. That's inevitable if it hasn't happened already.

"Yeah, yeah." Jess steps aside to let me pass and gestures to her face. "I've got this stupid sinus infection. I'm supposed to fly to Phoenix with Mom and the campaign on Friday but..." She closes the door behind me and finishes with a loud sigh. "I don't know if I'll be able to go now."

With two bedrooms and one bath, you can see the entirety of Jess's apartment if all the doors are open, as they are now. On my way into the living room, I scan the small space, searching for any sign of Amy. The coffee table is littered with tissues, a variety of boxes and bottles of over the counter medications, and a half-eaten sleeve of crackers— evidence enough she's ill—but Amy seems to be absent. She should be at school, but still, I can't risk that she might overhear the conversation to come. "Is Amy home?"

Jess flops down on the couch and pulls the blanket over her, tucking it under her chin. "No, she's at school. I swear, that kid never gets sick, and it isn't fair. All I've done is sleep for two days, and I still feel like day-old roadkill."

Lovely. That does explain why she didn't answer my calls, though. Not taking any chances she might be contagious, I choose the chair farthest from her. "If you need anything, you'll let me know?"

"I'm a big girl, Mac. I can take care of myself. Besides, I think you have enough on your plate these days without adding me to the list." She raises her brows, curiosity bleeding into her teasing tone. "What are you doing here, anyway? Shouldn't you be on TV reminding some cable news anchor how awesome my mother is or at home spoiling your very-pregnant girlfriend?"

"Gwen has a doctor's appointment this afternoon, so I can't stay long but...we need to talk." I feel like the world's biggest asshole, bothering her with this while she's sick, but *Seek*'s story will affect all of us. Even if I didn't need something from her, she deserves to know what's coming. "I'm sorry, but it can't wait."

"About what?" She pulls the blanket tighter under her chin, but she doesn't appear concerned.

"I've gotten a tip that a tabloid is working on a story about me. They're going to say I'm sleeping with...well, pretty much every woman I've ever met, including you and your mom. And they—"

I'm interrupted by the loud roar of her congested laughter. She almost sounds like she's wheezing. "That's ridiculous. No one will believe you're sleeping with me *and* Mom."

It does seem like they're overplaying their hand a bit. It'd be one thing to claim I was involved with one of them. Or even that I'd been with both of them at different times. Years apart. But mother and daughter at the same time? *Who does that?*

"Maybe, but that's not all." We've been lifelong friends, and there isn't much I can't talk about with Jess, but the words get stuck in my throat, anyway. Why is this so hard? *They're planning to say I'm Amy's dad.* See? Easy. Seven words that, providing we can insulate Amy from the gossip and fend off the political vultures, should be as funny as the idea that we're fucking. It's all ludicrous. But I can't quite form the words.

"What is it?" Jess pushes up on one elbow. The blanket falls away, and she pinches the skin at the base of her throat.

My hesitation is making this worse. *I'm* making it worse, and I don't even understand why. Ignoring the itch of trepidation crawling over me, I explain. "They think I'm Amy's father." Expecting more laughter or possibly anger, I pause, waiting for her response. It doesn't come, and an unfamiliar tension sucks all the oxygen from the room. *Did she not hear me? Or understand?* Whereas moments ago I struggled to get the words out, now they come tumbling from me in an involuntary rush. "They claim my name's even on her birth certificate. Obviously they or I guess their source faked it, so I figured the best thing to do would be to get the original so we can prove they're lying."

Their source. Why hadn't I thought about that until now? Probably because I already know who it is. Who it has to be. Dear old Dad. I have to admit, as much as I hate him and as little as I trust him, I never thought he'd do this. He must know there's a risk I'll expose him, although I'm not sure I will. I have to think this through. There are more important things at stake than even Kim's campaign or preventing my brother and mother from discovering the truth.

Things like Tris and Amy. I have no idea what Jess has told Amy about her paternity. I never had reason to wonder before. But if this comes out in the press…well, that's bound to screw with the poor kid, and that matters. A lot. Tristan too. What will he think when *Seek's* headline declares I have another kid? Gwen and I will have to prepare him for that. Somehow. Out of everyone else involved in this mess, he and Amy are the most likely to be hurt and the least deserving of that. We have to do everything we can to protect them.

"Mac." Jess's low voice draws my attention back to her. Sitting up, she leans forward, both arms clutched around her middle like her stomach aches. Without looking at me, she continues. "They aren't lying. I never planned to tell her... Well, I don't know—didn't know— what I'd tell her when she got old enough to ask. But the nurse kept talking about medical history and how important that is, and I thought..."

Anger thrums through me, and my hands tighten into fists in my lap. How could she do this? How could she ever think that was okay? But in its own way, it does make a strange sort of sense. I mean, it's inexcusable to do it without talking to me, but if the nurse was pressuring her, I can almost see why she did it. Still ... "You should've asked me before doing something like that."

She flinches, and there's a certain resentment in her tone that I've never heard from her before. "Would you have said yes?"

"I don't know." Except I do. It's been less than a year since Gwen told me about Tris, and it took me days to realize I wanted to be his dad. After all that angst over a kid who's actually mine, it's pretty goddamn safe to assume I wouldn't have agreed to let Jess put my name on Amy's birth certificate a dozen years ago. But I don't want to get into a conversation about it now. We can argue about her betrayal of my trust another time. Right this minute, the important thing is straightening this mess out as quickly as possible. "We'll need to get a paternity test. It's the only way to counter that birth certificate, and we're too close to the election now. We don't have enough time to make a counterargument and hope voters believe us. We need irrefutable evidence. I don't know how long those kinds of tests take. We probably can't get results in time to stop them from publishing. Hell, even if we did, they might decide to go ahead, anyway. But we'll need them as soon as possible so we can try and snuff this out before it has a chance to do lasting damage."

Jess turns her face to one side and chews her lower lip. She's going to regret that later. Her lips are already chapped enough from being sick. "Do you really think it matters? This has nothing to do with Mom or how good of a President she'd be. With Whitaker's third-party run, I thought Mom pretty much had this locked up?"

Frustration sizzles through me, but I take a deep breath, forcing myself to be patient. This is her life, her daughter, and it's all being threatened because of my dad. And sure, the choice she made is part of that too, but we can't change it now. All we can do is try and fix it. "We can't afford to take any unnecessary chances, Jess." Rubbing the back of my neck, I consider my words carefully before I continue. "And even if that weren't the case, we have to do this. I don't know what the legal ramifications of my name being on her birth certificate might be, but we both know I'm not her dad, and that needs to be corrected."

"That's the thing, Mac. You might be."

"What?" I don't know if it's her low tone—barely above a whisper —or the words themselves, but it's difficult to understand...or comprehend. *What the fuck is she talking about?*

"Do you remember Fourth of July that year?"

"Yes." An uneasy feeling ripples through me, and my blood's turned to sludge in my veins.

Between undergrad and grad school, I spent six years in Ann Arbor, and for the most part, all the various trips back home have run together, even the holidays. But a few stand out, and that's one of them. Kyle, one of our friends from high school, had a place on Rehoboth Beach—or rather, his parents did—and that Fourth of July, he hosted a legendary beach party. Truthfully, I was too wasted to recall every detail of that trip, especially after all these years, but I do know I spent the entire time pining for Gwen. We'd known each for less than a month at that point and both claimed we wanted to keep things casual, but I was already falling hard for a girl I hardly knew, and that's the whole reason that trip stands out from all the others. I didn't fuck anyone while I was home that week, and I especially didn't fuck Jess. Even then, Gwen was the only one I wanted. Just like she's the only one I want now.

"The last night we were at Kyle's parents place, out on the beach.

You—" Her voice cracks, and she puts her face in her hands. "We were all fucked up and we went skinny dipping." She pauses to drag in a ragged breath. Her hands are shaking. "God, we were fucking lucky no one drowned. It was so stupid. Do you remember?"

No. It sounds like the sort of reckless thing we might've done, though. But my mouth doesn't seem to be working, I can't form the words to tell her that. I can't even manage to shake my head. It's like I'm paralyzed.

She seems to understand. "It's okay. I know you don't remember a lot of that night." Wrapping the blanket around her shoulders, she gets up and paces toward the window. She keeps her back to me when she continues. "Someone brought coke, and you were really messed up. I'd never seen you quite like that before. Not that bad. And you know, I thought it'd be funny to hide your clothes. It was pretty hilarious, watching you stomp around the beach naked looking for your swim trunks, but the problem was, I was pretty fucked up too and couldn't remember where I hid them. We all looked for a while, but then everyone else got bored, I guess. You wouldn't give up, though, and I felt bad because it was my fault, so I stayed, thinking maybe I'd remember where I'd put them, or I could help you find them."

Until this very moment, I considered the night Gwen told me about Tris to be the most traumatic night of my life. It turned every-thing I thought I knew about myself and my life up to that point on its head. But this is so, so much worse, and I need it to be over. Clenching my hands on the arms of the chair, I speak through gritted teeth. "Go on."

"You kissed me, and you called me Gwen." Her voice catches in her throat. "You hadn't told me about her yet when you were sober. I had no idea who she was. But the way you said her name. God, I think I'd have given anything to have someone say my name like that. And you kept saying it, even when you…"

Her words trail off, or maybe they don't and I just can't hear them. All I know is somehow, I've found my way to the bathroom. Locking the door behind me, I bend over the toilet and puke until there's nothing left but regret and anger and shame. *So much fucking shame.*

~

MAC

"I'm so sorry, Mac."

I've barely gotten the bathroom door open, let alone stepped into the hall, when Jess's voice slams into me. Her tone is soft, plaintive, but every word hits like a baseball bat to the stomach.

"For what?" I shoulder by her into the living room, almost hoping she won't answer.

"For everything. For not stopping you that night." Her voice wobbles, and she's pinching her throat again. The skin is red and irritated like maybe she's been doing it the whole time I was in the restroom. "I know I shouldn't have let it happen, but I just...I thought I loved William, and he never treated me any better than he treated the rest of you, and I...I needed to feel like I mattered to someone."

In the intervening years, we've never talked about my father much. He'd hurt us both, and there was a certain comfort in simply knowing that, but we didn't need to rehash it every time we saw each other. Hearing her use his given name now brings me up short, though. Of course she would've called him William. They were intimate.

You fucked her too. You cheated on Gwen and fucked your dad's side piece and maybe got her pregnant, and you're such a shitbag you don't even remember it. My stomach cramps, but this time it's an empty threat because there's nothing left to purge, so I ignore it.

"He didn't care about me. But you did. I know, not like that. I didn't feel that way about you, either, but when you kissed me it felt... it felt like you did, and I was so desperate for affection, for sex that was more than just sex, you know? I couldn't make myself tell you to stop."

"I didn't fucking know who you were, Jess."

She flinches at my raised voice. "I know. I should've stopped it."

"What are the..." I know what I have to ask, but the words are jumbled in my head and I can't seem to put them together in a way that makes sense. "I mean, my dad... Did you... When was—"

Her brows draw together and she interrupts my floundering. "Are you trying to ask how likely it is that you're Amy's dad?" She waits for my nod and then sighs, her cheeks reddening. "I don't know. I was with your dad on Thursday, the night before we left for the beach, and you on Sunday."

I don't want to know any of this about my father, but I have to ask. "Did he use a condom?"

"No, never. He hated them."

What an asshole. If I ever have a daughter, that'll be the first thing I teach her about men. *Don't trust a man who whines about wearing a condom.* A flush washes over me, and my skin grows clammy. That might not be an "if I ever" scenario. I might already have a daughter. And I'm also a massive hypocrite. Tristan's very existence is proof enough of that. Although, at least I never complained about condoms —I just didn't use them sometimes with Gwen. Is that worse? I think maybe it is. And with that thought, another question occurs to me. One I hate having to ask and, worse, one I'm afraid I already know the answer to. "Did I?"

She shakes her head and whispers, "You pulled out, though."

Yeah, that sounds about right. That was my go-to maneuver with Gwen and apparently, I thought that's who I was with. Not that it's any excuse. A lot of women with unplanned pregnancies can attest to how fucking ineffective that is. Hell, I'm responsible for at least one and maybe two of them. *Could I be any bigger of a fuck-up?*

"God, the look on your face. I'm so sorry. Just..." She reaches out to touch my arm, I think, but I jerk away, and she pulls her hand back with a wounded frown. "Just don't blame yourself, okay? I was really fucked up, and I took advantage of you when you were so drunk and high you didn't even know who I was. That isn't your fault. And it isn't your fault that I didn't tell you the next day. Or when I found out I was pregnant."

I'm fairly clear on all the ways she's responsible. All the things she shouldn't have done or, in the absence of that, should've done differently. But she's wrong; I'm at least partly responsible. If I weren't such a stupid, self-indulgent asshole back then—and maybe still, if I'm being honest with myself—I never would've put myself in that position in the first place.

And while I sort of understand, as wrong as it was, why she might've had sex with me that night, I still can't quite grasp why she never told me, especially once she realized she was pregnant. For one thing, telling me would've taken the heat off her about the identity of the baby's father. My dad wouldn't have objected if she'd announced we'd been fooling around and she'd gotten knocked up. In fact, it would've taken the heat off him too. Win-win for everyone but me, who'd have never been the wiser. It doesn't make sense, but before I can ask her to explain, she's started talking again.

"I knew what I was doing with your dad was wrong, I knew he didn't care about me and that it wasn't healthy for me, but I'd gotten so wrapped up in him. He treated me like shit, and I still thought the world revolved around him. I was young and stupid and I kept going back for more. God, I was so fucking stupid. That night before we went to Kyle's, he'd picked me up at my friend's house. She used to cover for me when I was meeting him. Shelly. Do you remember her?"

I manage to croak out a yes, but I don't care. I don't even want to be hearing this, but now that she's started, Jess seems intent on spilling her guts and I can't seem to muster the strength to stop her.

"After we…" Her hands flutter in front of her and she starts again. "Afterward, William asked me for her phone number. I guess it was the first time he'd seen her, and he liked what he saw, but I was…" She shakes her head, frustrated with her younger self and maybe embarrassed too. "I was naive. Until that moment, I hadn't realized I wasn't the only one."

"He was married." *Seriously. What the fuck?* "To my mother."

"Yeah." She grimaces. "The only other one, I mean. I had no right to be, but I was jealous. He didn't like that much, and he ended it. We didn't speak again until I told him I was pregnant. He offered me money for an abortion, and I told him no, I wanted to have the baby."

This part isn't new; it's more or less how I remember him telling me about it too. "But you still didn't tell me."

"I should've, but…it was humiliating, Mac. The first time I saw you the morning after, you were in the kitchen eating breakfast with some of the other guys and telling them all about this girl you'd met at college and how anxious you were to get back to her. I've never forgotten what you said. 'Don't worry, boys, I'm never gonna settle down, but if any woman was ever worth it, she'd be the one.' They all laughed, but I knew you well enough to know how much you must care about her to even make a joke like that. So I was embarrassed that you didn't remember, and I didn't want to mess things up for you with Gwen if she did turn out to be something special."

She gives me a meaningful stare that seems to imply that was the right call, since Gwen and I are back together now. But I'm not so sure we will be after this. In fact, I'm almost certain we won't be, and I'm not in the mood for cutting Jess any slack. "That's bullshit. Gwen's got nothing to do with this, and we both know it. You were avoiding me, and Dad told me you were pregnant when I came home for Thanksgiving. She'd already split by then. I had no way to contact her and no reason to think I'd ever see her again, and I'd left a dozen pathetic voicemails for you whining about how broken up I was over her, so no, you don't get to use Gwen as some kind of fucking shield here."

That seems to have sparked her anger, and she glares at me. "I meant that's why I didn't tell you when I first found out. Yes, by then I knew it was over with Gwen, but you have to understand, when I refused to get an abortion, William suggested I sleep with you." I must look alarmed, because she hastily adds, "I never told him what happened with us. Never. But he said if I was determined to keep the baby, that's what I needed to do. He said you do most of your thinking with your dick and if I acted quickly enough and didn't tell you I was already pregnant, it wouldn't be any trouble to convince you the baby was yours. He even tried to buy me a plane ticket to go up to Michigan and see you." Her anger has burned itself out, and she's pensive when she adds, "I think that was the first time I realized what a horrible human being he is. I mean, what kind of person tells a woman she should trap his own son?"

"Except it wouldn't have really been a trap, would it, since she could be mine?" I've never been claustrophobic in my life, but saying those words aloud, the room feels like it's pressing in on me. Even the air is heavy. I have to get out of here. "I can't..." *Breathe.* "I have to go."

CHAPTER 9

GWEN

My doctor's appointment went as well as could be expected. Still textbook perfect, the babies and I are all healthy, and there's no indication that labor is imminent. All good signs, as long as I ignore Mac's absence.

Considering Stef's bombshell and where he was headed when he left home, I wasn't that surprised when he texted that he couldn't make it. Maybe Jess keeps Amy's original birth certificate in a safe deposit box and they had to go pick it up. Or maybe she lost it and they had to go to the Department of Health's office to pick up a new, certified copy. Whatever the case, I wasn't concerned. But something about the text message itself—*Sorry. Can't make it.*—bothered me, and it isn't until I'm back home that I figure out why.

Ever since our reckoning after the sex tape, he's ended every text conversation with a declaration of his love, even if sometimes he was in a hurry and it came in the form of a cheesy gif or a heart emoji. As far as I can tell, he hasn't even registered the fact that I have yet to say it back, and it hasn't impacted his willingness to share his feelings. But there was no emoji or anything else today, and it feels wrong.

I hate that I'm reading so much into it too. It's unfair of me to get wound up over a stupid text message he sent in a rush. *It's nothing. No big deal. Stop worrying.* But no matter how I try to convince myself, I can't shake the uneasy sense of foreboding that message aroused.

"Here's your salad." Willa offers me a bowl piled high with several kinds of lettuce, chicken, and just about every vegetable known to man. There are hard-boiled eggs and bacon bits too, and the whole thing is smothered in honey-mustard dressing.

I called her on my way home from the doctor's office and, as she has many, many times since I moved out of our apartment, she invited herself over for dinner. In the beginning, I thought she came over so much because she missed us. I still think that but, middle child or not, she's a mother hen and the closer I get to having the babies, the more she seems to hover. The fact that she's the one who made dinner for us even though we're at my place supports that theory. Resting the bowl on my belly—one of the few benefits of being this pregnant—I frown at it. "I'll never eat all this."

She's taken a seat across from me, tucking her legs under her and curling protectively around her own bowl, like she's afraid I might take it from her. "You said, and I quote, 'I want the biggest salad anyone has ever seen for dinner. I'm talking *Guinness Book of World Records* big, and don't skimp on the tomatoes. The acid reflux will be worth it.' I believe you even said something about literally dying if I didn't put enough dressing on it."

Yeah, okay, that does sound familiar, but now, with this enormous salad in front of me and worrying about where Mac is and why I still haven't heard from him, my appetite seems to have vanished. I do need to eat something, though, if for no other reason than to keep my sister from fussing at me, so I poke through the mound of lettuce, searching for the best bites. Bacon. Tomato. Bacon. Bacon.

Willa sucks on a cherry tomato like some kind of vegetable vampire before tucking it into her cheek so she can ask, "Are you sure your appointment went all right? You seem grumpier than usual today."

"Everything was fine. It's just..." I hesitate, unsure if I should confide in her. All the dirty laundry is about to get aired in a national tabloid. What could it hurt to tell her now, a few days early, when she'll find out about it soon, anyway? But Mac wouldn't like it and I think, despite our conversation with Stef earlier, he might still be holding out some hope he can keep a lid on this. I know I am. And if we can't, he'll want to control the situation as much as possible. I shouldn't take that away from him when these are his family secrets in the first place.

But Willa's always been my sounding board. Thoughtful and wise beyond her years, I probably started venting to her long before she was old enough to fairly do so. She never complained and, I think, in some ways she appreciated being included. To be honest, other than Mac, she's the only one I want to talk to about this, and he isn't here.

Mind made up, I glance toward the stairs to make sure Tris is still up in his room. The last thing I need is for him to overhear what I'm about to say. When I turn back to my sister, she's watching me with apprehension, so I start by reassuring her. "Everything's okay. I'm sure of it. But there's some stuff going on...with the campaign and Mac's family...and it's kind of upsetting. I feel horrible talking to you about this but...I don't know, I can't stop worrying and I'm sure I'm making a big deal out of nothing, but I guess I need you to tell me that."

Setting her bowl on the end table next to her chair, Willa leans forward, planting her feet on the floor and her elbows on her knees. "What's up?" Her serious expression belies the casual tone of her voice.

"You remember Kim's daughter Jess and her granddaughter Amy?" Willa hasn't spent a lot of time with us when we're working, not like Olivia did before she left for college, so in an effort to jog her memory I add, "They were here for the party on Memorial Day."

"Yeah, I guess." She shrugs, obviously wondering what this has to do with anything.

"Well." I stare at my food, nudging a chunk of cucumber around the edge of the bowl with my fork. Between my guilt over sharing a secret that isn't mine and worrying about her reaction, I can't look at her and I force the words passed a painful lump in throat. "On Friday, a tabloid is going to publish an article claiming that Mac is Amy's father. He isn't but, you know, the muckrakers will do anything for a story, especially connected to a campaign so close to an election. So he went to meet up with Jess, to get a copy of the birth certificate and figure out how to deal with this but now...he was supposed to be back in time to go to the doctor's with me, but other than a quick text to tell me he wouldn't make it, I haven't heard from him."

"Of all the things, why would they make that up? Where would they have even gotten the idea?" The doubt in her voice is hard to miss, but I appreciate that she's found a way to express it without explicitly calling Mac a liar or me an idiot for believing him.

"Amy's actual father is...not a nice person." Mac and I didn't discuss it earlier, didn't needed to. There's only one person who could be behind this. "He's trying to cause problems for anyone he can in any way he can."

"So you know who her father really is?" Out of the corner of my eye, I watch her relax back into the cushions, more at ease.

"Yes. It's...not a good situation." Having said that much, I hesitate. Knowing Mac, he'll still try to find a solution to this mess that doesn't expose his father. Not for Senior's benefit but for everyone else's. Willa's never broken my trust and she won't now. I'm as certain of her as I am of anyone. And yet...I can't tell her.

"But you won't tell me." When I shake my head, Willa sighs. "This must be so stressful. I'm sorry you're going through this right now. I mean, it would be awful any time, but now..." She flings one hand toward my stomach. "But I'm sure Mac will get it sorted out and everything will be fine."

"I know." My voice cracks and my nose stings with the futile effort it takes to hold back the unexpected tears that are already wetting my cheeks.

What the hell is wrong with me? She's right—everything's going to be okay. I'm being a ninny, and it's only more irritating after everything else I've been through. For more than a decade I was a single mother raising my son and my sisters, going to school, and working myself to the bone at dead-end jobs to support us all. That was adversity, and from where I sit now, nestled in my favorite chair in Mac's townhouse with money in the bank and a good support network, I've got nothing to complain about. So why do I feel so awful?

"Oh, honey." Willa's gotten out of her chair and come to lean over me, giving me an awkward hug. "It's going to be okay, but if it makes you feel better, when Mac turns up, I'll kick his ass for making you worry."

That coaxes a tearful laugh from me. "I'd do it myself, but you know..."

"Yeah," She smiles and pats my stomach. "You're gonna have to wait a little longer before you can administer any personal ass-kickings. But I've got you 'til then."

"You're the best." She straightens, and I grab her hand, communicating my thanks with a squeeze. "Will you stay until he gets home?"

"Obviously. How else would I beat him up?"

MAC

Sprawled on the couch in my office, one foot planted on the floor to keep the room from spinning, I raise the bottle of scotch to my mouth. It isn't the good stuff I keep locked in my desk for special occasions or the most important clients. This is the cheap shit that burns all the way down my throat, and I relish the sensation. It's the only thing I've felt in hours, much like the ceiling is the only thing I've seen. I can't even close my eyes, because then I see Gwen. Tristan. A barrage of ultrasounds. Olivia's mischievous grin when she was being a pain in the ass. Willa's calm and steady presence when...well, always. Even Diane with her sly smile and dry wit is there, and I can't bear any of it. *Nobody ever said wallowing in your own miserable existence would be easy.*

With a derisive snort, I mumble to myself, "Jesus, I'm fucking pathetic."

"I've never thought so before, but you're making a pretty good case for it now."

Alex has been leaning against the door frame watching me for...eh, I'm not sure. My grasp on time is pretty weak. A while though, and I've been ignoring him for just as long. If he wants to stare like I'm a zoo animal it's no skin off my nose, but if he's going to start talking, that changes things. The ungrateful shit hasn't spoken to me about anything but work in months, and I'm sure as hell not up for another battle with him about our waste-of-oxygen father. "Fuck off."

"You first."

I lift my head off the arm of the couch and squint, trying to focus my fuzzy gaze on him. *Christ, has he gotten taller since the last time I saw him?* "What are you doing here?" My throat is raw and my voice rasps, a consequence of cheap liquor and a lot of puking.

"Jess called me." His tone is so matter-of-fact the words don't register at first.

Once they do, it isn't hard to imagine how that conversation went. *I told your asshole older brother he might be Amy's father. He puked and ran out of here like a coward.* He's probably here to chew my ass for being such a fuck-up. He might even rub my nose in it. "So?"

"So...she said you were upset, and she was worried about you being alone and wanted me to find you. When I asked what could've upset you so much, she said I'd have to ask you, so you're going to have to tell me that part."

"I don't have to tell you shit."

"No, you never have, have you? Why start now?"

"Fuck. Off."

"You already said that. If this is how it has to be, could you at least be more creative about it?"

"Fuck you."

"I suppose I asked for that, didn't I?" Alex sighs and steps further into the room, his long strides bringing him to the couch with alarming speed.

It was a little weird when we were teenagers and he first outgrew me. I'm the older brother; I should be bigger, right? I got used to it pretty quickly, once I realized the benefits. Like, I never had to worry about other kids at school fucking with him. He wasn't any kind of fighter but with his size, no one was willing to take a chance on finding that out for themselves. But now he's looming over me like… like…the jolly green giant, and it's irritating. "Go away."

"No." Alex shrugs out of his coat and tosses it over the back of one chair before folding himself into the one nearest me. "You don't have to talk to me. In fact, I might prefer you don't. But someone needs to make sure you don't drink yourself to death, and I guess tonight that's me."

It's on the tip of my tongue to tell him I'm not going to die. In my misspent youth I drank…and smoked…and occasionally snorted…a hell of a lot more than this, and it all turned out fine. *Except, it didn't, did it?* Bile and scotch slosh in my stomach in answer.

"Before I allow you to sink back into your stupor, you need to call Gwen. She's worried about you."

He's right. It was a dick move to bail on her doctor's appointment with a text message and, even worse, I haven't responded to any of her texts since. *Everything went well with Dr. Williams. How's it going with Jess?* And, when I didn't answer that, a handful of messages asking me to call or text or something, anything. People say texts are terrible for conveying emotion. That it's easy to misunderstand typed words on a screen. Not so with Gwen's. The plaintive tone of her voice comes through loud and clear. She's worried, like Alex said, and the guilt of having upset her gnaws at me. "You've talked to her?"

"Yes. I stopped by the house to see if you were there first. Willa's with her, and I guess if you don't turn up, Diane's coming over too once she finishes her shift."

Good. Willa's good. She'll take of Gwen.

I must've said that out loud, because Alex scowls at me. "She wouldn't need to if you'd do the right thing and call Gwen back. Or even text her. Don't you think you owe her that much?"

Yes, and a hell of a lot more. But I can't do it. I can't tell her what I've done. And even if I did find a way to tell her, she'd never forgive me. Not after everything else. Not after I told her Amy was my dad's daughter. She never doubted me once, even when Stef told her about that damn birth certificate. And it was all a lie. There's no coming back from this and hard as it is, cruel as it might seem, the best thing I can do for her now is give her a clean break. Just like the one she gave me a dozen years ago. "I can't, Alex. I can't face her. Just… Can't you text her and let her know I'm not dead?"

"I already did, as soon as I found you, but she needs to hear from you. You're the one she loves."

She loves me. Did she tell him that? She hasn't said it to me, but I didn't need her to say the words to know it was true. She's so scared of being hurt, and it's hard for her to make herself vulnerable. Sure, it would've been nice to hear, but I know how she feels, because every morning, no matter what else was happening, she woke up and decided to stay. She was damn brave to take a chance on me and see how I've repaid her? I'm a chip off the old block, just like my dad.

"Jess says I might be Amy's dad." Hoping the scorch of cheap booze will dull the sharp edges of the words, which feel like they've sliced their way out of me, I follow my confession with another gulp of scotch. By the time I lower the bottle, Alex still hasn't spoken, and I crane my neck around to make sure he heard me. Did he fall asleep? Die of shock? No, he's dumbfounded but otherwise fine. And maybe… Jesus, is that bastard about to laugh?

"This was news to you?"

"Yes."

That, finally, seems to surprise him. He draws his brows together, studying me, and speaks slowly. "Then you didn't want to see it."

Tell him. This time, it isn't my dad's voice taunting me. It's Gwen's, and there's nothing taunting about it. I gulp from the bottle once again in hopes of chasing it away or drowning it out. No dice. Closing my eyes when I swallow is a mistake too; I can even see her face, her firm but gentle smile encouraging me. *Tell him.* "I thought she was Dad's." I've surprised myself by saying it and shift my gaze away, unable to watch his reaction. "She still might be."

"Don't be ridiculous. Dad and Jess never—"

His immediate denial pisses me off, and I interrupt him with an angry snarl. "Yeah, they did."

"But…" That single word holds so much hope, it makes my stomach clench. He doesn't want to believe me. It'd be easier to think I'm lying. That this is how I've rationalized my own failures.

As painful as it is to watch him grapple with this new information, I resent it too. He's still trying to make me the bad guy, to find excuses for Dad. "You always wanted to know. Well, that's the big secret. Dad and Jess had an affair for almost a year and, until today, I thought Amy was our half sister."

Alex leans toward me and snatches the bottle from my feeble grasp, raising it to his own mouth. He's always been more a wine-and-beer kind of guy and he coughs on the first gulp, but that doesn't deter him from taking a long, deep drink. It reminds of that night earlier this summer when I taught him how to smoke a joint and tried to find a way to make peace with him about our dad without sharing details he's better off not knowing. It didn't work, but maybe this time will be different. Lowering the bottle, he passes it back to me and says, "I think you'd better start at the beginning."

CHAPTER 10

MAC

I HATE WAKING up and not recognizing where I am. It's only happened a few times in my life, all when I was much younger and, I'd like to think, much stupider, but apparently that's not the case, because here I am, sprawled across an unfamiliar bed in the same clothes I flew home from Ohio in yesterday.

Fuck, I hope that was just yesterday.

Why is everything in this room white?

Where the hell am I?

There aren't a lot of clues. Stark white walls. A warm, fluffy, but also very white comforter. White bedside tables and an upholstered white headboard. It's too sterile, not to mention too difficult to keep clean for even a hotel. There are no personal effects, except my keys and wallet, which I must've discarded on the—yes, of course, white—dresser the night before. No knickknacks or vases of flowers. There aren't even any pictures. Ignoring the throb in my temples, I tip my head back to check the wall over the bed and... *Oh, Christ.*

Hanging prominently over the bed is a stretched white canvas framed in black. It isn't a painting or a photograph; it's just...blank canvas, and I know exactly where I am, which is only somewhat a relief.

Alex's condo. When he bought it, he hired an interior designer to decorate it for him, because my brother cares about that sort of thing. The results were...well, a lot like this bedroom, although I've never been in it before. There was never any need to stay over with my own place a few miles away.

Ignoring the parts of yesterday I don't want to think about, I pick through my hazy memories of the office. Going there because I couldn't face Gwen and had nowhere else to go. Alex showing up. Telling him...*Jesus, fuck. I told him everything.*

I started with the night I met Gwen. That she was a one-night stand. I didn't know her name but couldn't get her out of my head. How happy I was when I ran into her again. How happy I was that whole summer with her and how broken I was when she disappeared.

I told him about coming home that Thanksgiving. About Jess avoiding me and Dad telling me why and asking me to bully her into an abortion. Alex was confused and a little repulsed by the idea that Dad and I slept with the same woman. He didn't understand why I hadn't considered Amy might be mine or why I'd sleep with Jess when I was already gone for Gwen. But if I was going to tell him everything, I needed to do it in the order I experienced it, not the order it really happened. In my intoxicated state, it seemed like the only way he could understand.

I explained how it always was with Dad. How for as long as I can remember, he never liked me. And then, when I was still younger than Tris, I heard him arguing with Mom about another woman. Later, he didn't even try to hide his affairs from me. If I complained about it, he'd call me a self-righteous prick and insist I was no different. But even knowing all that, I was shocked when he told me Jess was pregnant. She was more than half his age and practically family. How could he have done such a thing, with her of all people? Any hope I had that we might someday repair our relationship evaporated when he asked me to convince her to get rid of it. He was a vile, worthless person, and I didn't want anything to do with him...except to protect Alex and Mom from him to whatever extent I could.

And I told him about Stef's visit. About *Seek* and the birth certificate. About going to Jess's and everything she told me. From there, my memory gets even fuzzier. We were both drunk by that point, and I have a faint memory of the sun peeking over the horizon as we stumbled out onto the street to hail a cab and come back here.

Wincing against the pain behind my eyes, I turn my head on the pillow and search for a clock but don't find one. I'm in hell. I must be. No, just Alex's condo, which is at least interior decorator hell.

My phone is across the room with my wallet, and I get out of bed to retrieve it with slow, deliberate movements that'd make the feeblest octogenarian look like an Olympian. The screen is too bright, though, and I sit back down on the end of the bed, squinting against the glare with a distressed groan.

"Does that sound mean you're up?" Alex asks through the closed door.

"No." I flop backward on the bed and regret it when the room tilts wildly.

"Too fucking bad." The door cracks open, and he pokes his head through. The asshole doesn't even have the decency to look hung over. "We have a lot to do today, and it's almost noon. You need to drag your lazy ass out of bed and come eat something so we can get started."

I do have a lot to do today, don't I? I should talk to Gwen. Explain what I've done. And Kim too. I'm not capable of planning the campaign's response to *Seek*'s article, but I have to let her know it's coming so she can put someone else in charge of managing the situation. Brian and Alex, probably. And then...then I want to be fucking numb. In fact, why wait? "Do you have any tequila?"

"Not for you." His admonishing tone is irritating and I'm on the verge of saying something ridiculous, something like "you aren't the boss of me," but he doesn't give me the opportunity. "Come on, Juana's waffles are getting cold."

"She's here?" I don't want to face the family maid today. She's too tied to the rest of them. Too much like family herself, and I'm too fucking ashamed to look her in the eye. Not even the buttermilk waffles she's been making since I was a kid can tempt me out there if she's waiting.

"No, but they were in the freezer. I just have to toast them. You know, like homemade Eggos."

Another time, I would've made fun of him for that. I'm by no means an expert in the kitchen, but I've managed to learn to feed myself. Alex, not so much. As far as I know, he'd starve to death if it weren't for Juana and the plethora of restaurants in D.C., but I don't have it in me to mock him today.

He also isn't going to go away until he gets what he wants, so I force myself from the bed and shuffle out to the kitchen after him. "I'm not going to eat. Don't think I could keep it down." Gingerly lowering myself into one of the chairs at his table, I glare at the waffle he's already placed on a plate in front of me. "But I'm up. Is that good enough for you?"

"It's a start." He pours himself a cup of coffee and leans against the counter, watching me. "So, here's where we're at. I've already called *Seek*'s in-house counsel this morning and threatened them with a lawsuit on any number of grounds. Honestly, some of it was a stretch, but—"

"What the fuck, Alex?" Is he out of his mind? The only legitimate standing we'd have for suing them would be defamation, and that doesn't apply if it's fucking true. Or if they had reason to believe it was true, and with the birth certificate, they've got that. My brother browbeating the publisher about their upcoming story and throwing around baseless legal threats gives it legitimacy. And if he didn't think to tell them the call was off the record, they'll have some juicy quotes from him to add when they go to press. *Not fucking good.*

But Alex talks right over me. "I told them I'd go back through every article they've ever published. I'd find every person they'd ever wronged and finance their lawsuits. *Seek* has plenty of victims out there, people who are in a better legal position than you are to bring suit but lack the resources. I told their counsel that if they went ahead with this story, I'd personally provide those resources and that I didn't care if I bankrupted myself in the process. It would become my life mission to end them. Professionally, personally. Fucking spiritually, if I can figure out a way to do it. So, they've decided it isn't in their best interest to run the story."

Holy fucking shit, my little brother's a stone-cold motherfucker. Brilliant, but tough and ruthless, and I'm the fucking idiot who never noticed before. Too stunned for anything else, I force a nod, and he continues. "With that threat neutralized, I called Kim. I told her we had a family situation and you and I would both be unavailable for the foreseeable future. Probably until after the election. She was concerned but didn't press, so you and Jess will still need to figure out what you want to tell her and when. Which brings me to my next point. I've scheduled the necessary appointments for a paternity test. I thought it might be important for the clinic to know there were two potential fathers who were themselves father and son, and it's a good thing I mentioned it, because they said in this situation the probability of a false positive is quite high if you aren't both tested. So, you have an appointment to get your cheek swabbed this afternoon. I've spoken to Jess and she's taking Amy in first thing tomorrow morning, and I've scheduled an appointment for Dad tomorrow afternoon."

"Does Dad know that?"

"Not yet, but I'll handle it. The clinic assured me the lab will have the results by Monday, which is the soonest I could find."

There's no fucking way Dad will agree to a paternity test. None. Although in fairness to Alex, I wouldn't have thought he'd be able to strong-arm *Seek* into killing their story either, so...maybe? But still, highly unlikely, and my head is spinning, not just from the hangover or my new worry about a false positive test result if Dad doesn't cooperate. Where the hell did Alex find the time and energy to do all of this? He might not have been as drunk as I was last night, but he was pretty fucking drunk. "How... I mean... When the hell did you get up?"

Alex shrugs. "My internal alarm clock is a bastard. I wake up at five-thirty no matter what. Today, I figured I could put that time to good use. So I took an aspirin, drank about a gallon of water, and got started." He gestures to the glass in front of me. "Now it's your turn."

"It isn't your job to fix my life," I point out before taking a tentative sip of the water. It settles fine, so I take a longer drink before setting the glass down. "You can't fix this."

"I'm aware of that." He straightens, his shoulders squared. "But I can help you fix it, so say thank you and eat your damn breakfast."

Yeah, he's done more than he had to already to help me out—more than I deserve—and he's right. I'm coming off like an unappreciative asshole. So I thank him, but as soon as those two words are out of my mouth, he leaves the room, abandoning me at the table like a toddler refusing to eat his peas. I have to respect that, because we both know I wasn't done arguing about the stupid waffle.

IN THE END, I ate the whole waffle and I'm still staring at the empty plate, surprised I got it down and even more surprised it hasn't come back up, when Alex returns, keys in hand. He holds them up, shaking them until they jangle, and the discordant sound makes me twitch. "Where are we going?"

"Where do you think?"

Home. Gwen. I should've gone straight back to her when I left Jess's apartment yesterday. The fact that I didn't is reason enough for her to never forgive me. But I don't know how to tell her what's happened, and until I do, we're in limbo. That isn't a great place for our relationship to be, especially when the twins could arrive at any time, but it's better than over, which is what we'll be once we talk. Frozen in my seat, I must seem like a deer in the headlights. "I don't know what to say to her."

He shrugs. "You'll figure it out. And we'll take the long way."

The long way? It's four miles. But I recognize the determined glint in his eyes, even if I hadn't realized before today how unrelenting he can be. From the look of him, if I resist, he's apt to try and wrestle me into the car. I narrow my eyes and consider that. He might be bigger, but there's no question I'm the better, more experienced fighter. I bet I—

"I know what you're thinking and yes, you probably could take me." He crooks his hand at me in a universal gesture that I instantly understand. *Bring it.* "But I don't think you want to do that. For one thing, you know I'm right. It's gonna suck, but there's no way around it and the longer you put it off, the worse it's going to be. And second of all, fighting with me isn't going to solve anything. It might even make things worse, especially between us, and you know what I think?" Struck mute, I shake my head and he continues. "I think you love me too much to blow things up now. That's why you never told me about Dad, right? Because you love me and were trying to protect me? Well, what good was all the fucking misery keeping it a secret caused if you're going to shit on me now, when it's my turn to try and help you?"

"You're right. I'm sorry." It's really something, realizing—on top of Jess's revelation—how selfish I've been. *Am being.* Like, I can recognize I'm acting like a dick but I don't know how else to be right now—I'm not even sure I know who the fuck I am anymore, in a world where I cheated on Gwen with a woman I thought of like a sister. That sure as fuck isn't something I ever thought I'd do. Is Alex as uncertain of me now as I am of myself? "You know I'd never hit you, right? I was thinking about it, like you said, but it was just—"

"Something else to think about. You were distracting yourself from all this other shit. I get it." He claps me on the shoulder and we walk toward the door together but he doesn't say anything else until we've reached the parking garage and we're both in the car, our seatbelts buckled. Turning the engine over, he gives me a sidelong look. "I've been thinking about some stuff too and I have a couple of things to say before we get there."

There's a strange note in his voice, and I can't tell if he's about to chew my ass or get weirdly emotional with me. Not that either one is a bad thing. He has every right to be angry with me and if he wants to have a heart to heart conversation, that's understandable too. But either way, I'm still so numb and uncertain of myself I don't know how to react or respond. *Why am I so bad at this?* Swallowing hard, I stare straight ahead, bracing myself for whichever way it goes. "Okay."

"I understand now why you didn't want to tell me about Dad. I get it. I still wish you had, but…" He pauses long enough to back out of his parking spot then shrugs, fiddling with the buttons on his steering wheel when he continues. "I wish you'd told me, but I might not have done it any differently if I were you."

"Thanks, man." That admission means more to me than he can probably imagine. I'm still not sure I did the right thing. But I chose a course of action and, sure or not, stuck to it because I didn't know what else to do. That my brother understands that and might have even done the same thing is huge and if nothing else, it means maybe our relationship can grow and become something better now that it's all out in the open. That's a silver lining I hadn't expected and right now, when everything else is falling apart, I need it.

He nods and throws the car into gear, easing through the parking garage with the caution of someone who's only recently learned to drive. "Do you think Mom knows?"

"She caught him once, when I heard them arguing, but that was close to thirty years ago. I have no idea if she knows he's still doing it. She doesn't act like it."

"She could be pretending not to know."

"That's what I've always assumed. I'm sure she doesn't suspect Amy is…" I stumble over the words but manage to correct myself. "Might be his."

"No, she assumed she's yours, like the rest of us did."

I'd always known that was the case. Or suspected it, anyway. Still, hearing him confirm it is strange. The way he's framed it, there's no equivocation or guessing. He knows exactly what Mom thinks, which means they've talked about it. "No one ever even asked me."

"I'm sorry." His voice is tight, like his throat's being squeezed, and the apology seems genuine. It isn't necessary, though, and in a way, it makes me feel worse. I knew what they thought and I never brought it up, either. I let them go on believing it because it was easier. Until it wasn't, and that isn't Alex's fault.

"It's fine." Clearing my throat, I turn toward the window before adding, "It turns out you all might've been right, after all."

"Yeah, about that." Alex hesitates, concentrating on the traffic before pulling out of the garage and onto the road. "When I called Jess about setting up a paternity test, she asked how you were. I told her you were fine but if she wanted to know more, she'd need to talk to you, if you were willing to talk to her."

That surprises me and I turn in my seat to stare at him. I mean, I'm not happy with Jess right now, and when—if—I ever manage to get my bearings again, there are a few things I'll have to say to her. I'll never trust her again, either, not like I did before. But cutting her out of my life seems like an overreaction. Besides, if Amy does end up being mine, I'll have to talk to Jess, won't I? "Why wouldn't I be?"

"Mac, what she did was…" His voice is strained, worse than it's been all morning, and I don't understand why he's gotten so tense. His shoulders are almost touching his ears, for God's sake.

"No different from what I did. We were both young and stupid and blitzed off our asses."

"Yeah, but…"

"But what? She kept it a secret all this time? I did that too. And so did Gwen, for that matter."

Alex blows out a frustrated breath. "My point was, however you want to handle the situation, that's up to you, and whatever you decide, I'll back you." He taps his hand against the steering wheel and looks at me from the corner of his eye before refocusing on the car ahead of us. "No, I guess that's not true. I'm not sure I ever want to see her again, and I'm not sure how I'll deal with that if she remains in your life in some capacity."

It's hard to think about the future when the present feels so much like a blackhole, but it's worse than that, because right here, in this moment, I can't quite grasp why he's so upset. And since he's apparently angry on my behalf, shouldn't I know why? "I don't get it."

"Obviously."

"Can you explain it?"

"I…honestly, I'm not sure I should."

What?

He frowns and starts pressing the buttons on his steering wheel again, the display cycling through his speed, tire pressure, and various other details faster than he could read it. Finally, he nods to himself and says, "Look, I think you're being hit with a lot of different things all at once, and that's making it hard for you to think through any of them. Maybe we should try and separate them out and focus on one thing at a time. Gwen and Tristan first."

He's turned down my street. I can see the front of my townhouse. My car is still at the office where I left it last night, but Willa's Camry is in the driveway, along with another car I don't recognize. Probably Diane's. Just seeing them there, knowing I'm moments away from facing Gwen, from having to explain to her what's happened, makes my pulse race and my stomach tie up in painful knots. "What am I supposed to say?"

"You're going to tell her the truth." He stops in the middle of the road and turns to face me. "Tell her exactly what happened. Exactly."

"I don't know if—" I'm interrupted by a honking horn behind us and I flip them the bird before finishing my thought. "I don't know if I can."

The corners of Alex's mouth twitch and he drives the short distance to my house, parking at the curb in front. "You can." Turning the car off, he twists in his seat to face me. "However she reacts, whatever happens in there, I'm here for whatever you need. Although, if you're going to stay at my place very long, you'll need to lay off the booze, because you snore like a motherfucker when you're drunk. I could hear you all the way down the hall last night."

I'll be occupying his guest room for some time yet, I'm sure, but even so, he's managed to do the impossible. He's made me laugh.

CHAPTER 11

GWEN

"THEY'RE HERE." Willa steps back from the window, letting the curtain fall into place, and twists her hands in front of her. I could almost believe she's more anxious about what's to come than I am. *Almost.*

Rising from her seat on the couch, Diane grabs her by the arm. It was very sweet of both of them to come stay with me last night, but there's nothing sweet about the way Diane is dragging my sister toward the stairs. "I'm sure Mac and Gwen would both like some privacy." She shifts her gaze to me. "We'll grab Tris on our way up and go hang out on the terrace. Text if you need us, okay?"

"Thank you." The words come out a little watery, and Willa's about to rush to my side. Diane catches her and gives me an encouraging smile before following her up the stairs, her hand planted between Willie's shoulder blades.

They've been a huge help, both with distracting me and helping with Tristan. Diane, especially, who seems to think of things I never would've. Like taking Tris to the roof. He's been in his room all morning playing video games, and that's where I'd have left him. But it's better this way. Willa and Diane will have eyes on him, so there's no need to worry he'll come downstairs for a drink and overhear something he shouldn't. Not that I have any idea what *that* might be.

Once Alex texted last night to let me know he'd found Mac, I was relieved to know he hadn't been in a car accident or something. He was okay. Except he wasn't, was he? Why didn't he come home? What could've happened to keep him away if it wasn't a physical event?

He was worried about *Seek* and their story, of course, but that wasn't any reason not to come home. I know what Diane thinks. Maybe even Willa too. But he said he's never slept with Jess and… God, maybe I'm an idiot, but I believe him.

At the sound of the front door, followed by footsteps, I take an involuntary step toward the stairs but manage to stop myself, rubbing one hand self-consciously over my stomach. I feel awful. Not just bad in all the ways I've weirdly grown accustomed to over the last few months, but in a new terrible way.

Mac crests the stairs with Alex right behind him, and his appearance doesn't do anything to calm my anxiety. His dark eyes are tired and pinched at the corners, his muscles tense and his neck corded. He's even chewing the inside of his cheek, which is something I've never noticed him do before. Whatever small hope I had that I've been blowing this out of proportion, that everything is going to be fine, is gone. As if to underline the point, one of the twins lands a hard kick against my ribs. *Even they know this is bad.*

"Hey." Mac's voice is subdued, and his gaze sweeps the room, probably checking for Tristan, before settling on me. His eyes fix on my hand, still gently rubbing the place I was kicked. "How are you feeling?"

Like my heart is breaking and I don't know how to fix it. He's stopped, Alex next to him, but they're still about ten or twelve feet from me; it feels like miles. Trying to keep my voice casual, as if nothing at all is wrong, I shrug. "As okay as I ever am anymore."

Satisfied by that bullshit answer, Mac nods and glances at Alex. To my surprise, Alex closes the distance between us and pulls me into a fierce hug. Over the last few months, he's been friendlier with me than he's been with Mac, but this is way beyond normal. His hushed voice isn't the kind for secrets but for funerals when he says, "I'll give you guys some space. Let me know if you need anything."

Too anxious for the conversation to come, I nod absently. "Oh, okay."

He leans closer still, and this time his voice is low enough that Mac won't overhear. "Just be patient with him, please. I know you have to do whatever's best for you, and for Tristan and the twins too, but he's…not okay right now."

I didn't need Alex to tell me that. Throughout our brief conversation, my eyes have never left Mac, and his misery would be clear to anyone. "Sure." Alex releases me, and I add, "Tris is on the roof with Willa and Diane if you want to join them."

Alex heads for the stairs, and I watch him until he's gone. I need those few seconds to try and gather my thoughts. As much as I need to know what's happened, I'm not sure I really want to, at least not yet, because whatever it is, nothing's going to be the same after this conversation.

Turning back to Mac, I force my voice to remain steady. "I told Tristan something came up last night. I think he assumed it had to do with work and he's used to that, so he didn't seem concerned you weren't here."

"Thanks. I'm sorry I disappeared on you like that. I know…I mean, I knew at the time it was wrong, but I just…" His voice cracks and he scrubs one hand over his face before trying again. "I needed some time to try and sort it all out in my head first."

"It's okay."

Mac arches one brow in that oh-so-familiar way of his, as if he's asking if I'm sure about that, and it makes how unfamiliar the rest of this is that much more striking. It's like simultaneously knowing him better than I know anyone else in the world and yet not knowing him at all. I'm so disconcerted by it, I fling one arm toward the couch and ask, "Do you want to sit down?" As if it isn't his own damn couch in his own damn house. *What is wrong with me?*

His faint smile indicates that the silliness of my question isn't lost on him, that in another moment, one that didn't feel so heavy and laden with things I don't understand, he might even have teased me over it. But that isn't what this is, so instead he turns to the furniture without comment.

He takes his usual spot at the end of the couch nearest the window, but he doesn't sprawl out like he often does, or even settle in and get comfortable. He sits on the edge of the cushion, bent forward with his forearms on his knees, and his eyes on the coffee table in front of him. "I'm sorry, Gwen, but I... Fuck, I don't know how to tell you this." His hands are clasped between his knees and he's gripping them so tightly his knuckles are white. Seeing him this torn up makes me sicker than I've felt in a long time, more nauseated than I was even in the throes of morning sickness, and I start to take a step toward him, wanting to comfort us both. But before I can move, he looks up and our eyes connect. "It turns out, I might be Amy's father after all."

What? No. How could that be? He said he's never been with Jess. And I believed him. Could I really have misjudged him so badly? Could he have done this? *No.* That isn't the Mac I know and love. He's always been so repulsed by his own father's cheating, there's no way he'd do it.

Unless he didn't considerate it cheating? I went on a few dates with other boys that summer in a foolish attempt to make Mac jealous, but I never slept with any of them. That was the only rule of our ridiculous non-relationship relationship.

"As long as we're fucking each other, we aren't fucking anyone else. Got it?" That's what he said the second night we were together. He'd taken me back to his apartment for the first time and we were so desperate for each other that we'd barely made it inside the door before he'd kicked it closed and pinned me to the floor, right there in his entryway.

My skirt was hiked up around my waist and his cock was already out, prodding against my thigh. And despite all the other ways he made me stupid, I was smart enough to recognize his demand for what it was—tacit acknowledgment we were about to fuck without a condom unless I said I wasn't on birth control or wouldn't agree to monogamy. Unless I said no.

It would've been the responsible thing to do, of course, and I'm as sure now as I was then that he would've respected that answer, but I didn't do it. We were both willing to gamble on a lot of other things, too many things, like babies and broken hearts, but STIs weren't one of them, and I'm struggling to accept that he would've put me in danger that way. And wasn't it only yesterday he was joking with Stef about immaculate conception? He didn't lie to me. *He didn't.*

He hasn't said anything else, but he's still watching me, like he can see all of my thoughts on my face as they cycle through my mind. And maybe he can, because he clears his throat and his voice is emphatic, his dark eyes pleading with me to believe him. "I didn't lie to you—not knowingly, anyway. I just…I didn't remember and, to be honest, I still don't."

"What happened?" I'm not sure I want to know, but the echoes of my own history with Mac are too striking not to ask. Maybe it's my penance for keeping Tristan a secret so long, that I have to listen to him tell me about Jess doing the same thing. The air of finality around him is so heavy it's unmistakable. This is a formality in his mind, telling me what happened and why we're over. I don't have a choice, and nothing I say will change his mind. But as long as I can keep him here in this room, talking to me, I don't have to acknowledge that reality. There will be time enough for that once he's gone, and if listening to every awful detail will delay that even a few minutes, that's what I'm going to do.

He hesitates. "Alex says I should tell you everything but I'm not sure he's right."

The mention of his brother loosens something inside me, and I finally move from the spot in the center of the room where I've been standing, frozen in place, since his arrival. *Alex is helping him.* Whatever the details of the situation are, it's pretty clear Mac doesn't want to lean on me and maybe, once he's told me, I won't want him to, though that's difficult to imagine. But he doesn't have to go through this alone. Alex will be there to support him through this. It's a small comfort after their recent estrangement, but it gives me the courage to say, "Please tell me."

"I don't know if you remember, but I came home for Fourth of July that year."

"I remember." I went back home for the holiday too. It was an awful weekend. I was so jealous, assuming he had a lot more fun with his friends than I did with my mother and her new boyfriend.

"I got really fucked up. We all were, Jess too. And we... I don't know, like I said, I don't remember."

"But she does?"

Another nod, and he looks even more miserable. "She says I called her by your name the whole time."

This is what Alex wanted me to hear. The realization is like a slap across the face. It hurts, and the fine hairs on the back of my neck stand on end. Even the twins sense my unease and shift restlessly in response. I smooth both hands over my stomach in an attempt to soothe them while my mind whirs with the ramifications of what he's said.

Alex isn't stupid enough to think this information would make me feel better. It isn't some grotesque consolation prize. *"Well, on the bright side, he thought he was with you!"* No, that isn't why he wanted me to know and, as I suspect Alex knew it would, it's made me feel worse. But he was right, I needed this information. The problem now is, I don't know what to do about it. Mac doesn't even seem to realize that he was assaulted and... *Fuck, this is awful.*

Awkwardly—because everything I do is awkward these days—I scoot forward in my seat and put my hand on his forearm. He tenses, the muscles in his arm taut beneath my fingers. "Mac, if you didn't know who you were with—"

"Jesus, Gwen, don't make this harder." He pulls away, sitting back in his seat, a physical manifestation of the gulf that seems to be widening between us. "Don't make excuses for me. We got fucked up like kids do and we fucked like fucked-up kids do. I cheated on you, the one and only rule we had, and I broke it and slept with someone else. Don't you see? How could you ever trust me again when I don't even trust myself?"

She violated you! I want to shout at him, to make him understand, because I do see. Better than he does. I'm not sure, but I think I might feel differently if they'd both been so wasted neither of them realized what they were doing. That's two fucked-up people fucking, like he said. That isn't what happened here, though. He was so intoxicated he thought he was having sex with someone else entirely, while Jess, however loaded she may have been, was still with it enough to realize that. Under those circumstances, it's clear as day to me that she took advantage of him. But maybe with as fresh and overwhelming as this all is, he isn't ready to face that yet. *Maybe he'll never be ready.* That's an uncomfortable thought, one I'm not yet ready to face, so I push it aside to ask, "Now what?"

He seems relieved and lets out a deep breath, like he's been holding it while he waited to see if I would push for more details. "Alex has convinced *Seek* to kill the story, so we don't need to worry about that, and he's set up a paternity test. I should have the results by Monday." Another deep, steadying breath, and he frowns down at his hands before meeting my eyes again. "I want you to stay here." He gestures at the room around us. "There's plenty of space for you and Tris and the twins. I know the stairs are a hassle, but..." He trails off with a helpless frown and shrugs. "I can stay with Alex until he gets sick of me. We can reevaluate later. Maybe I'll get an apartment, I don't know. I'm having trouble thinking about the future right now and I don't want to have to worry about you and the kids while I figure some of this out."

If we really are over, there's no way I'll stay in his townhouse long-term. If he were more himself right now, he'd know that. But I'm not as willing to give up on us as he seems to be, so I only nod. That he doesn't react to my easy acquiescence with shock or even mild surprise is further evidence that not arguing with him about it was the right call. There'll be time for that later, after he's come to terms with what's happened and is better able to make decisions about the future —our future—with a clear head.

"I'd also like to go to the rest of your doctor's appointments with you and be there for the twins' birth, if that's still okay with you." He leans forward, closing the distance between us, and reaches out, fingers splayed to palm my stomach. He pulls back at the last second, like he doesn't think he has the right to touch me anymore, to feel our babies move.

Every muscle in my body quivers with the need to hold him. To press his face to my neck and guide his hands to my belly and tell him I love him. My heart aches to stroke his back and promise this'll be okay. That we'll all get through it together. Convince him I'm not angry or upset with him, and I still want to be with him every day for the rest of my life.

But in some ways, right now I'm as lost as he is. Hyperaware of how much I want to comfort and support him but also how afraid I am of doing or saying the wrong thing. The last thing I want is to somehow unintentionally make things worse. So I stay in my chair and ignore the tremor in my voice when I say, "Of course that's all right."

"We'll need to talk to Tris at some point, but I'd rather wait until after I have the test results. It might be easier to figure out what to tell him once I know for sure about…that."

Unfortunately, I have to disagree. Whatever Mac is going through —whatever I'm going through—I won't lie to our kid, and he needs to know something is happening, even if we don't give him the details. "That's fine, we don't need to tell him anything about that part of this now, but if you aren't…if you're going to stay with Alex, we have to tell him something. He's too smart—he'll figure out something's up on his own, and that'll be worse."

Mac nods and glances toward the stairs. "Now?"

There are a lot of words and emotions jamming themselves into my throat, begging to be shared, but now doesn't seem like the time. For a man who's so often in control of other people's lives, publicly managing their crisis and privately guiding them through to the other side, I can't imagine how it must feel to have so little control of his own. Maybe giving him a sense of that back, that everything we do from here is up to him, at least as much as it can be, will help him find his center again? "Sure, unless there's anything else you don't want to say in front of him?"

"Probably, but I don't know what." He rakes one hand through his hair and he looks so tired, like he hasn't slept in days or even weeks.

The urge to comfort him rises again. I want to rub my fingertips over the deep lines in his face, smoothing them, and hold him while he sleeps. But regardless of how much I want it and I think he needs it, it's clear he wouldn't accept that from me now, so instead I say, "Well, if you think of something later—and you will, because that's how these things always work—you can text me or call me. Day or night." I hesitate, but I've held back so much in this conversation, I can't hold this back too. "Or just come home."

He nods and rubs his lip, his eyes narrowed in concentration. It feels like he's studying me, like I'm the most fascinating baseball game he's ever watched and he's trying to memorize every play. I wish there was some way to know what he sees, what he's thinking. If I wait long enough, will he tell me? No, evidently not, because what feels like several minutes pass in painful, awkward silence before he says, "Thank you."

"I'll text Willa and ask her to send Tris down." I don't know what everyone's doing up on the terrace, but once I've sent the text, Tristan wastes no time in joining us, his footsteps thundering down the stairs like an entire herd of elephants. It's hard to believe he's only one kid who weighs barely eighty pounds for the all commotion he makes.

Mac doesn't rise to meet him but turns toward the stairs, and with his attention somewhere else, his brow furrowed at some other knot he's trying to untangle, it's easier for me to read him, his uncertainty over what to say to our son and worry over hurting or upsetting him. Overshadowing that, though, is the love and antici-pation of seeing him again. They haven't been in the same room since the morning Mac left on his last trip with the campaign, almost a week ago, and the way his eyes light up when Tris swings around the bannister and bounces into the room makes my heart flutter.

"Dad!" Tristan pounces on the couch next to Mac with his usual exuberance.

Mac laughs, ruffling Tristan's hair and gently chastising him for jumping on the furniture before pulling him into a hug. It's such a natural moment—so damn normal—that for a split second I'm almost able to forget what's happened, especially once Tris starts babbling about a new video game he's adding to his Christmas list. Mac humors him, waiting for him to finish before making a vague comment about Santa that Tristan seems to take as a maybe but leaves me approximately one thousand percent certain no matter what else happens between now and Christmas, his dad will get him that game and anything else he asks for.

His tone has taken on a more solemn tone when he turns the conversation back to the reason for this visit. "I need to talk to you about something, but I don't want you to worry or be upset, because everything's going to be okay."

"Okay." It's a testament to how much Tristan has grown to trust his dad that his response is so unperturbed. And also to how much Mac loves him that he was able to lie so convincingly, because in his heart of hearts, he doesn't believe this'll be okay. Not yet, not now. But maybe he will. *I have to believe he will.*

"There are some things going on with me. It's kind of complicated and it doesn't have anything to do with you, so the details aren't really important. What you do need to know is that I'll be staying with Uncle Alex for a while."

"For how long?"

"I'm not sure," Mac hedges, no doubt figuring we should ease Tristan into what's a permanent change in his mind.

"Are you and Mom fighting?"

"No, no, it's nothing like that." Panic edges Mac's voice and he grabs Tris's hand, squeezing it. "I still love your mom. I always will. Just like I'll always love you."

"And the twins." It isn't a question, but a reminder, like his dad might've forgotten them. Mac and I both smile, and I wonder if he's thinking the same thing I am. *Tris is going to be a great older brother.*

"Yes, and the twins too. This is another one of those things that you don't have any control over, Tris. I'm really sorry about that, but it has to happen, and I want to do this in a way that changes as little as possible for you."

Tris considers that, then asks, "Does that mean we'll still go get..." He darts a glance at me, and changes course. "Will we still do our thing on Saturdays?"

Tristan wanted so badly to have something that belonged to only him and his dad, I'm not supposed to know about their Saturday trips for ice cream and plane watching at Gravelly Point whenever Mac was home on the weekend. Of course, Mac always gave me the highlights afterward, but Tristan was so pleased to share a secret with him that I happily played along. It's no surprise that this would be one of Tris's first questions.

"Absolutely. And just like when I was gone with work, you can always text or call me. Except it'll be even better now, because instead of being in some other state, I'll be up the road at Uncle Alex's. I might be pretty busy for the next couple of days, but once we find a routine, I bet you'll see more of me now than you did when I was traveling all the time for work."

"Can I come to Uncle Alex's too?"

"We can have sleepovers, yeah." That isn't what Tris was asking and in other circumstances, his question might've hurt my feelings. But I can see it for what it really is now. He's secure in his relationship with me; he knows I love him and I'll always be here for him. Things are still too new with Mac for him to be so confident about his dad. Even so, he's willing to accept that answer, and Mac presses on. "I have to go pretty soon—I have an appointment I can't miss this afternoon, but you can come upstairs and help me pack a bag real quick if you want."

Tristan agrees and as they make their way upstairs, he continues a barrage of questions about all the things they might or might not still be able to do together. It's the only sign that he's more uncomfortable with Mac's news than he's let on.

They're only gone a few minutes, but that's long enough for me to get a handle on some of the things I'm feeling, which is…a lot. For one thing, it's frustrating and disappointing to be dealing with more emotional turmoil. Since the drama with the sex tape and our subsequent talk, things have been going so well for us, I really thought maybe all of that was behind us for good. It's disappointing and frustrating to find ourselves in upheaval once again. It feels so unfair, and it isn't my or Mac's fault that we're in this situation.

That responsibility lies with Jess. I don't know her all that well, although after listening to Kim and Mac talk about her, it feels like I do, and it's so hard to believe she could've done something so awful. Mac's known her since he was literally a toddler, and that must make the betrayal feel so much bigger. How does Alex feel about that piece of this? He's known her his whole life too. Will he retain his relationship with her? I can't. Won't. I'm not without some sympathy for Jess. She's another victim of their dad. That doesn't excuse what she did to Mac, though, and I'll never be able to forgive her for hurting him.

As for Mac, I have to allow him to process this in his own way, in his own time. Of course I wish he didn't feel like he needed to stay at Alex's place to do that, but I can sort of understand it, given his misplaced guilt over his supposed cheating. If a little space will help him sort through this mess enough to realize the truth, I can live with it, at least for a while. But that doesn't mean I need to stand by helplessly and, as hard as it is to know what the right thing to do might be, I have to fight for him. And I'm going to start now.

At the sound of their approaching voices, I manage to heave myself out of my chair with a strength I haven't felt in months. It's amazing, really, what emotional upheaval will do for you, even when you're so pregnant you can barely move most of the time. But unexpected energy or not, I'm slow and clumsy, which means I'm still waddling toward the stairs when the three of them reach the landing.

"Do you need something?" Mac asks, his gaze drifting around the room, trying to anticipate what I've gotten up to do or get. Alex and Tristan's mouths are open too, like he'd only just beaten them to asking the same question.

"Oh no, I'm fine. I just thought I'd see you out."

"I'll be in the car. Why don't you come wait with me, Tris?" Alex gestures down the next flight of stairs, and Tris is torn about whether he should go with his uncle or not.

"Go on. Your dad and I need a minute. After they leave, you can come back up and I'll watch you play *Animal Farm* for a bit."

"Moooom!" His throws his thins arms up in exasperation. "It's *Animal Crossing*, not *Animal Farm*."

"Right, right. Sorry. *Animal Crossing*." Despite my blunder, that was the inducement he needed, and he leaves with Alex.

Alone again, Mac clears his throat and takes a single step toward me, one hand extended, and I know with bone-deep certainty I don't want to hear whatever he's about to say, so I don't give him the chance.

"I know what you're going through right now is…well, it's a lot, and I understand you need some time to come to terms with it. But you will, and when you do, the kids and I will be here waiting for you."

"Gwen—"

"No. Don't tell me not to wait. Because I…" *I love you.* It's on the tip of my tongue, pushing against the back of my teeth, but I can't tell him now, not like this. I thought I had all the time in the world to get used to the words, the weight and feel of them in my mouth. To save them for a special moment that'd let him know how deeply I feel them. I regret that now, but this isn't how I need to say them for the first time, either. I don't want to make him feel even guiltier than he already does or overwhelm him. On the other hand, I can't ignore the possibility that telling him might help. *But what if it doesn't?*

It'd be funny if this didn't feel like such a dire situation. Me, the queen of kneejerk reactions, suddenly plagued with doubt and indecision. Who'd have ever guessed? But maybe my indecisiveness is its own answer. We both—and especially Mac—have so much to grapple with already. Worrying about whether this is the right time to tell him how I feel can wait until all my other chaotic emotions have settled some.

But that doesn't mean I can't show him I love him or that there isn't anything else for me to say, either. "I know this is very hard for you. But you shouldn't be making long-term decisions right now, and I'm not going to allow you to close any doors you might later regret. When you're ready—whether that's to talk or come home—I'll be here."

He wants to argue with me. I can see it in his eyes, which is encouraging. Somewhere underneath all the trauma and grief, he's still the same Mac I've loved since I was eighteen. It's less encouraging when he says, "You can't wait forever."

I shrug and close the distance between us, wrapping my arms around his waist and pressing my face to his chest. He tenses, his breath hitching, but only hesitates a second before his hands are on my back and his chin's resting on top of my head. *How many times have we held each other like this?* Dozens? Hundreds? However many, it hasn't been enough, and I refuse to accept this might be the last time. My voice thick with tears I'm trying to hold back, I whisper-mumble the one thing I promised myself I wouldn't say into his shirt. "I love you." And then louder, but more wobbly, "I won't wait forever. I won't have to."

"Okay." Mac skims one hand over my belly and gently presses. One of the twins immediately rewards him with a gentle, rolling kick. I wish they hadn't been quite so accommodating, because then he kisses the top of my head and leaves.

CHAPTER 12

MAC

"Angie will call you with the results on Monday," the nurse explains as he slides the swab he's rubbed all over the inside of my right cheek into a narrow glass tube.

"Thanks."

"I've got everything I need." He drops the tube into an envelope and peels off the adhesive to seal it. "Do you have any questions before I let you get out of here?"

Everyone I've come into contact with at the clinic, from Angie the receptionist to Steve the nurse, has been polite and kind. In fact, they've gone out of their way to make me feel as comfortable as possible. But Alex made them aware of the situation, and it's impossible not to worry that despite their professionalism, they're all silently judging me.

"Uh, yeah, I was wondering..." There isn't any way around it—this sucks. And even though they already know about Dad, that doesn't make it any easier to ask. "My brother said he explained the situation when he set up the appointments?"

Steve picks up the thin file lying open on the counter and scans the page with an impassive expression. Even when he confirms that yes, there's a note in the file about that, he doesn't give anything away. It's impressive, and I hope I never meet him across a poker table. He'd clean me out.

"I guess I'm worried about the reliability of the results." *Among other things.*

"Right." He examines the file again then tosses it on to the counter and turns back to me. "Here's the deal. We swabbed the mother too when she brought the little girl in. It's weird, right, but it's helpful for the lab, especially in cases like this one. You don't need to worry about false negatives. If it's negative, that's because the kid has something in her DNA that she didn't get from you or her mother, and she had to get it somewhere, right? Positive results are trickier, and a false positive is a real risk since you and the other potential father are so closely related. But I see he's coming in tomorrow and, honestly, with both of your DNA samples for comparison, the lab will be able to nail it down."

"And if he doesn't show up?"

"Like I said, positives are trickier if we don't have a sample from everyone."

I am so fucked. That isn't Steve's fault, though, so I thank him for explaining it to me, check one more time to make sure they have my phone number written down correctly, and head back out to the car, where Alex is waiting.

"How'd it go?"

"Fine, I guess." Buckling my seatbelt, I ignore Alex's questioning expression and ask, "What's next on your fix-Mac's-life agenda?"

"I'm dropping you off at my place, and then I'm going to find Dad."

"The fuck you are. Not without me. Is he even in town?"

"I am very much going without you. And no. But Whitaker's campaign is in Youngstown, Ohio tonight. So my plan is to drive up there and bring Dad back myself for the test tomorrow."

Smart. Alex isn't going to call him and then trust him to find his own back to D.C. to get tested. That's what I'd do too. But it's a five-hour drive to Youngstown, and it's already nearly four o'clock in the afternoon. Between traffic and stops for food and gas, he'll be lucky if he gets there before ten. "Look, I appreciate that you're trying to spare me the confrontation with Dad, but this is my life. It's gotta happen sooner or later, and I'm voting sooner. Besides, it's a long drive, at night, and you don't need to make it alone."

He considers that and grudgingly concedes. "All right, but you should know, if you try to kill him I'm probably not going to stop you, so you'll need to proceed with caution if you don't want to be watching the twin's high school graduation—and college too, for that matter—on Skype from prison." My answering laugh feels unnatural but it seems to please Alex, so I ignore the instinct to smother it. And it begins to feel more genuine when he adds, "Are you good if we leave from here? I threw a bag in the trunk earlier in case you put up a fight and I needed to sneak out on you."

We went straight to the clinic from my townhouse, but I check the backseat, just to make sure my duffel's still there. "Yeah, that's cool. I wouldn't hate it if I had the chance to clean up and change before we confront him, though." It's probably ridiculous. I made Gwen, Tristan, and the clinic staff all suffer through my day-old funk, mostly because Alex assured me I didn't stink. But I'll need to be in top form—or the closest to it I can manage—when I see Dad, and it feels like a shower will help. Especially after adding a road trip to the mix.

"That'll work. He doesn't know we're coming, so I'm hoping we can surprise him. We can get a room at the same hotel, you can grab a shower, and then we can pay him a visit. Assuming this goes like I'm expecting, we'll drive straight back and hold him hostage in my condo until it's time to escort him to the clinic. If it goes better than I'm expecting, maybe we stay overnight and come back in the morning, but that's a pretty big maybe."

Digging my phone out of my pocket, I shake my head. "We've got to come back tonight. I don't want to risk leaving in the morning and getting stuck in traffic and missing his appointment. Plus, I don't want to be gone any longer than I need to be in case Gwen goes into labor."

"I thought she said they weren't coming anytime soon?"

"Well, yeah. Hold on." I hold up one finger and turn my attention to my phone, firing off a quick text to Gwen.

Mac: Thought I'd better let you know, Alex and I are taking a quick road trip. Will be back by morning. Sooner if you need me.

Turning my phone upside down on my thigh so I won't stare at the screen like a lovesick idiot waiting for her reply, I elaborate on my answer to Alex's question. "Even though the doctor said there were no signs labor was imminent at her appointment yesterday, that shit can change fast. I mean, honestly, we're fortunate she's made it this far. A lot of twin pregnancies don't."

"Maybe you shouldn't come with me." Alex gives me a sidelong look and starts fidgeting with the buttons on his steering wheel. As nervous tics go, it's not that annoying.

"No, I'm coming. She had a pretty long labor with Tris. Things can go faster the second time around, but with twins…" I shrug. "Basically, it's anybody's guess, but there are two things I am certain of. I'm not fucking around with this paternity test and a potential false positive, so I'm going to make damn certain he shows up. And I'm not going to miss the twins' birth." It might be wishful thinking that I can do both of those things without screwing up the other, or maybe Gwen has rubbed off on me. She's been insisting for months that the twins won't come until after the election. If she's right, I've got nothing to worry about.

My phone buzzes with an incoming text, and I flip it over to read Gwen's response.

Gwen: ????

Mac: Everything's fine. Just have to take care of something.

Gwen: Tell me later?

I don't want to make that promise. Depending on how this goes, depending on the results, depending on...well, a thousand things, really, I'm not sure I'll want to talk about it. Especially with her. Her stubborn refusal to recognize the writing on the wall is dangerous. It's too much like hope, and I don't have room for that right now. I'd be an asshole to allow her to continue to nurture it or, worse, somehow encourage her. But I also can't quite bring myself to say no.

Mac: Will you tell me the second you start having contractions?

Gwen: I've been having contractions since August. Consider yourself told.

Mac: Real ones.

The conversation bubble dances around on the screen for a long time. She's either writing a novel or can't decide what she wants to say.

"Gwen?"

"Yes. I wanted to let her know I'd be out of town overnight."

"Good thinking. How did things go with her today? Is it okay if I ask that?"

"Yeah, give me a minute to finish with the texts." I'm not trying to dodge his question, and I don't even mind it. He's worried about me, and I appreciate that. I'm worried too. And after as difficult as our relationship has always been, it's nice to be in this new place with him. But Gwen's answer has popped up on my screen, and she comes first. Always.

∽

GWEN

. . .

MY THUMBS FLY over the keyboard, typing out my fourth attempt at a response to Mac's text. *Why is this so hard?* Rereading my answer, I take a deep breath and hit send.

Gwen: You'll tell me what you're doing if I'll tell you when I start having contractions?

"Mom, you're not watching!"

Caught with my metaphorical hand in the cookie jar, I peek over my phone to find my son glaring at me. We're approaching hour five of *Animal Crossing: The Spectator Sport* and it's…well, okay, it's boring as hell. I mean, sure, some of the little animal villagers are cute and there's a certain amount of pleasure to be derived from Tris's enjoyment of it, but…it's a pretty low-key game and there isn't a lot to watch. Willa and Diane seem to agree with me, because they're supposed to be watching too and they aren't even bothering to fake it. *Why aren't they getting yelled at?*

"I am, I swear." Holding my phone aloft, I add, "But I'm talking to your dad too."

It might be a mistake bringing Mac up. Tris has been quiet about him since he left this afternoon, but I can tell he's worried, turning it all over in his brilliant little brain and trying to figure out why this is happening and what it means. But ever since I quit traveling with the campaign and Mac continued to go, it's been normal for the two of us to text like this, and I feel like maybe letting Tris know that's still happening will help him retain some sense of normalcy. *That could backfire if Mac doesn't come around.* Nope, not going to think about that right now. He'll see that what we have is worth hanging on to. He has to.

"Oh, okay." Tristan turns back to the TV to issue his demand. "You have to pay attention, though, or you might miss me catching a rare fish."

The horror. Willa snickers behind her book, and I consider ratting her out to Tris for her own lack of focus, but my phone vibrates with Mac's response, sparing her.

Mac: Exactly.

With a smile, I ponder how to answer. We've had a variation of this conversation a hundred times before, especially when we were younger. He prefers to call it negotiation, and I jokingly refer to it as blackmail or, sometimes, bribery, depending on the specifics, which almost always involve sexual favors for one or both of us. So, this isn't exactly the same but it's...similar. I want something from him, and he'll give it to me if I give him what he wants in return.

But how do I respond? My first instinct is to reply just as I would if the past thirty-six hours never happened, with light and fluffy banter. That's almost how this conversation feels already. Despite his reticence to tell me what he's doing, it's like I'm texting with another person entirely from the one who sat here a few hours ago and insisted we were over. I'm not getting the same sense of despair from him.

Maybe whatever he and Alex are doing has helped put his feet on solid ground again. Or he could be faking it, not wanting to get bogged down in an emotional conversation. Or I'm misreading the situation, because I'm not getting the full picture from text messages. But the thing is, if there's any chance he's feeling even a tiny bit better, I don't want to drag him back down. *Banter it is, then.*

Gwen: I'm just saying, historically, it's usually more fun than this when you blackmail me.

The receipt switches from delivered to read and then...nothing. Time drags while I stare at the screen, waiting for those bouncing ellipses to appear, but after five minutes they still haven't.

Shit. Was that the wrong thing to say? Have I upset him? Ugh. *Why did I say that? It was too flirty!* I set my phone down and pick it right back up. *Answer me, Mac. Please, answer me.*

But he doesn't. I need a distraction or I'll drive myself nuts worrying about this, but watching Tristan play a sedate video game isn't going to cut it. Sadly, since my burst of energy this afternoon, I've reverted to my turtle-stuck-on-its-back state of being, and I'll need help getting out of this stupid chair. "Someone help me get up."

"What are you doing?" Willa asks, but it's Diane who comes to my aid, pulling me out of this bottomless pit of a recliner.

Even with her assistance, it's a real effort, but I manage to get to my feet with an embarrassing, unladylike grunt. Fortunately, they're all willing to pretend they didn't hear it. "Making dinner."

"Why don't we order pizza?" Willa's suggestion is only motivated in part by concern that I might overdo it. Last night's salad excluded, she's a terrible cook but she'll feel obligated to help if I insist on making something, and she's reluctant to get up from her cozy spot on the couch.

"I kind of feel like cooking." I don't, but it's better than sitting around hoping Mac will text.

You can't mention pizza around Tristan if you don't plan on feeding it to him. Setting down his controller, he turns around to give us all puppy-dog eyes. He even manages to stick his lower lip out in a remarkable, if overdramatic, pout. "But I want pizza."

"What about homemade pizza?" Diane asks.

That's given Tris an idea, and he races from the room, shouting over his shoulder, "Hold on!"

Diane still has a loose grip on my upper arm, walking next to me as I totter toward the kitchen. "What do you suppose that's about?"

"No idea." We've reached the kitchen and she releases me so I can investigate the refrigerator. Thank God Mac invested in one of the fancy ones with the freezer on the bottom; otherwise, I'd probably need help with that too.

I'm still inventorying its contents—onions, peppers, ham...oh, there's even mushrooms—when Tristan returns, waving a thin square book over his head. "I think there's a pizza recipe in here."

I've made enough pizzas from scratch over the years as a cost-saving measure that I don't need a recipe anymore but... "Is that the cookbook your Aunt Willie got you for your birthday?"

Willa, now alone in the living room, can still be heard in the kitchen muttering with what I imagine isn't entirely fake dread. "Oh, no."

"Yes." Tristan opens the book on the counter and flips through the pages until he's found what he's looking for. He points and glances over his shoulder at me and Diane with a proud smile. "It does, right here!"

Closing the fridge, I move over to stand behind him, skimming the recipe overtop his head. Satisfied that we have everything we need for it, I call to my sister, "Didn't you buy this for him so you could do it together?"

"Maybe?"

Diane snickers. "Come on, babe. Or do I need to help you up too?"

Willa caves and joins us in the kitchen. Making pizzas—two, because mushrooms—is a team effort that takes most of the next hour. In addition to homemade dough and chopping all the ham and vegetables, we also made the sauce from scratch, even though there's a perfectly good store-bought jar in the pantry. It was included with the recipe in his book, and Tris insisted he wasn't skipping steps.

After dinner, Tristan returns to the living room to play video games again, this time without requiring an audience, thank God, and Willa starts on the cleanup. That's how it's always been. Olivia or I did the cooking, and Willa handled the dishes. So I'm content to sit on my ass and watch her do the work, but Diane doesn't seem to know the rules. Or maybe she feels like too much of a guest here not to help. She brings a load of dirty plates to the sink and Willie gives here an admonishing look. "I've got this, Di."

"You sure?" Diane sets the dishes down so she can put her hand on the small of Willa's back while they have one of those silent conversations couples have. It's such a private, intimate moment it makes my heart ache and I have to turn away. *I want that back.*

Hours later, when I've crawled into bed, I allow myself to check my phone, and there's a message waiting from Mac. It came in about an hour after my last text, around the time we were putting the pizza in the oven.

Mac: We did have a lot of fun, didn't we?

Gwen: I know it might not seem that way right now, but we still can.

He doesn't answer that, and at least this time it isn't showing as read. He's probably busy or asleep. Hard to say, since I don't know where he and Alex were headed. But I'm still clutching my phone in one hand, just in case, when Tristan's soft voice out in the hallway draws my attention. Although Mac's insisted on closed doors and knocking, I left it open tonight, anticipating Tristan might need me. He's been a trooper today, but he's still only eleven.

"Mom?"

I push up on my elbow and peer into the dark, trying to see him and gauge the situation. "What is it?"

"Can I sleep with you tonight?"

Oh. It's been a long time—years—since he's asked to sleep with me, and I bite my lower lip to contain the pained noise gathering in my throat. This is such an impossible situation for all of us, and poor Tristan understands it least of all. *I have to hold it together for him.* "Of course." Forcing a cheery voice, I turn on the bedside lamp and pull back the covers. "But you should be warned, I have a hard time sleeping lately, and I toss and turn a lot because I can't get comfortable, so I don't want to hear any complaints."

He shrugs and climbs up on the bed. "Does it bother Dad?"

"I don't know. If it does, he's never said anything." I'm lying on my side, my bottom arm stretched out across the pillow, and Tristan scoots closer to me until he can lay his head on my biceps.

"Then I won't, either." As I tug the blankets over us, he adds, "How are the babies?"

He was slow to warm up to the idea of being a big brother, but now that he has, he's all in, and it makes me smile. "Restless. Do you want to feel?"

He nods and lets me guide his hand to the right place, his lips tipping up when I find it. "Maybe that means they'll get here soon."

"Maybe."

"I hope so. I want to meet them."

"I'm glad you're excited. I am too."

"Is Dad?"

"Definitely."

There's a long pause in the conversation, during which one of the twins kicks me so hard my flannel-covered belly bulges at the point of impact. Tristan giggles and moves his hand to the same spot in case it happens again. When it does, he looks up at me with dark, serious eyes. "I used to think this would be scary, but it isn't. It's kind of cool."

"Mm-hmm, I remember." The first time he felt them, he yelped and jerked his hand away like he'd touched a hot stove. Mac laughed until his eyes watered. Then he told Tristan to try again, and when Tris placed a tentative hand on my stomach, Mac covered it with his own much-larger hand. The memory brings the sting of tears to my eyes, and I swallow hard in an effort to hold them in.

Tristan doesn't seem to notice, his gaze drifting back to my stomach before he says, "I'm sort of scared now too."

Fuck, this just keeps getting harder. Gathering him in both arms, I squeeze him tight.

Maybe a little too tight, because he makes an *oomph* sound and says, "Mom, I think one of the twins just kicked *me* in the stomach."

With a kiss on the top of his head and a watery laugh, because I'm definitely crying now, I relax my grip but only a little. "I'm scared too. But everything's going to be okay. I promise."

"How do you know?" His expression is so solemn it's like a kick to the gut. Or the heart.

"Because your Dad loves you more than anything and no matter what else happens, he's going to keep loving you." I have a lot of hope and not much else for how things will turn out between Mac and I, but this...this I'm sure of.

He seems flustered that I'm not understanding what he means. "But I want things to be like they were. I don't want him to stay with Uncle Alex. I want him to be here."

"I want that too, and so does he. But the problem is..." Careful of my words, I try to explain in a way he might understand. "Somethings happened to your dad, and it's nothing you need to worry about. He isn't sick or anything like that, and it doesn't have anything to do with you, but…someone else did something, and it's really upset him. It's going to take a little while for him to sort through all his feelings about that and figure out what to do next."

"Like how you felt when your mom left?"

I hadn't noticed until Joan came into our lives and he started calling her grandma that he's never called my mom that. I guess it shouldn't be surprising. He's never even met her, let alone had any kind of relationship with her. And for as perceptive as he is, it's sometimes easy to forget he's only eleven. "Yeah, a lot like that, actually."

"What made you feel better?"

You. I can't tell him that, though. This is hard enough on him without making him feel as if it's his job to straighten Mac out. It isn't even my job, as much as I might wish it were, and I can't—won't—put that kind of pressure on him. "I don't know. I guess life sort of went on around me, and eventually I realized I didn't want to miss it anymore. I know you want to help your dad and I think you're the biggest-hearted, bravest little boy in the world to feel that way, but we can't. He has to find his way through this on his own, and the best thing we can do for him in the meantime is keep loving him as hard as we can."

Tristan nods and snuggles closer. Our heart-to-heart must've eased some of his worries at least a bit, because a few minutes later he's fallen asleep. I can't reach the light without waking him, but that's okay. It'll be a while before I can sleep anyway and, with my phone still clutched in one hand, it gives me the opportunity to do something else.

CHAPTER 13

MAC

She sent me a picture.

The incoming text alert came through as I was getting out of the shower and now, I'm standing in the middle of the hotel room Alex rented in a fresh pair of pants, unable to look away from my phone.

Gwen and Tris are huddled up together in bed. She's wearing a flannel nightgown, the one she's always called frumpy but I think is adorable, and he's in his Captain America pajamas, his head on her shoulder, sound asleep. My own shoulders rise and fall with a deep breath, and I rub one hand over the hollow ache that's wedged itself under my sternum.

Fuck, I miss them. And I wish I was there, lying on the other side of Tristan, one arm over them both. The twins are always more active at night, and I'd be able to feel the rolling of their movements under my palm as I drifted off to sleep, holding my family.

I told Tris this new arrangement, with me staying at Alex's, would be better than when I traveled for work. I meant it at the time, but now I can see it for the lie it was. I always fiercely missed them when I was gone with the campaign, but it wasn't like this. In a few days—a week at most—I'd be with them again, and we'd share moments like the one Gwen captured tonight. But now? I'll never have this with them again, and my stomach churns with the realization. What's that old adage about quality over quantity? It's a common saying for a reason, and I'm the fucking idiot who didn't figure that out until now.

"You okay?" Alex comes to stand next to me, and I cant the phone toward him so he can see the screen, prompting him to add, "Ah, she's playing hardball."

She is, and I resent it a little, if I'm being honest with myself. She's only making this harder for both of us. But Alex and I have been over this already in the car on the way here. He thinks I'm being rash, that I'm making bad decisions I'll regret later when it's too late to fix them. And I'm not in the mood to defend myself again right now, not when we have other things we need to do tonight. I slide my phone in my pocket and grab a T-shirt from my duffel. "What's the plan?"

"Well…"

I don't like the sound of that. Tugging my shirt over my head, I come out the other side with a glare for my brother. "What?"

"I think I mentioned I wasn't able to track down his room number?"

I slide my hand back in my pocket to retrieve my phone again and shrug. "Yeah, so I guess we have to call him."

It isn't an ideal plan. Dad won't guess about the paternity test. Why would he? As far as he knows, he's the only one who could be Amy's father. But he'll figure out we've gotten wind of *Seek*'s story and guessed that he was the source. Why else would we show up here, five hours from home in the middle of the night? Because we fucking missed him? Obviously not. And calling to ask him to meet us ruins the element of surprise. It gives him the chance, however brief it might be, to concoct some half-assed cover story. Worse than that, it gives him the opportunity to sneak out before we can find him. But we don't have a lot of choices right now.

"Unless…" Alex hesitates, fiddling with one of the buttons on his shirt sleeve. "One of us could pretend to be him. If we go to the front desk and say we lost our key, they'll give us a new one, and they always write the room number on that little envelope they put the key cards in."

"That'll never work. They don't just hand keys out, Alex. They'll want to see… Ohhhhh." Realization dawns, and my glare deepens. "You little shit. You don't mean 'one of us.' You mean me." Because like my old man, my name is William Z. MacKenzie. As long as the clerk isn't the one who checked Dad in—unlikely at this hour—and doesn't notice that pesky Jr. tacked on the end of my name, it…might work. *Or, you know, I could spend the rest of the night in jail. No big deal.*

"Oh, you have the same name! I hadn't even thought of that." Alex's wide-eyed expression of faux innocence wouldn't fool anyone, and it isn't fooling me.

"You're a shit liar." The thought of pretending to be my dad makes my skin crawl. I've never wanted to be anything like him and if I hesitate, if I give myself a chance to consider what I'm about to do at all, I might back out. Grabbing my wallet off the desk by the window and jamming it in the back pocket of my jeans, I jerk my chin toward the door. "Let's go."

On the main floor, the elevators are situated in a hallway around the corner from the lobby, out of sight of the staff manning the desk. That's good luck. Even better, there's a single exterior door at the other end of the hall, meant to provide guests with easier access to their vehicles in the parking lots to the side and rear of the building. At this hour, they'll be locked for security and I won't be able to get back in that way, but I won't need to.

Stepping off the elevator, I head for the exit, but Alex doesn't follow. I turn around and throw both arms wide, exasperated. "Are you coming?"

"I was thinking maybe I shouldn't? It might seem suspicious, since I checked us in a bit ago. If the same clerk is still on duty…" He shrugs and shakes his head, shoving his hands in his pockets.

Oh, hell fuck no. "This was your fucking idea. If I'm doing it, you're coming with me, even if I have to drag you into that lobby by your ear which, by the way, would definitely be suspicious, so move your ass."

Alex sniffs and straightens his shoulders like he's offended, but he does in fact start moving. "Well, you seem to be feeling better."

Not really, but I'd prefer to get this over with. I'm not sure if conning my way into possession of the key for a hotel room that isn't mine constitutes breaking and entering per se. Maybe it's fraud or identify theft or, hell, maybe it's all three. Fuck if I know, but one way or another it's illegal. And there's the whole confrontation with my dad, making sure he shows up for the test tomorrow, all of it. I want it over so Alex will get off my ass and I can go back to wallowing in my own damn self-pity.

Outside, the air is brisk. Not quite but almost cold enough for us to see our breath, and we both hustle around the building back to the main entrance. The lobby's deserted, as I figured it would be, and I amble up to the desk, leaning on it with one arm.

The clerk on duty, a pretty young woman with a brown ponytail who can't be more than twenty-one or so, glances over my shoulder at Alex, who's lingering a few steps behind me, and then back at me with a smile so sweet it makes my teeth ache. *Goddammit.* Now I definitely can't get caught. I'll feel awful if this kid gets in trouble because of me.

"Good evening, sir. What can I do for you tonight?"

"I'm really sorry to bother you, but my friend here checked in earlier." I hook one thumb over my shoulder at Alex before turning back to her with what I hope comes off as an apologetic and slightly embarrassed expression. "When he got in, I went out with him to grab a late bite and a few drinks and, I don't know what happened, but it seems I've lost my room key somewhere along the way." I pat both front pockets of my jeans for effect, like maybe if I check one more time, the key might magically appear.

"Oh, of course." Her smile brightens even more, as though she's pleased my problem is one that's so easy to solve. "I'll need your name and ID."

"William MacKenzie," I answer. Slipping my wallet from my back pocket, I pull out my driver's license and extend it toward her, holding it over the desk with the pad of my thumb conveniently covering the suffix.

Still smiling, she leans toward it. For one fraction of a second, it seems like she's going to check it without taking it from me. Fucking perfect. Until she begins to raise her hand, and panic jolts through me. With a quick glance at the name tag pinned to her green polo shirt, I start talking. "I'm sorry to have to bother you with this, Melissa, and I really appreciate your help." On her name, she glances from my license to my face. *That's good. Look at me, sweetheart, and don't take the fucking card.* "I'm forever misplacing things. My girlfriend says I'm worse than our son."

She straightens, tipping her head to one side. "Oh, it's no big deal, Mr. MacKenzie. This sort of thing happens all the time. I'll have a new key for you in a second." Her hand falls back to the desktop, and my heart rate drops with it. "How old is your son?"

"He's eleven." Holding the card up, now facing me, I add, "Are you done with this?"

"Yup, you're all set." She's fiddling with the key card machine, but she pauses long enough to glance up at me with big green eyes when she adds, "I'll bet he's a cutie."

I'm busy putting my driver's license away before she can change her mind, but Alex decides to join the conversation. "Spitting image of his father."

"Aww, that's sweet." Slipping the card in a white envelope, she holds it out to me. "If there's anything else I can do for you, please let me know me, and I hope you'll enjoy the rest of your stay."

"I really appreciate this, Melissa, thanks." I take the card and make it four steps from the desk before I glance down at the envelope in my hand and...*fuck.* She didn't write the room number on it. *Goddammit.* Staying where I am, I spin back around and aim for a sheepish smile. "I'm sorry, this is so embarrassing, but we're with the campaign and we stay in an awful lot of hotels. It's hard to keep up from one night to the next. I'm in 317, right?"

Melissa raises one fist to cover her mouth and I guess hide her giggle, although it doesn't work very well. "You're in 233 tonight, Mr. MacKenzie." Her eyes spark with mischief and her cheeks are pink when she adds, "In Youngstown. Ohio."

A huff of surprised laughter escapes me. "Thanks, Melissa. You're a life-saver."

As soon as we're around the corner and out of her sight, Alex smirks at me. "I have to hand it to you, big brother. You make a very convincing himbo."

~

MAC

"Should we go in?"

"I don't know. Do you think he's out this late?" We knocked on the door of room 233 and got no answer, a possibility neither of us considered. I can't hear the TV or voices in his room, but that doesn't mean much. This seems like one of those hotels with pretty decent soundproofing, and I haven't heard anything from any of the rooms we've passed.

"He's probably asleep."

Doubtful. Alex might not have reason to know this from personal experience but as a teenager, Dad busted my ass sneaking in after curfew more times than I can count. If he was asleep, he'd have woken up when we knocked. "Well, what do you want to do?"

Alex shrugs and glances around the hallway. "I guess we could wait out here for a bit and see if he comes back?" His eyes drop to the keycard still in my hand, and he adds, "Or…"

I've never heard such a small word so weighted with meaning. Lifting both brows, I raise the key. "What, you want to just go in?"

"No, you're right. It's a bad idea." He pauses, his gaze drifting from me to the door and back again. "If he is asleep in there, we'd probably scare him to death. He might have a heart attack or something."

"He's too spiteful to die. He's going to outlive both of us." Tapping the card against my other hand, I consider our options. Alex is convinced Dad's in his bed, sleeping like a baby, but I think it's far more likely he's out on the town, at a strip club or some seedy bar. "If he isn't in there, I have to admit I kind of like the idea of seeing the look on his smug face when he returns and finds us waiting for him."

"Okay." He gestures to the door handle and swallows hard. "Let's do it."

Still, I hesitate. Wheedling the key from Melissa was wrong, sure, but as long as we didn't use it, that didn't seem so bad. Letting ourselves in, though? Definitely, incontrovertibly wrong and, whatever consequences Alex and I might face if we're caught, it'd be even worse for Melissa. *Then don't get caught, dumbass.*

What about Dad? Breaking into his room would be a serious invasion of his privacy. I'd be furious if he did something like that to me. But hasn't he already? He's the one who leaked the story to *Seek*. Wasn't that an invasion of my privacy? *I don't owe him anything.*

Mind made up, I slide the key into the slot and wait for the blinking green light. Time stands still as I turn the handle and ...all hell breaks loose.

"What the fuck!" Dad's outraged bellow rings in my ears but even so, I hardly hear it. He's sitting on the end of the bed, dress shirt unbuttoned and slacks around his ankles, with...a woman in his lap. *Why in the ever-loving fuck didn't I consider this possibility?*

Dad, Alex, and I all seem to be frozen in place by a combination of shock and—at least for Alex and me—horror. But the woman? She's unconcerned with our intrusion and, although I'm trying to avoid looking at her, it's kind of hard not to notice she's still bouncing in his lap. *Jesus Christ.*

Alex is the first to regain his wits. Leaning in front of me, he snags the edge of the door and pulls it closed again. With the snick of the latch, he mutters, "Well, that was a terrible idea."

"You think?" I ask, staring at the solid wooden door separating us from... *Ugh.*

"What now?"

"Why are you asking me?" I turn on him, only to find him peering back at me with bulging eyes and flushed cheeks, his mouth pressed into a flat line. Do I look like that too? *Probably.*

"You're the older brother."

It isn't difficult to guess where this conversation is headed, and while this might not be the ideal time for a sibling squabble, I'd rather bicker with my brother than think about what I just saw. Which is why I say, "It was your plan."

"Yes, but—" His mouth snaps closed with the click of the door handle, and we both turn toward it, bracing for whatever's about to happen next. *How did this night get so far out of fucking control?*

We step back from the door, and Dad's companion exits into the hallway, closing it behind her. It's hard not to see her now, what with her standing right in front of me. She's tall for a woman, almost as tall as I am, and older than me too, if I had to guess. Not by much, though. She's pretty enough with dark-blond hair and hazel eyes that aren't the least bit embarrassed when they meet mine. "Your dad said to send you in on my way out."

Huh. I wouldn't have expected him to tell her who we were. Not that it matters. She hasn't waited for either of us to respond, instead crossing the hall and letting herself into the room kitty corner to Dad's, which is when it registers that while her clothes were back in order, she wasn't wearing a coat or carrying a purse. She's another guest in the hotel and, while I don't recognize her, most likely someone working on the campaign with him. It's getting pretty fucking hard to ignore the parallels between his life and my own, and the shame that's been oddly quiet the past few hours returns with a vengeance, my gut tightening in discomfort.

"Ready to get this over with?" Alex asks. He doesn't wait for me to answer, instead plucking the card from my shaky fingers and opening the door himself. He goes through first too, holding it open for me and letting it swing closed once I've followed.

Dad is standing by the bed, his shirt re-buttoned and tucked into his pants, a tumbler of bourbon, I assume, in one hand. He's literally been caught with his pants down by both of his sons, yet the air of smug asshole that always seems to surround him isn't even dented, and he looks me dead in the eyes when he asks, "What are you doing here?"

Alex doesn't give me a chance to respond. "You've got ten minutes to pack your shit and call whoever you need to with the campaign and tell them you're taking a leave of absence."

Dad swings his gaze to Alex, both brows raised like he's only just now realized he's there. "What's this about?"

My brother steps forward, mouth open and ready to argue, but I stop him with one hand on his arm. *I have to do this.* "We know you're the one who leaked Amy's birth certificate."

Dad gives Alex one of *those* looks, the kind he's used to drive a wedge between us for decades, but Alex spits out, "Do you really think if I didn't believe him before—and I did—that walking in on you fucking some woman who definitely wasn't your wife and our mother wouldn't have convinced me?"

Realizing the game is up, Dad nods and crosses the room to the desk near the window. "That was unfortunate timing. There was a pack of little assholes running up and down the hall banging on doors earlier. When you knocked, I assumed it was them again." He shrugs and drops a few cubes of ice from the ice bucket into his glass then picks up the bottle to refill it. As he pours, he asks, "*Seek* hasn't run the story yet. How did you find out?"

That casual confirmation hits Alex like a sucker punch, and his complexion pales. After everything, some small part of him must've still been hoping for a solution. A reconciliation. If so, he knows once and for all it isn't coming now.

"Thanks to Alex, the story isn't running at all," I clarify. "And the dumbass reporter you were working with called one of my friends in an attempt to corroborate some of your lies. Fortunately for me, she's smarter than that."

"She?" Dad arches one brow and sneers at me, but I refuse to take the bait. Setting the bottle down, he raises the glass to his lips. At the last second, he stops, meeting my eyes over the rim of the cut-glass tumbler. "I have to admit, I was surprised to see your name on the birth certificate. I didn't think Jessica had the good sense to follow my advice." He stops, taking a drink, and when he lowers the glass again, he's wearing a befuddled smile, like he's working on a puzzle he can't quite fit together. "I was never quite sure if she had, you know. You paid an awful lot of attention to the baby, but I couldn't decide if that's because you thought she was your sister or your daughter. Your mother was quite upset about it those first few years. Of course, I told her boys will be boys and you could hardly be blamed if you didn't want to get tied down to a girl like Jess, but I can't tell you how many nights she cried herself to sleep, insisting she'd raised you better than that."

He really doesn't know what happened between Jess and I at the beach. Relief that she was telling the truth about that is overshadowed by the shame and regret that I'd caused my mother so much pain. But I'm confused too. "No. If you thought I believed she was mine, why would you have asked me to convince her to have an abortion?"

"Because I wasn't sure and I wanted to be. That's why I asked you to do it. When I suggested Jess try and trap you, she had a fit, but sometimes women need to think about these things. You know how they can be." He shrugs and glances from me to Alex and back, as if we're all sharing in some secret knowledge about women. "Anyway, I thought for sure your reaction would give you away once I told you I'd fucked her. You've always been so damn sanctimonious, even as a kid, and I didn't think you'd be able to contain your outrage upon discovering you'd had my leftovers. And you were predictably outraged, especially once I mentioned abortion. Why should you have cared about that unless you thought it might be yours? But as I said, I was never certain, so the birth certificate was a nice surprise."

He's said so many revolting things, I don't even know where to start. Like the casual misogyny of his "women, am I right?" attitude and how it's inconceivable to him that I might believe a woman has the right to choose whether she'll have a baby regardless of my involvement in the situation. But there's no point in mentioning any of that, is there? It's not like I'm going to change him. And even with his scummy reasons for telling me, it doesn't make a lot of sense, since he was trying to keep the whole thing quiet. That's the part I'm stuck on. "Telling me was a huge risk. I might've told someone."

"You didn't, though, did you?"

Each word cuts through me like a knife and his confidence is a fist, grabbing and squeezing my lungs until I'm left gasping and choking on nothing. All this time, and he never worried I might blow his cover. Never even considered the possibility, never once doubted whether I'd keep his secret. *Because the apple didn't fall all that far from the tree, did it?*

"How did you even get the birth certificate?" Alex asks, still trying to piece some of the details together for himself.

Dad arches one brow, a sly half smile curving his lips. "How did you get a key to my room?"

"*Touché,*" Alex mutters. We've all apparently broken a few laws in this mess; better not to go into the details. Glancing at his watch, he raises his voice to add, "You've got about three minutes left. If you don't want to abandon your shit, I'd suggest you start packing."

At least one of us is holding it together. It's almost funny, isn't it? The brother I always thought of as a doormat has a titanium spine, and I'm the one who's a worthless mess.

Setting his glass aside, Dad begins throwing the few bits and pieces of clothes he's unpacked into his open suitcase, offhandedly asking as he does, "I don't suppose either of you is going to tell me where we're going?"

I would've preferred not to tell him, at least not right now, but I'll have to face his reaction eventually. Might as well get it over with. "Back to D.C. for a paternity test."

"So you did fuck her." He hasn't stopped what he's doing and doesn't even bother to glance at me, but his voice oozes smug satisfaction when he says, "Well, it's good to know for sure."

CHAPTER 14

GWEN

WHAT IN THE ACTUAL FUCK? I've read Mac's text four times, and I'm…
Well, I have no idea what to make of it, so I read it again.

> **Mac:** Might've committed a little light B&E but it appears we've
> gotten away with it. Almost back to D.C. Should be at Alex's within
> the hour if our hostage continues to cooperate.

Okay, yeah, the fifth time isn't the charm. Might've? Light
breaking and entering? Hostage? No, seriously, what the fuck? And
the conversation bubbles have begun dancing around on my screen
again. Apparently, he has more to say, and I'm honestly not sure I
want to know what that might be.

> **Mac:** I hope I didn't wake you up.

I'm still in bed, but his texts didn't wake me. The twins, as usual,
are to blame for that. And I'll have to get up in a half hour anyway to

get Tris ready for school. But...*light* breaking and entering? What does that even mean? And *might've* seems like a lot of ambiguity around an activity that, to me at least, seems pretty fucking straightforward. And they've taken a hostage? What am I supposed to do with this information?

Gwen: Already up, but it's Owen/Charlotte/Zachary's fault, not yours. Also, you can't say you MIGHT'VE committed LIGHT (wtf, dude?) B&E and have a hostage (!!!) then leave me hanging.

Mac: Why three choices?

Sure, of course that'd be the thing he focuses on. We haven't spent a lot of time having conversations dedicated to baby names. Instead, we throw them out in conversation as a way to simultaneously run them by the other person and also test how they sound. Usually we do it in gendered pairs, or sometimes suggesting four names all at once, two each, so I get why he might wonder about three but, I mean, that's so not the point right now. Smothering my irritated growl so I won't wake Tris, who's somehow managed to spread his tiny frame out to occupy the entirety of Mac's side of the bed, I respond.

Gwen: I thought we could use Zachary for a boy or a girl.

Mac: ...

Gwen: I'm serious!

Mac: I hate Zachary. Owen's okay, I guess. Charlotte's nice.

Gwen: But Zachary is your middle name!

Mac: I haven't forgotten that. How are you feeling?

Gwen: FOCUS. You need to tell me about your new life of crime before we talk about anything else.

Staring at the screen with an intensity that might crack it if I'm not careful, I await his response. Several minutes pass before he sends a photo of…his dad in the back seat of what I'm pretty sure is Alex's car. I guess that answers at least part of my question, because there's no doubt Senior is the hostage, but…

Mac: Suspect has been apprehended and is being brought in for a paternity test.

The peal of laughter that escapes me is too loud, and Tristan stirs, mumbling and pulling one of the pillows over his head. He's kicked the covers off and is on his stomach with one leg of his pajamas pulled up to his knee. It's adorable, and I snap a picture and forward it to Mac before replying.

Gwen: Oh, well, if that's your hostage, I'm good with it.

I tap out a second message asking how he's feeling, my finger hovering over send. Treating his confrontation with his dad like a madcap criminal adventure is meant to make me laugh and deflect from his actual state. It's a distraction. And if I'm right about that, I already know how he's doing. *Not good.*

Really, this isn't all that different from the way everyone constantly asks me how I'm feeling. They mean well, but it's annoying, in part because if I happen to be in one of those rare moments where I've managed to forget or distract myself from my discomfort, it reminds me, bringing all my aches and pains back to front and center of my thoughts. As much as I want to support him, I won't risk doing that, and I'm backspacing over my message when he responds.

Mac: Your appointment's at 11 tomorrow, right?

Gwen: Right

Mac: I'll pick you up at 10:30

Gwen: Okay!!!

Three exclamation points is overkill, for sure, but I half expected him to say he'd meet me there. This is a good development, and as much as I'm agonizing over everything I say to him, I'm not going to put myself through the torture of over-analyzing punctuation too.

Depositing my phone on the nightstand and stretching one leg out, I nudge Tristan with my foot. He bats at me with one arm, but there's too much space between us and it doesn't connect. "It's time to get up and get ready for school."

He flails all four limbs, seeking the blanket. He manages to snag it with his fingers and pulls it all the way up until it covers him and the pillow he's still holding over his head. From beneath the enormous pile of bedding he's buried himself under, he says, "I don't want to go to school today."

Well, that's new. Not entirely unexpected, though, and there's a part of me that wants to let him play hooky. I'm a firm believer that everyone needs a mental health day once in a while. Why not now? We could spend the day in bed, cuddling and watching silly movies, and nursing our bruised hearts together. But sometimes you have to pick yourself up and carry on, even when you don't want to, and I think this might be one of those times.

"Come here, Tris." I tug at the blanket until he throws it and the pillow off to give me a mutinous look. Yeah, I'm not giving in to that attitude. "Remember last night when we talked about how to help your dad? Well, I think one of the ways we can do that is to go on with everything like normal, so he doesn't feel like he needs to worry about us. That way he can focus all his attention on the other stuff."

Tristan nods but still sounds skeptical. "I guess."

"Besides, you like school, and it'll make the day go by faster than if you hang around here with boring old me all day." To be on the safe, I add one more inducement to the list. "And we'll have tacos tonight for dinner."

That does the trick and a few minutes later, he's gone upstairs to take a shower and get dressed while I head downstairs to make his breakfast. Mornings were usually too rushed for anything more than toast or a bowl of cereal, but since I quit traveling with the campaign, I've been making him a more substantial breakfast two or three mornings a week. Today is a pancakes-and-bacon kind of day, if I ever saw one.

I'm sliding the tray of bacon into the oven when Willa comes in. "You're up early."

"Work," she grumbles before disappearing into the refrigerator. She emerges with a cup of yogurt. "What are you making?"

"Pancakes and bacon. Want some?"

"You had me at bacon." She returns the yogurt to the fridge. "Anything I can do to help?"

"No, I've got this." I pause to mentally recalculate the pancake recipe and throw her a teasing smile. "I'm not completely helpless, you know."

She shrugs and frowns down at her nails, picking at her cuticles. "You sick of us already?"

"Who? You and Diane?" I shake my head and scoop flour into the bowl. "No. But I feel bad you've both stayed here the last couple of nights. You guys can go home; Tris and I will be fine. I promise."

"I know, but..." She pushes off the counter and comes closer to peer over my shoulder into the bowl, her voice overly casual. "I worry, okay? What if you go into the labor and you're home alone?"

"Then I'll call someone. Mac, you, Alex, Joan, Cece...I have lots of options." That thought almost sidetracks me. It wasn't that long ago that I didn't have anyone but my sisters to depend on. Somehow, without my even noticing it was happening, my support network has gotten a lot bigger, and that's an encouraging realization among all the upheaval. "Or, I guess, an ambulance if it came to that. I mean, don't get me wrong. I love having you here, but you have your own life. You don't need to babysit me."

"But I kind of want to. Is that weird?"

Is it? Maybe. My relationship with my sisters has always been out of the ordinary, at least from what I've observed in media and among my friends and their siblings. For a lot of years, I was as much Willa and Olivia's mother as I was their sister, but the lines were always a little blurry, a little more confusing with Willa because she was older. She didn't need me the same way Olivia did. Then again, given the way Alex seems to have taken over Mac's life in the last day and a half, maybe this is what siblings do? As long as Willa doesn't feel obligated, as long as she's here because she wants to be, I'm not going to send her away. "I don't think it's weird, and I like your company too much to kick you out. I just…I don't want you to feel like you have to stay."

"I kind of do, though." I must make a face at that, because she laughs and adds, "Not like that. It isn't some crazy sense of duty. It's just that you've always been there for me and Liv, and I love you and want to be here for you too."

Willa's being so earnest and the last sentence was so heartfelt, a lump forms in my throat, causing me to sniffle. I jam my wooden spoon into the bowl and give her a teary glare. "Stop it. Nobody wants tear-flavored pancakes."

"Sorry, I didn't mean to make you cry." Her own eyes are shining a little and she pinches the bridge of her nose before she adds, "Anyway, I'm glad that's settled. I feel better having talked it over with you."

"Does that mean you're staying?"

She nods. "At least until that man of yours sees the light."

I didn't tell Willa and Diane everything Mac told me yesterday. What happened between him and Jess is far too personal for me to share it with anyone. That's up to him. So I gave my sister and her partner a slightly more detailed explanation than the one Mac gave Tris. And the very best thing about my sister? She didn't need all the intimate details. She trusts my judgment, and if I'm not ready to give up on Mac, she isn't either.

～

MAC

No one was able to sleep in the car on the long drive back from Ohio, which isn't to say we spent the time working out our differences. Other than the occasional discussion about stopping for gas or food, we rode in silence. Alex and I took turns driving with Dad trapped in the backseat—child safety locks for the win—and there wasn't much to say.

By the time we got back to Alex's, we'd been up all night, and everyone went straight to bed. I gave up the guest room in favor of the couch, under the theory that if Dad tried to sneak out while we were sleeping, I'd hear him and wake up. That—along with locking him in the backseat, if I'm being honest—was possibly over-cautious. Dad hasn't done anything to make us think he'd make a break for it. Still, with the paternity test hanging over my head like a guillotine, I'm not taking any chances.

Dad's appointment at the clinic isn't until three, and I set the alarm on my phone for one o'clock with back-up alarms at one fifteen and one thirty, but after a few hours of fitful dozing on Alex's godawful couch, I give up on the possibility of actual restful sleep and start scanning the news on my phone. *Old habits die hard.*

It's nearly eleven when Alex emerges from his room. He heads straight for the coffee pot. "You can't sleep, either?"

"Your couch blows, man," I complain, throwing my legs over the edge and sitting up.

"It looks nice." He pauses in pouring a pitcher of water into the pot to frown. "And it was expensive."

"Fuck that. Couches are meant to be comfortable."

He shrugs and goes back to preparing the coffee. "I've been thinking, after this we can't go on working with Dad. Or, I don't know, maybe we can but I don't want to."

Despite Alex's change of heart about Dad now that everything's out in the open, I didn't really expect this, or maybe I haven't been able to think enough about what comes next yet. But I'm not keeping secrets anymore, so I admit, "I've been planning to leave the agency for a while now."

"Right, I forgot. You'll be working in the White House if Kim wins."

"No. I mean, that's what she wants, yes, but I'm not going to do it."

He presses start on the coffee maker and turns to face me with a vague gesture toward the guest room. "You'll regret it if you turn her down because of this."

"It isn't because of this, or not only this. Obviously it'd be an honor but...it's a demanding job, and I don't want to give that much of myself to it right now. I have other priorities."

"Gwen and the kids." He nods with understanding. "What will you do then?"

He's at least half right, but that's close enough. Correcting him will lead to another lecture about rash decisions, and I'm too tired for that right now. But I don't have an answer for his question, either. I've been thinking about it for months and had almost decided to start my own shop, but the last couple of days has me doubting the wisdom of that. "I haven't figured that part out yet."

The sound of a door opening prevents Alex from responding, and we both turn toward the hallway, waiting to see if Dad appears. If we're lucky, he got up to use the restroom and he'll go straight back to bed once he has.

My hopes are dashed when Dad comes to stand in the mouth of the hall, both brows raised in question. "I thought I smelled coffee."

How does he do that? He waltzes into the room like we're a normal family and he hasn't done everything he could think of to ruin my life and pit Alex and I against each other. It makes me uneasy, like skin-crawling and stomach-cramping uncomfortable, because even though I've dealt with him my whole life, I don't understand how someone can be so confident, even knowing everyone else in the room hates him. I'm not competent to diagnose anyone, but that sure seems like the behavior of a sociopath to me.

Still standing by the coffee pot, Alex crosses both arms over his chest and leans against the counter. "It'll be ready in a few minutes."

Dad nods and folds himself into the chair perpendicular to the couch, where I'm still seated. I inherited my stature from him and we're about the same size, although he's put on a few pounds in recent years. His presence is deceptive, making him seem much larger than he is. Larger than life, really. I used to resent it, the way he could command a room and everyone in it, including my brother. Like a god King in a fantasy novel, no one can resist. *Except me.* "What do you want?" Some of my resentment has crept into my voice, and I resent that too.

"Alex said there's coffee." With a glance in my brother's direction, he adds, "And I imagine there are still a few things we need to talk about."

He still thinks he's in control. He's gone along with our plan, coming back to D.C. without complaint, and I'm not sure why, because he doesn't seem to realize that finally, something has changed. Anger slides through me and I sit up straighter, squaring my shoulders, but Alex beats me to it, his voice terse. "All I want to know is why."

"Why what?" Dad asks, and as much as I hate to agree with him on anything, I'm wondering the same thing.

"Why did you always treat us so differently? You've done every-thing in your power to make him miserable." Alex uncrosses his arms to wave one hand in my direction. "And you've spent my entire life alternately ignoring me or treating me like a third-rate lackey. Why?"

Oh, well, that's a fair question, one I've wondered about myself. But ultimately, I'm not sure it matters. He was a shitty father to us both, just in different ways, and from where I'm sitting, it seems like Alex should be grateful he drew the indifference card instead of the one for inexplicable cruelty. Although, indifference is its own kind of cruelty. This hasn't been easy for either of us.

"Your brother was a trap," Dad explains, crossing one leg over the other and smoothing the wrinkled fabric of his trousers. His words tighten my gut, but everything about his posture and expression is casual, like we're talking about the weather or last week's football game. "I had no intention of marrying your mother. We were having a good time, that's all, and her family connections were good for my young business. I didn't see my mistake until it was too late, because she wasn't content with that, and when she got pregnant, her father—your grandfather—threatened to run me out of town if I didn't marry her. He could've done it too. Could've ruined everything I'd worked so hard for because I'd been foolish and let myself become reliant on him and his friends. But that's where all the money was, protecting rich snobs from the consequences of their actions, so I did the only thing I could, I married her."

His gaze swings to meet mine, and there's so much contempt in his eyes it pushes me back in my seat. "But I've hated you since the moment she told me I was going to be a father, because you gave them —her and her father—the leverage to force my hand." His eyes shift to Alex, and he waves one hand in dismissal. "By the time she wanted another baby, it didn't matter anymore. They'd already gotten what they wanted, and it benefited me to keep her happy, or happy enough, so I agreed."

That explains a lot but not everything, and judging by Alex's strained expression, he's too stunned and hurt to respond. It'd be best to let the subject drop, and yet I can't stop myself from asking, "You think Mom got pregnant on purpose? To trap you?"

Dad shrugs. "I don't know whether she did it on purpose or figured out how to turn an accident to her advantage. Either way, it's the same end result."

That's why he told Jess to trap me. Or part of the reason. There's no denying it would've been to his benefit for everyone, including me, to believe I was the father of Jess's baby. But he would've delighted in it too. The son who was used to trap him, himself trapped. Even I can see the symmetry. It's disorienting and appalling to realize I understand his revolting thought process, and a hot flush crawls over me. *I'm not like him.* "You aren't getting out of my sight until you've taken that test this afternoon, but after that? I never want to see you again."

He's unconcerned. "That's going to be difficult, since we own a business together."

"Only because Mom made you do that too," Alex chips in, and there's a certain discomfort in Dad's expression at the reminder. He'd be nothing without Mom, and he knows it. But Alex isn't finished. "We're going to buy you out of the agency." He glances at me, unsure, and amends his statement. "Or I will on my own if I have to. Whatever it takes so neither of us ever has to deal with you again."

Dad's brows draw down, a crease forming between them, but his tone is dismissive. "You can't force me to sell, and even if you could, you couldn't afford to do it."

Unfortunately, he's right on the first count. Alex and I each own twenty-four percent of the company, and he has the other fifty-two percent. It was made clear from the time we joined the firm that even if we combine our shares, we'd never be able to outvote him.

He might be right on the second point too. Everything Alex and I inherited from our maternal grandparents is tied up in trusts. Grandpa might've been a cutthroat old bastard, like Dad says, but he was smart too, and there's literally no way for Alex and me to spend ourselves into financial trouble.

We each received two trusts. One designed for our education and other major life events, like buying our first home. I've already transferred that one to my kids. The other provides a modest annual allowance. It's meant to provide security, but it isn't enough to finance buying Dad out, and the principal is untouchable. All of which means, without selling my house or time to plan, I'm not sure I could come up with enough liquid cash to buy Dad out in a lump sum. Alex is probably in a little better shape than I am. He still has that education fund for one thing, and he might be able to convince the administrators that this qualifies as one of those major life events to take a special disbursement, but I don't even know if that'd be enough.

Alex seems to reach the same conclusion, because he says, "You can't force us to continue working with you. If you won't sell your shares, you can buy us out."

Dad laughs as if this is nothing more than a game, and I guess maybe to him it is. "I'm not buying you out. If you don't want to come to work anymore, don't. I'll run the agency, and you'll still get your piece of the profit."

Does he not have the money, either? He should. Granted, he admitted to being dependent on Mom and her family in the beginning. But the money he's made from the agency for the last thirty years isn't insignificant. He should be in a much better position, with more liquid cash, than either of us. If he isn't, we can use that to our advantage, and with that realization comes another. "How much do you think the MacKenzie Agency will be worth if Alex and I set up our own competing agency? How many of the clients do you think would go with us?"

Most of them. He seems to know it too, because there's a glint of doubt in his expression, but Alex is the one who goes in for the kill. "That's right. It might be tight at first, but we could do it. Those profit-sharing checks you'd have to send us would go right back into our new venture. It's up to you, Dad—buy us out or don't—but either way, your money's going to fund D.C.'s newest PR firm and your biggest competitor."

Red-faced and angry, Dad is out of his chair, shouting at Alex through clenched teeth. "You fucking little weasel. At least your brother's always had the courage to come at me straight on, but not you. You're like a snake in the grass, lying in wait and striking when there's finally something in it for you. If you think—"

"That's enough." I jump up to stand between them. Alex hasn't moved from his place in the kitchen, his expression stoic, but I don't trust Dad, especially when he's this agitated. How I'm the one who ended up playing the referee will forever be a mystery, though. "Those are your choices. Take a few days and think it over. I'll have my lawyer reach out next week to see what you've decided."

CHAPTER 15

GWEN

BY THIS TIME NEXT WEEK, I'll probably have newborn twins. It's a little hard to wrap my head around, even after all this time and all the many ultrasounds they've taken where I can clearly see both babies on the grainy screen.

Today's doctor's appointment went like the last. A series of tests followed by an ultrasound—all of which showed that the babies and I are doing great. But there's no indication they plan to arrive anytime soon. At least not on their own.

"Why don't you want to be induced on Tuesday?" Mac asks when we're back in the car. He's been unusually quiet today—not that I blame him—and other than exchanging pleasantries when he picked me up and a little bit of small talk in the car on the way to Dr. Williams's office, he hasn't had much to say, so his question takes me a little by surprise.

Honestly, it's been a strange day so far, although nothing out of the ordinary has happened. But neither of us has mentioned or even alluded to the current situation, and he's so somber he isn't even interested in Kim's campaign. I raised the subject of the recent polls—all showing Kim with a comfortable lead—while we were waiting for the doctor to come in, and he said he hadn't seen them. It's so weird, because while he's still reluctant, he's so much more open in texts, and I have no idea why or what to make of the obvious difference.

All of which means I'm more than a little relieved he's showing interest in something, even if I do sort of dread answering his question. "I've agreed to be induced on Thursday if they still haven't come on their own yet. What difference does two days make?" I'll be thirty-seven weeks on Tuesday, which has been our target date all along, but when Dr. Williams suggested inducing me that morning, I resisted, and he agreed to wait until Thursday.

"None, I guess." Mac shrugs and starts the car. "I'm surprised. I thought you'd be more anxious to evict them."

I'm ready for this pregnancy to be over, so I can understand why he'd think that, but... "I'm kind of used to it and I've made it this far; I can hack it a few more days. Besides..." I hesitate, aware I'm probably going to get an earful from him when I admit this, or rather, hoping I will, because that's what would happen under normal circumstances. "I haven't voted yet and the polls don't open until six on Tuesday morning, but if I were getting induced that day, I'd have to be at the hospital really early too and I wouldn't be able to vote first."

Half backed out of the parking space, Mac slams on the brakes and throws the car in park before turning in his seat, one eyebrow cocked in disbelief. "I thought you were voting absentee."

"I never said I was for sure. I said I'd think about it." It's not *my* fault if he took that for agreement and forgot to follow up later. "Have you already voted?" He's probably going to say yes and be super smug about it. Hell, I'm so desperate for him to be his normal, familiar self that I *want* him to be insufferable about this.

"Yes." He doesn't sound super smug. If anything, he sounds baffled that I didn't do the same. Not exactly what I was hoping for but still, this conversation is going better than any of the other stilted exchanges we've had today. "You keep saying the twins aren't coming until after the election, but you can't know that. What if you go into labor Monday night and you don't get to vote at all?"

"I'll vote on Tuesday. I'm not going to miss it. I promise. I just… I like the ritual of going in on Election Day and casting my vote and getting that little sticker." I know it sounds stupid. It *is* stupid, especially in my present situation, but it's the truth. And it's too late to do anything else now, anyway.

Realizing there's no point in badgering me about it, he turns back to the road and resumes driving. Or maybe not. Giving me a sly sideways grin that makes my heart thump wildly out of control, he says, "If you're wrong and you aren't able to vote, you'd better hope Kim wins. Otherwise, I'm never going to let you hear the end of it."

Success! That's the Mac I know and love. I almost make a joke about being able to live with that if it means he'll be sticking around, but I refrain, too worried about how it might land. He's so different in texts, more himself, which seems promising if I ignore how reserved he is in person. I need to find a way to convince him to open up again without pushing too hard. It's daunting, but part of that means keeping him with me as long as I can. "I'm kind of hungry. Do you have time to stop for lunch before you take me home?"

Mac glances at the clock on the dashboard and his disappointment seems genuine when he shakes his head. "Alex and I are meeting Mom for lunch." He pauses, rubbing his lip and narrowing his eyes as he refocuses on the car ahead of us. "Do you… Would you like to come with me?"

Yes! But instead of blurting out my enthusiastic first reaction, I have to know more. "Is this about…everything?" He nods and I sigh, realizing it's probably not a good idea. I want to be there to support him through what is sure to be a difficult conversation, but I feel like my presence will make the whole thing more uncomfortable and awkward for Joan and Alex. Especially Joan. If she doesn't know anything about the things Mac and Alex are about to share with her, it's going to be…unpleasant, and I'm not sure she'd appreciate having me there to witness the whole thing. "I'm not saying no. If you need me there—or want me there—I'll go. But I'm worried it might be weird for your mom if I do."

He considers that before saying, "I don't think she'll mind, and I think...well, I guess I hope she already knows some of this, but maybe that's wishful thinking."

Awkwardly leaning across the center console, I put my hand on his knee. "Okay, I'll go."

He doesn't say anything, just swallows hard and nods stiffly before dropping one hand from the steering wheel to lace his fingers with mine.

~

MAC

ANGER IS A POWERFUL EMOTION, and that's what got me through the confrontations with my dad. Things are more complicated with my mom, though, and the only emotions I can summon for our lunch date are worry and anxiety, neither of which will hold me together the way anger did.

Things have been better with Alex the past few days. He's been great, actually, but this'll be as painful and uncomfortable for him as it will be for me. It wouldn't be fair to lean on him when he'll be dealing with his own tumultuous emotions. But I'm not sure I can do this without...well, without Gwen. Because if I'm being honest, I don't want just anyone to hold my hand and reassure me. *I need her.*

Asking her to come with me after I've told her I don't see a future for us as a couple is enormously unfair. She wants to help me, and I'm taking advantage of that. Worse, I might be giving her the wrong idea. Or rather, might be giving us both the wrong idea. If I'm going to let her go, I need to do that, don't I? But as we walk up to my parent's front door, I can't regret bringing her.

"Will your dad be here too?" She's staring straight ahead, but the slight wobble in her voice is unmistakable.

"Not as far as I know." After his appointment at the clinic yesterday, he went his own way, I assume to rejoin Whitaker's campaign, although I can't be sure of it. Alex and I considered asking Mom to meet us at a restaurant or at his condo in case Dad decided to make an appearance at home, but in the end we didn't think we ought to do this in a public place, and it seemed unlikely he'd show his face. Here's hoping we weren't wrong about that.

She catches my fingers and gives them a gentle squeeze. "Whatever happens, it's going to be okay."

I can't find the words to answer, mostly because I'm not as certain as she appears to be. I mean, how am I supposed to tell my mom about Dad's cheating? About Jess and Amy and all of it? And how will she react to that? But I do appreciate Gwen's confidence—isn't that why I brought her?—so I nod before disentangling our fingers to hold the door for her.

Once inside, Mom and Alex's voices drift through the house, guiding us to the kitchen. Gwen and I both saw Alex's car in the drive —we couldn't have missed it, since I parked right behind him—but even so I stupidly say, "Alex is already here."

She nods and recaptures my hand, lacing our fingers. It reminds me of the first time I brought her here, when I told my family about Tris. I hadn't wanted her to come that day, but she'd insisted, and in the end, I was so damn glad she did.

As soon as we enter the kitchen, Mom, who was in the midst of an animated monologue about her latest charity project, stops talking and turns to face us. Her already bright smile gets even bigger when she sees Gwen, but she follows it with an admonishing frown for me. "You didn't tell me Gwen was coming."

"Sorry, last-minute decision after her doctor's appointment this morning. I hope you don't mind?" I glance at Alex to gauge his reaction too, but he only shrugs.

"Of course not." She sounds offended that I thought she might.

"Ruth left us plenty of food." Mom gestures to the table, already set with several plates of sandwiches and bowls of various salads in its center. "She's at her granddaughter's preschool this afternoon, helping with the Halloween festivities."

Right. With everything else, I've managed to forget tomorrow's Halloween. Now that Tristan's in middle school, they don't do much to mark the holidays, not like they do for the younger grades. But he's been looking forward to trick-or-treating for weeks. I'll have to remember later to ask Gwen if I can tag along tomorrow night.

It's strange to think that a few days ago this is something the three of us were planning to do together. Not because we talked about it and made plans—although Tristan did both…a lot—but because we're a family. Of course Gwen and I would take our kid trick-or-treating together. What else would we do? But it won't be like that now; none of the holidays will be the way I've been imagining them over the past few months, and that's difficult to accept.

Mom gives us both a hug, whispering something I don't catch about her pants to Gwen. I'm not sure what that's about, they're just black yoga pants, but whatever it is, Gwen finds it hilarious and her eyes are sparkling when they break apart.

With the greetings out of the way, we all sit down at the table, Gwen between Alex and me, and Mom across from Gwen. Mom resumes talking about her charity event while we all fill our plates. She's in a great mood, cheerful and unsuspecting that we've all come here for any other reason but a happy visit, and it makes my stomach clench with discomfort. I hate that I have to do this. I don't want to do it. But if she doesn't already, Mom deserves to know. No matter what my intentions were, it was wrong of me to have kept it from her so long.

Alex seems to be equally ill at ease, because as soon as there's a lull in the conversation, he throws himself into it, his fork clattering on his plate. "We have to talk to you about something important, Mom."

Both brows raised at his grave tone, she sets her own fork down and folds her hands in her lap. "Oh?"

Having launched the first grenade, Alex apparently doesn't know how to continue, because he turns on me with a slightly wild-eyed expression. Gwen's hand finds mine under the table and she holds it, her thumb stroking the back of my hand.

Focusing on that soft caress, I take a deep breath before saying, "It's about Dad. He—"

"If you're about to tell me he's having an affair, don't bother." Gazing down at her plate, she continues with a steely voice, "It isn't his first, and I'm sure it won't be his last. I don't think he's been faithful for a day of our marriage. Before that, even, for that matter."

Gwen and Alex are both wide-eyed with shock as we glance between one another, trying to figure out what to do next. I don't know if I appear quite as stunned as they do. Probably not. My predominant reaction is…relief. Deep down I always knew I should've told her—it was a matter of health and safety for her—but I was too chicken to do it and part of me thought maybe she already knew. It's hard to say if I really did have some kind of sixth sense about that or if that's what I told myself to justify my inaction, but either way I'm glad to know it never mattered.

Alex finds his voice first. "Why have you stayed all these years if you knew?"

"Because I loved him, I still love him, and I didn't know what else to do." She shrugs and refolds the napkin in her lap before shaking it out again. "And I always thought it was best for you boys if we stayed together. William doesn't make loving him easy, but I hoped the two of you would eventually form some kind of relationship with him. I still hope that, and I don't think you should let his wandering eye get in the way of that. That's between me and him and has nothing to do with either of you. And if it makes any difference, there's… I have someone I see too."

Whoa. Did my mom just admit to also having an affair? Of all the things I imagined happening today, that wasn't one of them, but I'm not going to judge her for it. To be honest, most of what she's said makes me sad for her. It must be incredibly difficult to love someone like my dad. I might not understand why she does, but I believe what she says, and if she's found some measure of happiness, I won't begrudge her that. But she doesn't know everything yet, and maybe once she does, that'll change things for her. Or maybe it won't, and I'm going to have some difficult decisions to make. Pushing those thoughts away, I lean one elbow on the table and grip Gwen's hand even tighter with the other. "There's more, Mom. We have to talk about Amy too."

That does seem to surprise her, and she raises both brows. Giving Gwen a meaningful glance, she asks, "You want to talk about that now?"

Gwen nudges my thigh with our joined hands as if to say, *it's okay, tell her.* With that encouragement, I nod. "Yeah, Mom, I do. Because the thing is, I know you think she's mine, that everyone thinks that, and she might be, but she might be Dad's too." I didn't know until this very moment exactly how much I'd tell her, but her stricken expression makes the decision for me. Even with as mixed up as I've been with my own emotions lately, I'm not so self-absorbed that I don't have sympathy for her and giving her all the details wouldn't serve any purpose but to hurt her. "I don't want to go into it all and it's kind of complicated how this went down, but neither of us knew about the other at the time, and he was the one who told me she was pregnant. He said he was the father, and I took that at face value, but it's all come out now because he leaked it to a tabloid that I was Amy's dad, I guess to try and hurt Kim's campaign." I know better than that, of course, but if I tell her his primary goal was hurting me and she denies it or defends him? I'm not sure I can deal with that right now.

"But you let everyone believe she was yours." Her expression hardens and her voice sparks with anger. "He told me she was yours. He claimed he tried to convince you to step up and take responsibility for her, and you refused."

She's angry at Dad for lying and there's nothing I can do about that, but she's also angry at me for going along with it. "I'm sorry, Mom. It seemed easier to let people think what they wanted."

Alex clears his throat and taps on the table. If we were in the car right now, he'd be frantically pressing all the buttons on his steering wheel. "So, Mac and Dad have both taken a paternity test and we'll know for sure on Monday. Other than that, we've pulled some strings and gotten the tabloid to drop the story, so you don't need to worry about the gossip columns."

"Kim still doesn't know the truth, and I don't know what if anything Jess plans to tell her once we have the test results. But I know you two are close and I... I'm sorry I didn't tell you all this sooner."

Mom rushes to take the blame. "No, it's my fault. I wanted to protect you boys from your dad's less-admirable qualities. It was foolish of me to think I could, and by keeping it all a secret, I made things worse."

That makes two of us. Reaching in front of Alex, I grab her hand and give it a gentle squeeze before letting go again and sitting back in my seat. *Now for the hardest part.* "I've decided..." I thought I knew what I wanted to say but I hesitate, trying to organize my thoughts as clearly and kindly as I can. Telling her what happened in the past was one thing. Difficult and upsetting, but none of us can change it now. Telling her how we intend to go forward...well, that's worse, because there will be very real consequences for her based on the decisions Alex, Gwen, and I make. My gaze finds Alex's, and he nods in silent encouragement, so I push on. "We've decided we're done with Dad. As far as I'm concerned, I don't ever plan to see him again. More importantly, he's never going to see my children again. Tristan loves you and you've become an important part of his life. I don't want that to change, but you'll need to understand I won't risk an inadvertent run-in with Dad, and that's going to complicate things." I didn't talk about this with Gwen ahead of time. I should've but judging by the way she's nodding along next to me, she agrees, and it almost feels like we're still a team.

"I understand." She sounds more shellshocked than anything, and I'm not convinced she really does grasp what I'm saying.

But Alex forges ahead. "As far as the agency is concerned, Mac and

I are probably leaving to start our own shop. So far he's refusing to buy us out, but—"

"He can't. He's broke." Mom's found firmer ground now, and she squares her shoulders as she continues, "He's terrible with money; he always has been."

"What?" Alex and I ask simultaneously and I gesture for him to go ahead. "I've never gotten the impression money's a problem for you."

Mom leans toward the table and if I didn't know better, I'd say she's...smirking. "Money isn't a problem for me. I might've been a stupid lovesick girl, but your grandfather was no fool. When we married, my dad forced William to give me half of the company, and you must understand, those early years when the business was young and you boys were tiny, money was tight. At one point not long after Alex was born, William had to swallow his pride and ask Dad for a business loan. Dad refused because he didn't trust William to pay him back, but he offered to buy ten percent of the agency to give your dad the cash infusion he needed. When your grandfather died, his shares came to me, so until you boys joined the agency, I had sixty percent of it and your dad had forty percent. And like the trusts you two received from my parents, everything I inherited from them is under my control. Your dad can't touch a penny of it without my authorization."

"But you were the one who made him offer us a place with the agency. He made you give up your shares for us, didn't he?" If I know anything about my dad, it's that he never would've given up even more of his stake in the company for Alex and me.

"Yes, exactly." Mom's definitely smiling now. "Don't you see? I had sixty shares and I gave up forty-eight—twenty-four for each of you. But I still have twelve shares."

"Holy shit." It's Gwen, but it's safe to say she speaks for Alex and me too, because we all seem to be having the same realization at the same time.

"Between the three of us, we have sixty shares?" Alex is dumbfounded, like he can't quite believe it and his eyes widen further when Mom nods. "That's enough to force him out."

With sixty shares, we have a controlling interest and can do anything we damn well please, up to and including shutting the business down, liquidating its assets, and starting fresh with something that's never been tainted by our dad. For the first time in three days, I'm able to imagine what my future might look like, or part of it, and it's...not entirely awful.

CHAPTER 16

MAC

IT'S late afternoon by the time Tristan and I get back from our weekly trip for ice cream and plane-watching. I'm not sure the ice cream was a wise decision, since he's already pretty wound up in anticipation of trick-or-treating tonight, but I couldn't bring myself to say no. I keep turning the poor kid's life upside down; the least I can do is be consistent about that.

Everyone else has gone upstairs to change—Gwen, Willa, and Diane are dressing up too—and it's a little weird hanging around my own living room like I'm a guest. But I guess I sort of am, at least for now.

Gwen is the first one back downstairs, having swapped her jeans and oversized sweatshirt for a witch's costume. She's carrying the stereotypical wide-brimmed pointed black hat in one hand as she comes toward me, but that isn't what's caught my attention. It's the dress. The jagged hemline hits the top of her knees, and the generous skirt drapes from the high waistline that sits under her breasts. It doesn't disguise her baby bump, that'd be impossible at this point, but it manages not to draw extra attention to it, either. The scooped neckline is the real showstopper, revealing the top curves of her breasts and a mouthwatering amount of cleavage. *Fuck me, her tits are amazing.* Add in the black fishnet tights and black patent leather ballet flats that complete the outfit, and I'm shifting in my chair to hide the rock-hard erection pressing against my zipper.

"I look stupid, right?" She's stopped a few paces in front of me, and her pleading tone draws my attention to her face. I don't know what she sees in my expression, but whatever it is, her cheeks flush and she glances away. I dislike that she feels insecure in her outfit or, well, ever actually. It doesn't matter if she's eighteen or thirty, pregnant or not, she's gorgeous, and she ought to be confident of that. But there's something charming about the way she seeks reassurance from me—that my opinion matters to her—and it makes me ache for all the mornings we got ready to hit the campaign trail together and with that same uncertain smile, she'd turn to me and ask how she looked. Fuck, but I miss that. Or maybe it would be more accurate to say I just miss her.

"No." My voice cracks like a damn teenager, and I clear my throat before trying again. "No, I like it."

"Thanks." She chews her lip for a minute before gesturing to her breasts. "I ordered it from a maternity website, so I didn't think it'd put the girls front and center like this."

It's more skin than she's shown in recent months, but not so much that it's obscene or inappropriate. "It's fine. You look great. Honest. Just, maybe don't bend over if you don't want to fall out of it."

That coaxes a laugh from her, and she comes closer, stepping between my spread knees and putting her cool hand on the suddenly hot skin of my forehead. *Jesus, her tits are right in my face.* My throat feels tight and scratchy and I clench my hands to prevent myself from grabbing her by the hips and pulling her into my lap. "What are you doing?"

"Checking you for a fever." She slides her hand from my forehead to my cheek, cupping it. "It's pretty out of character for you to warn me about my dress instead of waiting for the free show. Are you feeling all right?"

No. "Yes."

Her eyes grow wide and she parts her lips, but unlike her uncertainty when she first came downstairs, which was genuine, this is all for show. For me. She even bats her eyelashes. "Then what's the problem? You don't like my breasts anymore?"

As if on command, my gaze drifts from her face to her chest. It'd be so easy to snag the neckline with one finger and tug it down. Her breasts would spill out, and I could get my mouth and hands all over them. She'd sit crossways in my lap, one leg thrown over the arm of the chair, my hand between her thighs. Sexy as they are, I'd be impatient with her tights and tear a hole in them in order to push her underwear out of the way and get my fingers inside her. And she'd—

Stop. I have to stop fucking thinking about it. It can't happen, not now when Diane and Willa and Tris could come downstairs at any moment, and not ever, because she deserves someone better than me. Someone she can trust. "This can't happen."

She leans even closer, her mouth near my ear, and she must be able to feel my breath blowing fast and hot against her collarbone. "It can. You just have to decide you still want it."

"I do," I admit. The column of her throat is there, right in front of me. I'd barely have to move to nip the side of it, where her pulse jumps under her skin. Forcing my eyes closed so I'm not tempted, I continue, "You know I do. But—"

"Mom!"

By the time Tristan reaches the bottom of the stairs with Willa and Diane trailing behind, Gwen has teleported to the other side of the room, a feat I'd appreciate more given her current condition if I weren't still trembling with the need to touch her. She was, however, kind enough to leave her witch's hat ever-so-conveniently in my lap, and the wide brim crumples in my rough grip as I hold it over the very-inconvenient bulge in my jeans.

I expected ending our relationship and continuing to co-parent with Gwen might be challenging, but I had no idea it'd be like this. I mean, of course I can't turn my feelings for her off with the flip of a switch, but I never dreamed she'd try to…whatever that just was.

It's my own fault; taking her with me yesterday to my mom's was a bad idea. As much as her calm and steady presence made things easier for me, it gave her the wrong idea. That wasn't fair. And it'd be doubly unfair to give in to my own desire for her, even if she wants it too.

Tristan, dressed in a Captain America costume, complete with mask and shield, is hopping around in front of his mother, but Gwen stares right over him at Diane and Willie. "Where's Tris?"

"Mom!" His impatient squeal makes everyone, including me, laugh. "I'm right here!"

"Oh!" Eyes wide, she puts one hand on her chest. "I didn't recognize you, I thought you were Captain America."

Tristan rolls his eyes. "You know I'm too old to believe that now." Grabbing her hand, he pulls on her arm and adds, "We've got to go. It's starting to get dark."

"Your dad and Willa and Diane are going to take you. Someone has to stay here to hand out candy," Gwen explains, pulling her hand free of his grasp.

"But I want you to come." Tristan might be old enough that he didn't fall for Gwen pretending not to recognize him, but he isn't too old to pout.

"I'll slow you down. You'll hit more houses and get more candy if I stay here."

But Diane—dressed as the cheese to Willa's cracker—intervenes. "You should go, Gwen. Willa and I can stay and hand out candy."

Gwen chews her lip and considers it before caving. "All right." Turning to me, she adds, "Are you ready?"

Not really. I have no illusions that Tristan's going to stay with us. Gwen is slow, and in his quest for mad amounts of free candy, he's going to run ahead. After what just happened, I'm not sure I'm prepared to be alone with her again so soon, even if we are in public. And there's also the matter of my really fucking inconvenient boner.

"Let's go." Adjusting myself behind the shelter of Gwen's hat, I stand and follow them downstairs.

~

GWEN

I'M A FUCKING GODDESS.

I don't know where I got the confidence, but I had Mac on the ropes tonight. Maybe it was my hormones or the scorching heat in his eyes, but if we hadn't been interrupted, I'm almost certain I could've closed the deal.

To be honest, it's probably for the best we were interrupted. He still has a lot to work through, and I don't want to rush or pressure him. But I can't lie, I felt sexy as hell when I had him pinned in that chair. And even though I was on my best behavior for the rest of the night, his eyes kept straying to my cleavage. It was just the boost I needed, because I really did feel a little silly when I first came down in my costume. But between our brief encounter in the living room and all those stolen glances while we followed Tris around the neighborhood, I've been stupid horny all night, which it turns out is a great distraction from how stupid uncomfortable I am.

Mac stayed long enough to help me sort through Tristan's candy and stole all the tootsie rolls, the weirdo. We had a nice evening together, like we might've before all the revelations of the past few days. It was great but also...kind of terrible, because it made me miss him even more. But maybe this is what he needs. I feel like he still needs space to process everything that happened, especially with the way Jess betrayed his trust and violated him. Maybe while he's doing that, the best thing I can do is show him it doesn't have to change us. The three—soon to be five—of us can still be a happy, loving family.

Once he left and Tris went to bed, I came straight up to the master bath for a little me time. I was never much of a bath person, preferring showers, but these days, relaxing in Mac's enormous tub is my favorite way to end a long day. Nothing can make me feel the way I did before I was pregnant, but the weightless sensation of being in the water and the soothing heat on my sore body is pretty damn close.

Grabbing my waterproof vibrator off the edge of the tub, I sink down in the water and spread my knees. I don't even have to consider what I'll fantasize about as I slip the vibrator beneath the surface. It's Mac, of course it's Mac, and it isn't entirely a fantasy. The past few months, when I started taking more and more baths and sex was becoming increasing awkward, he'd sit on the edge of the tub and finger me. He liked to tease me, drawing it out until my orgasm hit like a gale force storm and I thrashed, sending tsunami like waves of water all over the bathroom. Afterward he'd get a towel and clean up, teasing me for that too.

I tuck the vibrator between my leg and the side of the tub. I don't need that yet, instead using my fingers to slowly stroke my folds, like he would. With my other hand, I cup my breast, rolling my nipple between my thumb and forefinger. It makes me shiver, and I bite my lip, resisting the urge to go faster. If the only Mac I can have right now is the one I can imagine, I want to make it last.

Sometimes, after I came, he unzipped his pants and jerked off. It was the hottest thing I'd ever seen, his big hand sliding up and down his thick shaft while he told me in that deep, rasping voice how much he wanted me. It was almost as hot as—

A muffled buzz distracts me from my trip down sexytimes memory lane. Did I accidentally turn the vibrator on? Nope…I pull it out of the water, and it's as silent as ever. Which means it's my phone, buried under a pile of towels. For a split second I consider ignoring it, but it's after ten and there are only three people who'd text me this late at night. Willa, Olivia, or Mac. Since Willie's downstairs with Diane and Olivia's at college doing things I probably don't want to think too hard about, I like my odds.

Hooking one arm over the edge of the tub, I pat my hand around, feeling for my phone and cursing myself for using so many towels. Fortunately, I find it under the second one and squeal like a teenage girl when I see Mac's name on the screen.

Mac: How are you feeling? Didn't overdo it with all the walking, did you?

Of course. He fussed at me the whole time we were out trick-or-treating with Tris. I should've expected he'd follow up. But I'm in a dangerous mood, and by dangerous, I mean incredibly turned on. Without considering how he'll react, I open my camera app and take a picture of my toes peeking out of the water and send it to him. That's innocent, right? *Unless he starts thinking about what we used to get up to at bath time too.*

Mac: You're trying to kill me, aren't you?

With a grin, I sink lower in the water and tap out my reply.

Gwen: No. You're no good to me if you're dead.

Mac: Definitely not dead.

Did he just... Does that mean what I think it means, or am I reading too much into it? Maybe he's simply pointing out that if he's texting, he's obviously alive? Everything isn't about sex, right? Even if I am so frigging horny, I think it should be. But that's the kind of innuendo-laden thing he would've said before. I can even imagine the smirk that would be on his face if he were here.

Gwen: I'm gonna need to see some proof of life.

He goes silent long enough that I wonder if he isn't going to answer. Then the picture comes through, and I let out a startled bark of laughter that echoes off the tile. He's on a bed with a snowy white comforter, and all I can see of him is his legs and bare feet. He's still wearing jeans and his legs are crossed at the ankles like he's stretched out on the bed relaxing, but my gaze keeps going to his feet.

I've never understood the whole foot-fetish thing. No judgment. Everyone likes what they like and that's fine, but I didn't get it. Except, I might be starting to now, because Mac's feet are sexy as fuck. How did I never notice that before? I'm not even sure what's so sexy about them. Is it the lightly tanned skin, or the way the denser hair on his legs gives way to a sparse dusting on the tops of his feet? Or maybe it's his toes. They're long and narrow with neatly manicured nails, but something about them is so...male. Factor in the raised tendons that line the tops of his feet and that one prominent vein near his ankle and whew. It's a lot. But it also isn't what I asked for.

Gwen: That doesn't prove you're alive.

Mac: What would?

Gwen: You are not this dense. You know what I want to see.

As soon as I've hit send, I start second-guessing myself. Was that too bold? I mean, it's not like I came right out and asked for a dick pic, although I think it's pretty clearly implied. But maybe that's the point. What if he understands what I'm getting at and he's trying to politely shut me down?

He doesn't leave me in doubt for long. The receipt changes from delivered to read, and seconds later my phone rings. I take a deep breath to push down my sudden bout of nerves and answer with what I hope is a sultry "Hello."

Mac's deep voice rasps over the line and he doesn't return my greeting, instead offering me a piece of morbid trivia. "Did you know sometimes a corpse can still get an erection? It can be a sign of sudden, violent death."

"I... What? Ew, no. How do you know that?" Halloween or not, I wasn't expecting this macabre turn in the conversation.

"I don't know. I must've read it somewhere."

"Well, thanks for ruining the mood, I guess."

"I wasn't trying to ruin anything. I thought calling might be better since, as far as I know, corpses can't talk."

"They can't text, either. Did it occur to you maybe I just wanted to see your dick?" *Oh, shit. Why did I say that?* I'm not sure I've ever said something so brazen in my life. Certainly not when I wasn't sure how it'd be received.

"Yeah." He pauses to sigh, and the heavy sound of it makes my heart ache. "I just don't think it's a good idea."

He doesn't have to say more than that; I already know the rest. He doesn't think we have a future and he doesn't want to lead me on. But he's wrong. After everything else we've been through, how could we not get through this too? He had every right to toss me to the curb when he found out about Tristan. Keeping our son a secret was unforgivable, and I'll regret it for the rest of my life. But if we could come through that together, how can this—something done to him, more than something he did—be the end? How do I tell him that without making him feel like I'm pressuring him, though?

Considering my words carefully, I set my phone to speaker and lay it on the edge of the tub leaving my hands are free for anxiety-induced wringing. "I get it, Mac, I do. I'm trying hard to give you the space you need. I don't want to push you into something you aren't ready for, but maybe... I mean, we've spent a lot of time together—most of our time together, really—avoiding talking about the future. Maybe we could do that again? Just for a while, until you've dealt with some of the other stuff? That way I can still be there for you when you need me, like going to your mom's with you yesterday, and you can be there when I need you. But it'll be without expectation or labels. Like before."

Is it weird that going backward would almost feel progress? Maybe. Probably. But the thing is, I don't regret that we began with a casual relationship. Sure, it went on longer than I would've liked, but we both were—are—kind of messed up, and I'm not sure either of us ever would've been ready to commit if we hadn't eased ourselves into it. Why can't it work that way again?

"And what you need right now is to get off?" he asks gruffly.

"Well, yeah, that's what I was trying to do when you texted anyway. I don't think you appreciate how hot you were in that henley you wore today." It was heather gray and fit him so well, like it was made for him. The way it stretched across his chest and showed that delicious triangle of skin at the base of his throat, no one else should ever be allowed to wear one like it.

"Is that so?" The words come on a chuckle, but there's an edge to it, like he's still a little uneasy and something else. Self-conscious, maybe?

"Yes. And then you sent me that stupid picture of your feet and I… I wondered how I never noticed how handsome they are before."

Finally, an honest laugh. "You really are in a bad way if you think my feet are handsome."

"I am, and it's all your fault, so you're basically obligated to help me." It's on the tip of my tongue to ask him to come over, but my instincts tell me not to. That'd be pushing him too far, too hard. It'd be too much. So instead I ask, "Are you still wearing the shirt?"

"Yes."

Quickly drying my hands on one of the towels, I pick my phone back up. I'm still not sure he's willing to go along with this but if he does, I'll be ready. "Show me."

He makes a disgruntled noise and I don't think he's going to do it, but then a message pops up on my phone informing me he's requested a switch to video call. After hitting accept, I prop the phone against a shampoo bottle and settle into the water. From this angle, he can only see my head and bare shoulders, although I don't think he can see even that from the way he must be holding his phone. That clit tease has aimed the camera directly at his chest, gray fabric filling my entire screen.

I'm about to complain and demand he tilt his phone so I can see his face when he does just that. He offers me a reluctant smile, one brow cocked as he asks, "Happy?"

"Not yet."

He laughs and his eyes move over me. Well, over the image of me on his screen, I guess, but his gaze is so heavy I can feel it. Like he's really here. *God, I wish he was here.* Dipping his head, he rubs one thumb over his lip. "Well, if it's any consolation, you weren't the only one having filthy thoughts earlier."

"Tell me." My skin prickles with hot anticipation and I slide one hand over the swell of my stomach and between my thighs.

"I wanted to pull you into my lap so I could get my hand under your skirt and my mouth on your nipples. It would've been so easy—your breasts were on the verge of falling out of that dress already, and I wouldn't have been able to resist."

"I wouldn't have wanted you to." The bath water's still plenty warm, but I shiver anyway and pinch my clit between two fingers. "It wouldn't have been enough, though."

"Not for me, either," he admits.

When we converted the call to video he was sitting up, his back against the headboard, and he still is, but he's slid down some and he's doing something off screen with his other hand. I'm about to ask what when the metallic jangle of his belt buckle followed by the snick of his zipper answers my question, and I bite my lip to contain the throaty moan of anticipation that almost escapes me. Redirecting my thoughts, I ask a different question. A better one. "What would be enough?"

"Nothing. It's never enough. I always want more of you." His biceps flex and he lets out a low, rough groan that makes the tiny muscles in my center clench. It's a familiar sound and I don't need to see him to know what he's doing, but he flips the phone around, showing me anyway.

He's pulled his shirt up, enough to show the stretch of skin below his navel, and he's pushed his pants and boxers down around his thighs. He's stroking himself slowly, with a grip that's much too loose to accomplish anything, and I mimic his tempo with my fingers between my legs.

"I would've wanted you inside me."

His cock jerks and he blows out a harsh breath, letting me watch as he gives it a firmer, faster stroke. But then he turns the camera around again, his dark eyes tracing the lines of my face. "I wouldn't have been able to resist that, either. If everyone else hadn't been coming downstairs any minute..."

The simmering arousal in my core tightens, and I circle one finger around my clit, starting in a wide arc that quickly narrows. I'm torn between my physical need for a fast, hard release, and the fear that once it's over he'll hang up and the distance between us of the last few days will return, or worse, grow. But I can't ignore the way he left that last sentence hanging. I need to know. "How?"

He hums, his gaze drifting from his phone toward the ceiling while he thinks about it, and I reach for my vibrator, sliding my thumb over the button until the surface of the water ripples from the disturbance. His eyes come back to me like he somehow knows what I'm doing, and he licks his lips before saying, "Probably turned you around in my lap so you could ride me. Take what you need."

Spreading my thighs as far as I can, I press my vibrator against my opening and imagine it's him. With gentle pressure, as though I were lowering myself onto him, I slide it home. My eyes close of their own volition, and I'm unable to contain a shuddering moan when the rabbit ears settle over my clit.

His hoarse voice commands me to look at him, and I blink, surprised to realize I wasn't. Focusing on the screen, on the flex and pull of his arm and his dark, heavy-lidded eyes staring back at me, I roll my hips. The water sloshes around me in gentle waves, and the pulse of the vibrator, too strong for a slow build, pushes me closer to the edge.

"Fuck, I love the way you sound." Even over the ragged gravel of his voice, I can hear the friction of his hand on his cock. I want to watch too, while he strokes his hard length until his cock pulses and he comes. But I need to see his face more. The way his brows slant in concentration like the pleasure is dancing right on that line between too much and not enough, his gaze softening and lips parting as he pants and gasps for air. God, I love his face. *I love him.*

My breasts feel heavy, achy and needy, and I arch my back until my throbbing nipples break the surface of the water. They're so sensitive they draw even tighter in the cool air of the bathroom, and I close my legs to hold the vibrator in place so I can roll and pinch them between my fingers. I'm like a bow string, taut and vibrating with energy held in suspense, waiting for that exquisite, explosive moment of release.

"Do you want to come already?" His voice hitches on the last word. He's close too.

My answer is a garbled yes and my inner muscles clench, squeezing the shaft of the vibrator, imagining it's him.

"Go on, do it. Come for me."

It's as if my body was waiting for his permission, and my orgasm arrives with a sudden, powerful burst in my core. Intense and wild, it's a little bit mean, the way it grabs hold of me, refusing to let go, forcing me to enjoy every last fluttering spasm. And through it all, I can't tear my eyes from my screen. From Mac. His head tipped back, digging into the pillow, I know the exact moment he comes, because it's accompanied by a sharp intake of breath, followed by a gasped curse that makes me quiver with recognition.

In the aftermath, pleasant tremors still rippling through me, I remove the vibrator and turn it off. We're both still breathing hard, and Mac's staring up at the ceiling when he lets out a shaky laugh. "I think I needed that as much as you did."

"Call anytime." The water in the tub is still warm-ish, but the cool air feels good on my overheated skin, even if it does make me shiver, so I sit up a little straighter before adding, "I mean, you know, for anything, not just that."

He turns his head toward the phone, his expression inscrutable. "Thanks."

Feeling awkward, I reach for my phone, holding it closer so he can only see my face. "I guess you probably need to clean up."

"Little bit, yeah." He laughs again, but this time it's more of a stilted huff, like he's floundering too. Why does this suddenly feel so strange?

I hold one hand close to the camera lens so he can see the wrinkled pads of my fingers. "I'm pruning."

"I'll let you go, so you can get out of the tub." He glances away and back again, at a clock, I think, because he says, "It's getting late anyway, and you need your rest."

"Okay. I guess I'll see you Tuesday for my next appointment?"

"Yeah, I'll pick you up again if that works for you?" He waits for my nod of agreement then frowns, adding in a cryptic tone, "If you make it 'til Tuesday. All the books say—"

"I will," I insist, interrupting him before he can tell me about whatever he's read. I don't want to hear it. "In fact, if you don't have anything else going on, you can pick me up early, say around eleven, and take me to vote before my appointment at one."

"That's a deal, but ten would be better. Lines might be long at the polls. If we have extra time, we can grab lunch before your appointment." Despite his agreement, he still seems pretty doubtful that any of this planning is going to come to fruition.

"All right." I hesitate before adding, "I miss you."

"I miss you too." He sighs and rests one splayed hand on his chest, over his heart. I'm overcome by the need to tell him I love him. I've thought about it so much lately, but I've come to the conclusion that it's better to wait a little longer. It's true that knowing how I feel might help him, but I'm still too worried about overwhelming him, or worse, making my love feel like a burden. I want him to come home, I want us to be a family, but not until he's ready, and pushing him would be counterproductive. That's what I keep telling myself, anyway. Still, I almost say it. It's like I don't even have control—the words are just there—but before I can blurt them out, he says goodnight and disconnects the call.

CHAPTER 17

MAC

"Maybe we should get out of here. Go get a late breakfast or—"

My glare is enough to bring my brother up short, but just to be sure, I tell the lie too. "I'm fine."

Alex nods, and I turn back to the TV and the twenty-four-hour news channel that's been on since I woke up. It's almost ten o'clock on Monday, and my anxiety has reached incomprehensible levels. Like, this is worse than what I've imagined it'll be like when Gwen goes into labor. My stomach aches, my skin feels like it's too tight, and my knee keeps bouncing up and down no matter how many times I remind myself to sit fucking still.

It isn't just the unbearable wait for the clinic to call with the tests results that's making me so restless, either, although that's a big part of it. Other than a few texts back and forth checking in on each other yesterday, I haven't spoken with Gwen since our ill-advised phone sex on Saturday night. When she suggested we try going back to the way things used to be, I gave in because I'm a selfish, greedy bastard. But we opened Pandora's box when we imagined a future together, and there's no closing it now. Things have changed again, and we can only go forward. I just haven't figured out how to do that yet.

I thought the election coverage might distract me from both of those problems, but I was mistaken. With less than twenty-four hours before the polls open, the talking heads' endless blather feeds my anxiety. It's the helplessness of being out of the fight in these crucial last hours. The Republican vote is split between the incumbent and Whitaker's independent candidacy. The polls are good for Kim. Really, really good. But I won't be able to relax until every vote's been cast and she's been declared the winner. Especially since Whitaker and his camp are taking pot shots at her every chance they get, and she isn't fighting back. That's a bad call this late in the race. Someone needs to tell her she can fight back with dignity. Without sinking to his despicable level. *I should call her.*

I've already unlocked my phone, thumb hovering over Kim's name in my contact list, when I change my mind and toss the phone on the couch. What would I even say? After Alex's cryptic call telling her we were leaving the campaign, she'll be worried. There's no way she'd let me get away with barking a bunch of advice at her and hanging up without some kind of explanation.

My phone is still skidding across the cushion when it begins to ring, and Alex gives me a sharp look. "Is that the clinic?"

I snatch it back up and stare at the caller ID in confusion. *Olivia?* What would make her call me instead of one of her sisters? Adding Gwen's youngest sister to the long list of things I'm worried about, I shake my head for my brother's benefit and answer my phone. "Hey, everything all right?"

There's a slight pause followed by the sound of barely suppressed laughter. "I'm fine, Dad."

"We've been over this. You aren't allowed to call me that, even in jest."

"Whatever." Her sarcastic response, which I'm one hundred percent certain was accompanied by an eye roll, helps me relax a little. Still, she doesn't ever call me just to chat, so I'm not surprised when she adds, "I was calling to ask a favor. You know that credit card you gave me?"

"Yeah." I gave it to her the day we dropped her off at school over Gwen's halfhearted objections. I wanted her to have it for miscellaneous school expenses and in case of an emergency. She used it to buy her books at the start of the semester and hasn't used it since, so I'm not exactly concerned about her abusing it.

"I was wondering if I could use it to buy a train ticket to come home tomorrow morning? I was planning to hitch a ride with one of my friends tonight, but now this last-minute study-group thing has come up, and I don't want to miss it."

Of course. "Let me guess, you didn't fill out your absentee ballot, either."

"Oh, you haven't voted yet? That's perfect." Now she sounds really excited. "The train gets into Union Station a little before ten. Could you pick me up, and we could both go vote on the way home? But you can't tell Gwen and Willa. I want to surprise them."

"I have voted, actually, and that won't work. I have to pick your sister up at ten to take her to vote before her doctor's appointment." Trying very hard not to sound like the dad she accuses me of being, I add, "Don't you have classes tomorrow?"

"Yes, but I already talked to my professors, and they were super understanding about it. Especially once I mentioned that my sister, who's basically the most important person in my life, is due pretty much any minute with twins. I don't have to be back until Thursday, so fingers crossed there will be babies before then."

Olivia isn't always subtle about her manipulations, but damned if it doesn't still work on everyone, including jaded college professors who've heard every excuse in the book and, of course, me. Maybe this is the distraction I need, though. "Why don't I come down and get you? You'll have to be ready pretty early so I'll be back in time to get Gwen, but I could take you both to vote."

"You'd do that?"

"Sure, why not? Except if Gwen goes into labor between now and then. If that happens, you're on your own, kid."

"I'll use this nice shiny credit card of yours to buy a train ticket or rent a car or do what-fucking ever I have to do to get back if that happens."

"That's fair."

I spend a few more minutes on the phone with Olivia, working out the details for the morning. After I hang up, Alex is giving me a questioning look and I'm halfway through bringing him up to speed on my conversation with her, my phone still clutched in one hand, when it rings again. I expect it to be her calling back about some detail she forgot, and I don't even glance at the caller ID before answering.

The chipper voice on the other end of the phone isn't Olivia's. The woman asks for me by my full name without identifying herself. It could be a scammer or a solicitor. Or it could be a healthcare worker, cognizant of privacy concerns. My money's on the latter, and the words feel strange in my mouth when I say, "This is William MacKenzie, Jr. How can I help you?"

"Hi, Mr. MacKenzie. This is Angie from Pentagon City Health. I'm calling with your test results."

It must be difficult making calls like this one. If I weren't on the verge of throwing up all over my brother's perfectly styled living room, I might be impressed by how well Angie's handling it. Calm, professional, but with undeniable kindness. Me, on the other hand? Barely able to choke out a coherent response. "Sure, uh, of course, go ahead."

"The tests conclusively determined that you're not the child's father."

I blink against the sound of my own blood rushing in my ears and try to focus on her words. Her tone is confusing me, like she doesn't know if this is good news or bad news, but either way, she's sympathetic and on my side. "I'm so sorry. Could you repeat that?"

"You're not the child's father, Mr. MacKenzie."

"Oh, that's…that's…" I stutter, staring across the room in a daze until my eyes land on my brother. His questioning expression snaps everything back into focus. "I understand. Thanks so much for calling."

Angie informs me I'll receive a copy of the results in the mail, and we end the call. Alex can hardly contain himself. "Well?"

I shake my head and, just to be sure there's no misunderstanding, croak out the answer he wants. "She's not mine."

"That's great!" He jumps to his feet, ready to celebrate, I guess, but he notices I'm still frozen on the couch and frowns. "It is great, isn't it?"

"Yeah, I mean…yes, definitely, it's good. I just…" Without a doubt, I'm relieved, but there's something else there too and I can't quite put my finger on it. I lean forward, forearms on my knees, and frown at the floor, trying to figure it out. "I don't know."

He sinks down next to me in a squat and ducks his head, forcing me to make eye contact. "You've had a lot of shit thrown at you lately; it's understandable that you're still overwhelmed."

"What are you now? My therapist?" I'm joking, but it's apparently gone over Alex's head, because he furrows his brows and leans back.

"Have you thought about that?"

"What? A therapist? What the hell for?"

He nods and straightens to his full height again, probably so he can peer down his nose at me. "The fact that you're even asking why is…" He doesn't finish the thought and throws his hands up in frustration. "Look, I'm not telling you what to do, but maybe it's something to think about. Hell, I've been thinking about it the last couple of days, and I'm not even the one who— Just fucking think about it, all right?"

"Sure, yeah," I agree, more to placate him than anything else, because he seems angry all of the sudden. No, not angry, agitated, and that's as baffling as everything else that's happened today.

It seems to do the trick, and he changes the subject. "I really am hungry. I don't suppose I can convince you to go out to get something now that you're not waiting around on pins and needles for them to call?"

"I'm thinking about going over to see Gwen." I need to share the test results with her and I suspect she's going to think this changes things, but it doesn't really. While I'm relieved Amy isn't my kid, I still cheated. I don't trust myself, and she shouldn't trust me. How can I even ask her to? It's tempting to give her the news via text and avoid a hard conversation if I can. But that's cowardly. I owe her a face-to-face conversation. Alex nods and wanders away while I tap out a text message.

Mac: You busy?

Gwen: Girls day with Diane. She took me for a manicure and pedicure. After this we're getting lunch and maybe going to a matinee. What's up?

I'm in the midst of typing out my response, asking her to let me know when she gets home so I can come over, when another text comes through.

Gwen: OMG, I forgot it's Monday. Did you get the results?

Well, shit. I can't very well leave her hanging when she's guessed what this is about. And I'm not going to ask her to cut her day short with Diane over good news. If the results had come back the other way, it might be different, but as it is, it isn't so bad to tell her by text, is it?

Mac: Yeah. I'm not Amy's dad.

Gwen: Wow! You must be so relieved.

Gwen: How are you feeling?

Gwen: Are you okay?

Gwen: Do you want to talk? We're almost done here, and I can come right home.

Her rapid-fire texts and the questions they contain make me smile.

It's like she's blurting her thoughts out as quickly as she has them. But I don't want her to cut short her fun for me. I'm all right, even if the news is still sinking in, and there's no urgency to whatever conversation we might have. Besides, if anyone deserves a day of pampering right now, it's Gwen.

Mac: I'm definitely relieved but yeah, I'm good. No need for you to change your plans. Have fun and maybe I'll come over later, after Tris gets home from school.

Gwen's response is a thumbs up. Not an emoji but an actual photo of her own hand, her short fingernails freshly painted with a glittery purple polish.

$\sim$

GWEN

"I THINK YOU SHOULD CALL MAC." Willa's announcement, which she's making for roughly the hundredth time, is accompanied by a mulish frown.

"I'm not calling Mac again." I've already talked to him once, after Diane and I got home. He seemed fine. Better than fine, compared to most of the last week—those test results must've lifted an enormous weight off his shoulders—so I only feel a tiny bit guilty about discouraging him from coming over.

"With Tris, her water broke at work." Willa gives Diane a meaningful glare that seems super accusatory from where I'm sitting.

Defensive and more irritable than usual, I say, "So what? He wasn't born for another eighteen hours. I had plenty of time. I *have* plenty of time. If this is even the real thing, and I don't think it is."

Diane and I decided against a movie this afternoon and went shopping instead. It was good to stretch my legs a little, even if it was at a snail's pace, but all that walking around the mall, I'd definitely overdone it and by the time we were on the way home, I was having contractions. But they didn't feel any different than the ones I had on Halloween, when I'd also overextended myself traipsing around the neighborhood with Mac and Tris in search of an epic candy haul. On Halloween, all it took was a half hour chilling in my chair with a big glass of water while Mac started checking Tristan's candy over, and they went away. That's how it's worked ever since I started having them in August. And they didn't even come back after my bath time fun with Mac. Why should today be any different?

Except, I have to admit, it is. It's almost midnight. Diane and I have been home for almost ten hours, and I've done my very best to relax, but…the contractions haven't stopped. So this might be the real thing. Maybe. But they're also irregular and more annoying than painful, so I'm not convinced. Besides, I refuse to give birth before I vote tomorrow.

"Do you think you could sleep?" Judging by her tone, this question is coming from Dr. Diane Neuhaus rather than Diane my sister's girlfriend or Diane my friend.

"Maybe?"

"Then you should go upstairs and lie down."

"Seriously?" Indignant, Willie glances between us and throws her hands up. If it weren't for Diane's presence, I'd be wondering if I fell through a time warp or something. Willie's acting a lot less like the calm, intelligent, competent adult—who also happens to be a nurse—that I know her to be and more like the anxious preteen she was the last time I was pregnant.

"Seriously." This is still Dr. Diane talking, and she gives Willa a sympathetic but no-nonsense smile before adding, "Even if this is the real deal, it's not time to go to the hospital. Until it is, the best thing she can do is try and get a good night's sleep so she's well rested when the time comes."

"Okay, sure, but she should still tell Mac what's going on."

Diane shrugs. "I have no medical opinion on that."

Willa's eyes widen, both eyebrows soaring toward her hairline and her lips smashing together in a frown. It's a comically over-exaggerated expression that's made funnier by the fact that she isn't doing it on purpose, and I have to force myself not to laugh.

"There's nothing to tell him right now. For all I know, it'll stop soon. And if it doesn't, if things get worse, I'll call him. But it's the middle of the night and he's had a rough week, and I'm not going to bother him with this until I know for sure."

"Fine." It isn't agreement so much as acknowledgement that I'm not going to budge on this, so further arguing is pointless.

A few minutes later, after reassuring Willie that I'll text her if I need anything, I've managed to make it upstairs and into bed, but sleep is elusive. Part of the problem is my discomfort, but more than that, I miss Mac and wish he was here. It's been long enough now since he's slept in our bed that his pillow doesn't even smell like him anymore. Which makes my refusal to call or text him extra stupid. But what if this isn't labor? I'll be embarrassed if I drag him out of bed and make him come over here in the middle of night for a false alarm. And he has enough to worry about right now without adding me to the list, at least until I'm sure.

Part of me had hoped if he got the test results and they were negative, that'd be the push he needed to come home on his own. It isn't that simple, though; it never was, because Amy was never the problem. The discovery that he might be her father was shocking, but in other circumstances he never would've left me over it.

No, the real problem is Mac believes he cheated on me and until he's able to recognize that he didn't choose what happened that night and therefore couldn't have cheated, he isn't going to come back. For the first time since he told me, my confidence wavers. Secure in the belief that he'd eventually realize that, I've tried hard to give him the space he needs to work through this while supporting him in whatever way he'll allow. But what if I'm wrong? What if he never accepts that he was assaulted and continues to believe he cheated?

Another creeping doubt, this one accompanied by pangs of guilt, grips me. Am I being selfish to hope Mac will recognize what happened to him for what it was? I've been fortunate that I've never been violated in that way, but I've known other women who have been, and the aftermath can be devastating. Is he better off if he never has to face that? Maybe continuing to believe he's a cheater would be easier for him than acknowledging reality?

Tears sting my eyes, and I rub one shaky hand over my belly. I have so many regrets where Mac is concerned. Disappearing on him, keeping Tris from him, being too cowardly to tell him I love him. I don't want this to be another way I've wronged him. I just don't know what the right thing to do is anymore. And I'm scared.

CHAPTER 18

MAC

"I HATE YOU." Olivia's declaration as she slides into my car and slams the passenger side door would be convincing coming from someone else. From her, it's just...normal.

"You don't. You love me." Throwing the car into gear, I pull away from the curb in front of her dorm and give her a sidelong look. "Or you should, since I'm the gullible asshole who got out of bed at three thirty this morning to drive down here and get you." It's six thirty now, and after about ten gallons of coffee on the drive to Williamsburg, I'm starting to feel human. Well, human-ish.

"I hove you. I late you. I have you. I lote you." She scrunches up her face, rejecting all her options for a new blended word that reflects both sentiments, and lapses into silence. She apparently hasn't ingested enough caffeine to be human yet.

It takes about ten minutes to reach the highway, and so far it's clear sailing. But we'll be passing through Richmond at the start of rush hour and approaching D.C. in the thick of it, so that'll probably change soon. And, honestly, I-95 always has the potential to be a shit-

188

show, even in off peak hours. Without traffic, it'd be almost exactly two hours and fifteen minutes from Olivia's dorm to my townhouse. With traffic…well, I've got three and a half hours before I have to pick Gwen up. Most days, that'd be plenty of time, and today had better be fucking one of them.

We're almost to Richmond when my phone buzzes with an incoming text message. I was too groggy when I left Alex's condo this morning to plug it into my car, and now it's rattling around somewhere in my center console along with my wallet, a bunch of loose change and, inexplicably, three of the dozen magnetic darts that came with the dartboard hanging in Tristan's bedroom. After a quick glance to make sure she hasn't fallen asleep, I break the silence. "Can you find my phone please?" I nudge the compartment between our seats with my elbow before adding, "It's somewhere in there."

"Sure." Olivia turns sideways and starts digging around for my phone. She's mystified by the darts too and momentarily waylaid by my wallet, which she flips open.

"It's not in there and you've already got my credit card, so there's nothing else you need in there, either," I point out in an effort to get her back on the task at hand.

"Oh, fine." She tosses my wallet down and holds my phone up next. "You want me to plug it in?"

If she does, the car will read the text to me over the sound system and she'll overhear, so I might as well save a step. "Just read it to me. The security code is—" *Not needed.* Olivia has leaned across to shove my phone in my face, triggering the facial recognition. Surprised, I jerk my head away in an attempt to keep my eyes on the road, but she's already settling back in her seat, my phone cradled in one hand.

"It's Willa. She says… Oh."

"What?"

"'Diane left for work a little bit ago. I'm leaving now and dropping Tristan at school on my way. I'm ninety-nine percent sure Gwen's in labor and in denial about it. Since she's going to be here alone, I thought you should know.'"

"What?" In response to that, Olivia takes a deep breath and starts again, but I cut her off. "I heard you. I just… What the fuck? She was supposed to call me."

"Eh." Olivia shrugs. "Gwen might be in denial. Or Willie might be overreacting. It could go either way, so I wouldn't freak out yet."

Too fucking late. My stomach has transformed into a mosh pit for nervous butterflies, and I grip the steering wheel even tighter to keep my hands from shaking. "No way. Willa's the most levelheaded of the three of you." It doesn't occur to me until I've already said it that I might've insulted Olivia, so I hastily add, "No offense."

"None taken. It's totally true. Except…" She pauses, like she's thinking something over before continuing. "When Gwen was pregnant with Tris, Willa got really weird toward the end. I think it was a middle-child thing or something. Like, it hadn't been that long since our mom left and even though she was still a kid, Willie was old enough to worry about what would happen to us if something happened to Gwen, you know? She's always been a big bucket of anxiety—she's just better at dealing with it now—and I don't think it'd be that strange if Gwen's pregnancy has made her relapse a little."

Okay, yeah, I can see that, and it makes a lot of sense, but Gwen has a far more established habit of dismissing reality when it doesn't suit her. Exhibit A, she tried to pretend we'd never met before her job interview, and she maintained that farce for weeks afterward. Plus, whatever impact their childhood might still have on Willa, she's a nurse. Which reminds me that Diane's a doctor. "Text her back. Ask her what Diane thinks."

Olivia nods, her brow furrowing in concentration as she taps out the message on my phone. Willa answers right away. "Diane thinks she's in labor but says it's still early and there's no need for panic.'"

I loosen my grip on the steering wheel a little. That's good. Great, even. Not only is Diane a doctor, but she wouldn't be impacted by the traumas of their childhood. She's able to see the situation with a more clear-eyed view than Willa, and if Diane doesn't think there's any need to panic—

"Maybe you should let me drive?"

Instinctively, I check the speedometer. *Huh.* I'm going eighty-seven. Yeah, that's a little fast. Anything over eighty-five on the highway is an automatic reckless driving in Virginia—a criminal charge instead of a traffic violation. Since the last thing I need to deal with right now is a fucking court appearance, I back off the gas and set the cruise control for seventy-eight. "Sorry, I'm fine."

She isn't convinced, but I'm relieved when she lets it go. It's not that I don't trust Olivia's ability, but right now I need the distraction. Driving requires concentration, a lot of it in the heavy traffic that flows between Richmond and D.C., and that focus is keeping me from completely losing my shit.

Gwen's in labor. Probably. After promising her that no matter what else happened between the two of us, I'd always be there for her and the kids. And now I'm not there. I can't stop thinking about that picture she showed me the night she told me about Tris. The one from the hospital, right after he'd been born. A young single mother, barely more than a baby herself, already responsible for two younger sisters and now a new baby. She was so alone, so simultaneously terrified and happy, that Olivia had coined one of her made-up words to describe Gwen's expression. *Happified.*

It isn't my fault that I wasn't there that day, but ever since we discovered she was pregnant again, I've made it my own personal mission to ensure this time would be different, that she wouldn't be scared and alone. I wanted her to be free to celebrate the twins' birth without fear or worry, with nothing but happiness and love. *And now I've fucked it up.*

Diane says there's no need to panic yet, and if she's right and traffic cooperates, I should be able to make it back before the situation becomes urgent. *Hopefully.* But that doesn't negate the fact that I've broken my promise in other ways. And maybe that's what's been nagging at me ever since the clinic called me with the test results. Yes, it's a huge relief to know Amy isn't my daughter, but that fact doesn't change what happened with Jess that night at the beach.

"I cheated on your sister." My unexpected—even to me—confession seems loud in the quiet car. Not as loud as Olivia's response, though.

"What? When?" She continues in a slightly quieter tone, "Is that why you've been staying at Alex's?"

I didn't think Gwen would tell anyone what's going on, so I'm not surprised Olivia doesn't know anything more than that I've been staying with my brother. I haven't shared all the details with anyone but Alex and Gwen either, but…well, I sort of started this, whether I meant to or not, so I guess I have to tell Olivia something. It might as well be the truth, and once I've started talking, I find the whole story pouring out, not just the parts about Gwen and Jess and Amy but all of it.

Olivia listens quietly, staring out the passenger side window, but by the time I've finished she's turned in her seat, her eyes boring into the side of my face. It's unsettling.

"What? Why are you staring at me like that?"

"I just… What the hell, Mac? First of all, the thing with Jess was a long fucking time ago. My sister loves you, and there's no way she'd hold that against you. Especially because, you know, you didn't cheat. You were raped."

There. That's the thing Alex and Gwen have both been dancing around for days. I wondered what they were trying to get at, but now that Olivia's said it aloud, I'm certain this is it. And it does give me pause that all three of them have reached the same conclusion, but… that doesn't mean they're right, does it? I would know, wouldn't I? I take one hand off the wheel to rake my fingers through my hair, trying to make sense of all the weird, unfamiliar thoughts racing through my mind. "No, it wasn't like that. I was really drunk and—"

"How do you know what it was like? You don't even remember it. You thought you were with someone else. You consented to sex with someone else, not with her, and you wouldn't have done it if you were sober and aware of who you were with. But she went ahead anyway, knowing all of that."

"Jess was fucked up too, we all were, and—"

"So? She still knew what was happening, didn't she?" Olivia's tone is a strange blend of empathy and anger, and I'm not quite sure what to make of it when she goes on. "Look, I'm one thousand precent certain that if I'd gotten in the car this morning and told you the exact same thing happened to me at a frat party or something, except I was you and some guy at school was Jess, you wouldn't have left campus until you found him and dragged him to the police station yourself."

Or beaten the ever-living shit out of him then *turned him in to the police.* But it isn't the same. "Jess didn't mean it like that. Dad really screwed her up, and she just... I don't know." Frustrated by my inability to put my thoughts to words, or even pin them down in a way that makes sense in my own head, I frown at the tailgate of the blue pickup truck ahead of us.

"Yeah, but see, it is the same, and I don't see you denying how you'd react if it were me instead of you." Her voice softens and she reaches over to squeeze my shoulder. "I get that there's probably some self-preservation wrapped up in this whopping case of denial you've got going on here, but I think you're making the situation worse. I mean, I'm a college freshman studying political science so this is, like, way outside my wheelhouse, but I don't think you should blow your whole life up and sacrifice the people you love over something you didn't do, and you definitely didn't cheat."

"I put myself in that position. I chose to get so fucked up on—"

Olivia cuts me off with a curt nod. "Right, right. Your skirt was probably too short too."

A terrible sense of...something I can't quite put my finger on slithers through me. Hurt? Anger? Betrayal? Confusion? It's all of that and so much more. A maelstrom of emotions I can't categorize and don't know how to cope with, but...she's right.

I'm not sure I'm comfortable with calling what Jess did rape, but maybe that's my own hang-up, or like Olivia suggested, self-preservation. Or maybe I'm just intimately aware of how my dad can fuck with a person's head. But Jess did take advantage of me and the situation—I can see that much now. The problem's still the same though. How can I ask Gwen to trust me when I don't trust myself?

Maybe Olivia was right about that too, with her sarcastic little crack about short skirts. It is kind of like victim blaming, isn't it? But being able to recognize that on a rational level isn't the same as applying it to my own feelings. Maybe Alex was right. Maybe I do need therapy. It wouldn't be so bad, would it? I should quit drinking too, at least until I can figure how to trust myself again. And then, once I've done all that, maybe Gwen and I could...

That thought is interrupted by a loosening in my chest, a sense of certainty that feels out of place among all the other things I'm feeling. That's what Gwen has been trying to show me in her own quiet way for the whole last week. I have shit to deal with, but I don't have to wait or sort it all out alone. That's why Gwen, usually so quick with the knee-jerk reactions, hasn't wavered. Why there've been no tears or arguments between us. She believes in me—in us—and she wants to support me while I reckon with the past and face the future together. *How could I have been so fucking stupid?*

"I'm going to quit drinking," I blurt into the silence that's fallen in the car.

"I mean, that's fine, but that isn't what I meant about—"

"Wait," I interrupt her, changing lanes before I continue. "I need you to drive."

"Uh, okay, whatever you want." Her eyes have gone round but she doesn't argue, and I pull off at the next exit so we can switch seats in a Target parking lot.

We're still about an hour from home, assuming traffic doesn't get worse. That doesn't give me a lot of time and I have a lot to do, but at least it's after eight now, so businesses are starting to open. After buckling my seatbelt, I grab my phone and open the web browser.

Once she's merged back onto the highway, Olivia gives me a worried glance. "Can I ask what you're doing?"

"I'm looking up..." I change my mind at the last second, shaking my head instead. I love Olivia, and I'm not sure she can possibly realize how much I appreciate the things she said this morning, but I can't tell her yet. Not until after I've talked to Gwen.

GWEN

.   .   .

I'M DEFINITELY IN LABOR. That much has been clear for a while. When I went to bed, the contractions were still irregular and not painful, but that changed sometime around three. First they became consistent, arriving every fifteen minutes, and not long after that they became stronger too. Still, I managed to hold it together until Willa and Tris left for work and school at seven fifteen. The contractions were coming every ten minutes by then, but I fooled Willa or she never would've left me home alone.

Now I'm standing in the nursery adjacent to the master bedroom —formerly Mac's office—leaning on the edge of one of the cribs with each contraction. *This is fine. Everything is fine.* Dr. Flores and Dr. Williams both said I should go to the hospital when they're coming every five minutes, and Mac's supposed to be here in less than an hour. Forty-five minutes, to be precise. That's plenty of time, as long as I ignore that the contractions went from nine to seven minutes apart in the last hour. If I continue to progress at that rate...

God, I wish he was here already. It was possibly stupid to let Willa leave, but it'd seemed like the right thing to do at the time. The only person I wanted was Mac and if I couldn't have him, I didn't want anyone. That was also stupid because I could've called him, but two hours ago, I still felt like I had all the time in the world. Now...well, now I'm not so sure.

But I can call him now, can't I? By the time he gets ready, he might not be much earlier than already planned, but that doesn't matter. I need to hear his voice. I need him to know what's happening. I need Mac.

Before I can follow through on that thought, I have another contraction. According to the app I've been using to time them, it's been seven minutes again, but this one feels worse. Maybe. They're all sort of starting to run together, and I'm not sure I trust my own judgment anymore. But worse or not, I brace both forearms on the crib's railing and squeeze my eyes closed until it passes. As soon as it has, I dial Mac.

He picks up on the first ring and instead of saying hello, he asks, "Where are you?"

What a strange question. Why would he ask me that? I'm at home. Where else would I be?

"Where are you, baby?" Repeating his question, there's an unfamiliar edge to his voice, and I must be losing it, because I imagine I can hear it not only through the phone but distantly in the house. As if he were here. And he called me baby. We're going to have another baby. No, babies. Today. *Oh, shit, I don't know if I can do this.*

My throat tightens, and somewhere along the way I've started crying. Still holding my phone to one ear, I use my other hand to wipe my damp cheeks and when I lower it again, I blink twice, not sure I'm seeing clearly, because Mac is here, striding across the room, folding me into his arms, stroking my back and murmuring all sorts of soothing words.

I drop my phone and fist both hands in the front of his shirt. Pressing my face to the base of his throat—God he smells good, why does he smell so good?—I sob, "You're really here?"

He chuckles, squeezing me even tighter. "I'm here. Can you tell me where we're at?"

I don't know how he knows I'm in labor. Maybe he can tell by looking at me. If my appearance resembles the way I feel, that's probably it, but I don't care. It doesn't matter how he knows, only that he does and he's here. I keep my answer short and to the point. "The contractions are seven minutes apart, and they suck." I pause to sniffle then add in one long, rambling sentence, "Also, I love you and I'm sorry I never told you before and I don't know if now is the right time to tell you but we're probably having babies today and I need you to know that first."

Grinning, Mac brackets my face with both hands, wiping my tears with his thumbs. "This is the perfect time to tell me. I've got some stuff to tell you too."

I nod and hiccup as I say, "Okay." It's a garbled mess, but he seems to understand.

"I love you so damn much Gwen. More than I ever imagined I

could love another person. And I love our kids." He slides one hand around to palm my stomach, glancing down at it before continuing. "And I'm so sorry for the last week, because you needed me to be here and I wasn't. But if you'll forgive me, I want to be with you and our kids, and I'm going to put in the work to prove to both of us that it'll be worth it. I'm going to quit drinking, at least for a while, until I can get a handle on everything that's happened. And I've already scheduled—" My gasp and the tightening of my belly under his hand brings him up short, his eyes widening. "Is it a contraction?"

"Yes, but please don't stop talking." I like the things he's saying, I really like them, but the sound of his calm, steady voice would be enough regardless.

"Okay." He accepts my weight, letting me lean into him instead of the nearby crib, and rubs my back. "I think I need help figuring out how to deal with all the shit with my dad and…well, everything. And I want to be the kind of partner you deserve. So I've made an appointment with a therapist for later this week and I'm going to keep going, for however long it takes, even if that's the rest of my life. And, speaking of the rest of my life, I want to spend it with you. We'll get married, and if it's important to you, I've pulled some strings and found someone who can make that happen today, before the twins are born." He sounds skeptical about if there's really time, but it's the first hint of doubt I've been able to detect, and I can't blame him for that. I doubt I'll have time to vote, let alone get married, which I'm not sure I want to do anyway.

The pain has crested and I'm on the downside of it, but it's still pretty intense, so I shake my head against his chest and force the words out. "Not today."

Mac kisses the top of my head. "Okay, not today. Do you want me to keep talking?" He waits for my nod. "I've been thinking about names for the twins too. I'm starting to come around on Zachary. I get that the reason you like it so much is because you love me, and from that perspective, I like it a lot more too."

The contraction has passed but I'm still trying to catch my breath, so I pant a little when I ask, "Even for a girl?"

He doesn't hesitate. "Whatever you want." Then he laughs, a little nervous, before adding, "We might be in trouble if it's two girls, because I don't have any other ideas there. But if they're both boys, or a boy and a girl, I was thinking maybe Oliver Alexander."

"Oliver and Zachary." I like the names together, and I like the feel of them in my mouth, but it isn't until I repeat them again, this time using the nicknames Ollie and Zach, that it hits me. "Oliver Alexander, for Olivia and Alex?"

"Yeah, if you like it, I figure it's the least I can do since they're the ones who finally made me realize how monumentally I've been screwing up the last few days. It won't really work for a girl. We can't have two Olivias, and all the Alexandras I've known go by Alex, which would also be confusing. That's why I thought it'd be better as a middle name for a boy."

"Yeah, plus if Alex ever has a kid, he might want to use..." *Wait. What did Olivia do to help Mac?* I haven't talked to her since Halloween, when I texted her a picture of Tris in his costume, and I didn't tell her anything about what's been going on, other than that Mac was staying with Alex for a bit. "When did you talk to Olivia?"

Mac's lips part, but it's Olivia's voice that answers. "We had almost three hours in the car this morning, so there wasn't much else to do."

We both turn toward the open door, and there's my baby sister with a big grin and misty eyes, undaunted by the fierce glare Mac is throwing her when he says, "I told you to wait downstairs."

She shrugs. "There was no way I was going to miss that, and I mean, you can be mad at me if you want, but I think that was the sweetest thing I've ever seen so I'm not sorry."

She's so unrepentant, it's impossible not to laugh and... *Oh, shit. I'm crying again.* I can barely get the words out. "You brought me my baby sister?"

He's still scowling at said baby sister. "It's a long story, but I didn't have much choice. You aren't the only one who forgot to early vote."

That reminder makes me cry harder. "I haven't voted."

Mac sighs and turns back to me. "I know, baby. We still have some time before you have to go to the hospital. So if you still want to vote we need to get going."

I don't know what I want to do. I mean, I do, I want to vote, but I'm unsure if I should. Our polling place is about a mile away and, in theory, I still have a little time. But the line will be long, and things seem to be going a lot faster than they did with Tris. With him, the contractions weren't this close together or this intense until hours after my water broke. "I don't know. I don't know. I don't know." I repeat it three times to be sure they both understand how very uncertain I am.

"That's okay." He looks from me to Olivia. "Can you grab her hospital bag? It's in the closet, under my tie rack." As soon as she's gone, he grabs me by the back of the neck and pulls me close, dipping his head until I can feel his warm breath against my ear. "You're overwhelmed right now. Don't think about what you should do or what you have to do. Stop thinking ten steps ahead—think about the next step and let me worry about steps two through ten, okay?" He waits for my response, but I only nod, and his strong fingers flex, his thumb caressing the sensitive spot under my ear. "Take a deep breath and tell me what you want to do, and I'll do everything in my power to make it happen."

I don't know how he's so cool and in control right now. I would've expected a little more panic, at least if fathers-to-be in the movies are anything to go by. But whatever the reason, his strength and composure bolster my own rattled confidence. "I want to vote."

"Okay." With a gentle squeeze of my neck, he brushes his lips over mine. It barely counts as a kiss, but butterflies take flight in my belly anyway and, seriously, who'd have guessed that could even happen right now? Olivia's returned, clutching my bag in front of her with both hands, and Mac presses his forehead to mine and smiles. "Now, let's go vote and have a couple of babies."

CHAPTER 19

MAC

WE WERE STALLED in the bedroom by another contraction but as soon as it's eased, Olivia leads the way down the stairs while Gwen and I follow at a much slower pace. So slow that she has another contraction halfway down the last flight of stairs. We'd passed Gwen's phone and therefore also the app for tracking Gwen's contractions off to Olivia, who's standing in front of the open door, Gwen's bag and purse at her feet and phone clutched in one hand.

How long? I mouth the question over top of Gwen's head, which, by the way, she's pressing against my chest so hard it feels like she's trying to burrow into my sternum.

Olivia holds up seven fingers, and I let my shoulders relax a little. Christ, but this is intense. And if I feel that way, how must Gwen feel? In other circumstances, I might've chastised her for not calling me, but to be honest, as things worked out, I think it would've been worse for both of us if she had, since I wouldn't have been able to get to her any faster, anyway. Score one for Gwen's stubborn streak, I guess.

As soon as she's able, we finish the last few steps and make our way to my car. I leave Gwen long enough to toss her bag in the trunk, assuming both sisters will get in while I do. But when I close it, I find them standing in the driveway on the driver's side of the car, staring at me. *Why aren't they in the car yet?* I clap my hands like a douche and point at the car. "Come on, both of you, get in."

Gwen's lower lip quivers. "I don't know where to sit."

The way I see it, it doesn't matter much where she sits. It's not like she's going to be comfortable in either location, but if she's in the passenger seat, at least I'll be able to keep an eye on her. "We're only going a mile. Get in the front."

She nods and starts around the car. Olivia's opened the rear door already, but I grab the little eavesdropper by the arm before she can climb in. With my face close to hers, I keep my voice whisper-soft so Gwen won't overhear. "I know you're freaking out a little right now. I am too. But she—" I jerk my chin toward Gwen, "—needs us to hold our shit together. If you can't do that, you need to stay here."

She answers with an equally low voice. "Are you sure there's time to vote?"

"Nope, but here's the thing. If she doesn't get to vote, she'll regret it, and she might not ever admit it to either of us, but I know there are things she regrets about the way Tris was born, and that's not happening this time. So we're going to vote, and if that means the twins are delivered right there in the middle of the polling station, well I guess we'll all have a story to tell." I wish I was half as chill about not making it to the hospital as I've made it sound. Just saying the words makes my stomach churn. But that doesn't change the point I'm trying to make, which is still true even if I am more anxious about it than I'm willing to let on.

"I hove you!" Olivia throws her arms around my neck in a quick there-and-gone hug, and then she's diving into the back seat and shouting, "Come on, let's go!"

I dash around the car to help Gwen get situated and then return to the driver's side. I'm fastening my seatbelt when she grabs my arm, her fingers digging into my biceps, and stomps her feet against the floorboard. My gaze flies to the rearview mirror to find Olivia holding up six fingers. *Fuck.*

I'm torn between comforting Gwen and getting us to the polling station ASA-fucking-P, but Olivia leans between our seats and puts one hand on Gwen's shoulder. She gives me a grimace I interpret as *what the fuck are you waiting for?* and says to her sister, "What can I do to help?"

Right. Let's go. The good news is we don't have far to go, but there's bad news too. Mainly that there are about three million traffic lights in the mile between my house and the polling place, and I hit every single fucking one of them red. So of course, I'm pulling into the parking lot, and Gwen's nails—which are shockingly sharp for as short as they are—start digging into my arm again. Bracing her other hand on the window, she whines, "Ow, ow, ow, ow!"

Does that count as talking? I don't remember now if one of the doctors told me or if I read it somewhere, but supposedly if she can still talk through the contractions, it's not that bad yet. When I first got to the house, she definitely could, although she preferred listening to me instead, but things seem to be getting worse.

"Maybe we should go to the hospital?" Olivia asks, but she isn't quiet enough, because Gwen hears her.

Whatever uncertainty she was feeling earlier, it's gone now, and she shakes her head. "I want to vote. Sitting down makes it worse—I need to get out of the car. I need to move."

That settles it. The line is long, as expected, which is also both good and bad news. High turnout is good for Kim and her prospects, but not so great for my laboring girlfriend. We've joined the end of the line, and if I had to guess, it'll take us an hour, maybe more to get to the front. *Not good.*

Olivia is having similar thoughts. "Maybe I should go ask one of the poll workers if they can bring you a ballot?"

"No, I'm fine, and I don't want to make a big deal out of this. Everyone else has waited so long, I'd feel like a jerk jumping ahead."

Olivia's eyes bug out a little, but she doesn't argue, and I won't, either. There's a hospital two miles from here. Granted, it isn't the one we planned to use, but it gives me the confidence to ride this out a little longer.

When her next contraction comes, the line hasn't moved at all. Looping her arms around my neck, she leans into me and sways her hips. I wish there was more I could do for her besides hold her and whisper whatever random vaguely encouraging thoughts pop into my head, but at least she does seem to be feeling better now that she's out of the car. For the moment, that's encouraging, but it's not a great sign for the ride to the hospital.

Fifteen minutes and two more contractions later, the line, still growing behind us, has shifted some, and I'm starting to think we might be okay. There's still a long way to go before we reach the front, but things seem to be holding steady. At least they were until the next contraction, when Gwen lets out a soft moan, and the woman in line in front of us turns around, one brow raised.

"Is she all right?" She's an older woman, and the corners of her green eyes are wrinkled with concern.

Once again attempting to hollow out my chest like the Tauntaun in *The Empire Strikes Back*, Gwen doesn't answer, and as much as I hate the idea of announcing the situation to everyone within earshot, I don't really see that I have a choice. Conscious of my volume, I answer, "She's in labor, but she wants to vote first."

The woman chuckles and lowers her voice too, leaning closer to Gwen. "Well, I guess I know who you're voting for. I'd have done the same thing in your shoes. I'd have done anything to be here today."

Gwen doesn't lift her head from my chest, but she makes a weird half laugh, half groan sound and extends one clenched fist in the other woman's general direction. The woman frowns in confusion, but Olivia provides the necessary clarification and a demonstration. "You know, fist bump?"

"Oh!" Delighted, she taps her knuckles against Gwen's and offers me a warm smile. "I'm Shirley, by the way." She tugs on the sleeve of the tall Hispanic man next to her. He's been so quiet I didn't realize they were together. "And this is my husband Charlie. If she needs anything, let me know. We're happy to help."

"That's very kind of you, thank you. I'm Mac." Patting Gwen between her shoulder blades, I add, "This is my girlfriend, Gwen, and her obnoxious little sister, Olivia."

Shirley laughs, Olivia glares, and the three of us fall into casual small talk punctuated by the occasional grunt from Charlie or groan from Gwen. Another twelve minutes passes that way—I can tell time by Gwen's contractions and Olivia's reassuring nod after checking the app—but the last one seemed worse, judging by Gwen's restless swaying and soft sounds of distress. My suspicions are confirmed when she peels her face from my shirt to stare up at me with wide, worried eyes. "I think my water broke."

Shit. Olivia glances down at Gwen's yoga-pants-clad bottom. "I mean, yeah, either that or she peed." She turns the phone screen toward me and smiles brightly. "But we're still at six minutes."

"Six minutes!" Gwen's voice is high and shrill. "I thought it was seven!"

I didn't want to worry her or distract her, but that may have been the wrong choice. "I'm sorry. I would've told you if you got to five."

She's already over it, or at least has other things on her mind. "I need to go home and change. Liv, you stay here and hold our place in line so Mac can take me— Ow, ow, ow!" Both hands on her stomach, Gwen scowls down at it with an expression of betrayal that would be hysterical if I weren't on the verge of panic. *That didn't feel like six minutes.*

Pulling Gwen closer so she can lean into me again, I look at Olivia and my heart rate skyrockets. She's staring at the timer with eyes as big as dinner plates. "That was only three minutes."

Three? What the fuck happened to five and four? "Are you sure? Maybe you hit the wrong button or the app malfunctioned or—"

Olivia interrupts me with a stiff shake of her head. "It was three minutes, Mac."

My heart slams in my chest while I run through our options. We should leave and go straight to the hospital but...voting was important to Gwen, and I still want to make that happen for her if I can. There's no way we can continue to wait in this line, though. "Liv, you need to go find a poll worker and see if they'll bring her a ballot."

"I've already sent Charlie to get someone. They're coming now."

In all the excitement of the last few minutes, I honestly kind of forgot Shirley exists, but sure enough, Charlie's coming toward us with a poll worker at his side. Well, the name tag the kid is wearing indicates he's a poll worker. I have my doubts. I mean, he must be at least eighteen, but his floppy blond hair and goofy smile aren't convincing.

"Hi, I'm Joey." He gestures to Charlie. "This gentleman said you could use some assistance?"

"Yeah, thanks, Joey. My girlfriend's in labor. She'd really like to vote before she goes to the hospital, but I don't think we have time for this line. Is there any way you could bring her a ballot?"

Joey's gaze drops from my face to Gwen. Her contraction has passed but she remains pressed to me, her face in my shirt. He couldn't have missed her, hanging off me like a Remora attached to a shark, but it's the first he's really looked at her and I can see the exact moment he notices her wet pants, because his eyes go wide and his face pales a little. *I feel you, buddy.*

Meeting my eyes again, he's recovered some, his expression apologetic. "I can't bring it to you here, but we have a place for drive-thru voting. It's meant for senior citizens, but there aren't any rules about who can use it or anything, and it's right around the corner." He leans closer, lowering his voice conspiratorially to add, "There's no waiting."

Fucking perfect. After thanking Shirley and Charlie for their assistance, we make our way back to the car. Gwen has two more contractions in the time it takes to walk to the car and drive around to the designated curb for voting. The sharp edge of worry has severed my entire concept of time, but Olivia assures me they're still three minutes apart.

Joey is there, leaning down to speak through Gwen's open window as soon as we arrive. "Sorry, I should've asked for your IDs before. I have to check y'all in before I can give you ballots."

Olivia passes both her ID and Gwen's between the seat. Gwen, who has her eyes closed, doesn't take them, so I lean in front of her to pass them to Joey. Anticipating that he might ask for mine and not wanting even the small delay of additional conversation, I explain, "I early voted, so it's just for them."

Joey nods, salutes me with their IDs, and jogs off to do whatever official business it is that's required of him. He's gone long enough that Gwen has another contraction while we wait and by the time he does return, IDs and ballots in hand, I'm on pins and needles expecting another. *No way she gets through that ballot first.*

And indeed, she doesn't. She's a little slow because she's distracted and in pain and she's being extra cautious too, double- and triple-checking her choices on the clipboard she's holding against her stomach, which adds up to not one but two contractions in the time it takes her to vote. Joey bails during the first with a rushed promise to "be right back," and the arrival of the second prompts me to twist around in my seat. "Still three minutes?"

Olivia's nod isn't reassuring this time, because Gwen's writhing in her seat, and she reminds me with an apprehensive tone, "She did say it's worse sitting down."

Gwen is still trying to catch her breath and give her ballot one last review when Joey returns. This time he comes around to my side of the car. Confused, I roll my window down, and he thrusts a grocery sack through the opening before I can ask what he's doing. "Here, I noticed her teeth were chattering. She can have my sweatshirt if that'll help, and there's a bottle of water and a granola bar in there too."

Taking the bag, I blink at him. Confused and grateful and impressed by the kindness of a complete stranger who's a kid himself, I can't figure out how to respond. But Gwen trades me the ballot for the bag and takes out his sweatshirt. It's navy and more of a jacket, really, with a zipper up the front. She opens it wide, spreading it over her like a blanket. "Thanks so much, Joey." She tucks the sweatshirt around her shoulders before ducking her head to peer out my window at him. "Is that short for Joseph?"

"Yeah, why?"

Her brow furrowing in concentration, Gwen doesn't answer, so I collect Olivia's ballot and pass them both through the window to Joey then gesture to her—or more accurately, her stomach. "I'm pretty sure Zachary just got his middle name."

"Oh." A beat later, when it's sunk in, "Oh! That's so cool!"

With that, we're on our way—fucking, finally—to the hospital. There's a brief argument about which hospital that should be, with Olivia and I advocating for the closest while Gwen insists we stick to our original plan. We chose the hospital we did because it has a Level-IV NICU and is the highest rated in the area. With twins and the risk of premature labor, that seemed important. Now, they're no longer premature and apparently hell-bent on arriving really, really soon, so that doesn't seem so critical. Besides, the closer hospital still has a Level-III NICU and a great reputation. But ultimately, Gwen's emotional comfort is worth a lot, and if she'll feel safer and more confident at the original hospital, that's enough for me. Besides, it's not like it's *that* far away. Nine miles. Sure, traffic is always a concern, but it's the middle of the day. Barring a horrific accident or something, the worst-case scenario is, like, half an hour. That still seems doable.

We've crossed the Potomac and are passing the Tidal Basin when Olivia informs me Gwen's lost another minute between contractions. Ten more minutes, and I'm pulling off 395 onto New York Ave NW as Gwen makes a noise that...honestly, I have no idea how to describe it. I've never heard another human make a sound anything like that before.

Panting hard, she follows it by grabbing my thigh and gasping, "I feel pushy."

Olivia, who's gotten pretty quiet in the backseat, pipes up to ask, "What does that mean?"

Ignoring her sister, I focus my attention on Gwen and rest my free hand on her belly while I cling to the steering wheel with the other like this is an action movie and I'm dangling from a cliff. "Not yet, baby. I can literally see the sign for the hospital. You only have to hold on, like, one more minute, maybe two." It's a bald-faced lie. I mean, I *can* see the hospital, but it's not like she can start pushing the second I pull up at the entrance.

"T-T-Talk to me."

She wants to be distracted. I can do that. Hell, I need it too. "I've been thinking, maybe next year after things have settled down a little, I should sell the townhouse." She makes a strange noise, and I have no idea what it means or if it has anything at all to do with what I've said, but I pretend it's disagreement and state my case. "Once the twins start walking, it'll be a lot better if we don't have so many stairs. And it'd be kind of nice to pick a place out together, don't you think? Tristan could help too. We'll pick it out as a family, you know? We could even get a place with a backyard so you and Tris can have that dog I know you both want. We'd have plenty of space for Willie and Liv to come back whenever they want. Who knows, maybe we'll even want to have another baby someday and—"

Thankfully I've pulled up in front of the entrance, because Olivia leans between the seats to smack my arm really fucking hard. "If you're at all serious about that last part, now's not the time to suggest it."

What last part? Whatever. It doesn't matter. We're here. Throwing the car into park, I jump out and rush around to help Gwen. By the time she's on her feet, a security guard has come over with a wheelchair, but Gwen shakes her head and holds up one hand, like she's warding him off. "I can't… It feels like… I really want to push, and I don't think I can sit down again."

"It's okay, baby, we'll walk. I've got you." With one arm around her waist, we start toward the door while Olivia parks my car. It's slow going, and we've just made it through the revolving doors when the security guard returns with two nurses and a stretcher.

Gwen's relief is palpable but short-lived. Still in the lobby, she sobs, "I have to push."

One of the nurses, a middle-aged man with salt-and-pepper hair, responds with a clipped, impatient "You have to wait," but it's too late. Gwen's body has waited long enough, and I don't think she could stop it now, even if she wanted to.

They're rolling her onto the elevator when she grits her teeth and groans, very obviously pushing.

"I said—"

The other nurse, also a male but a much kinder person, cuts his coworker off. "She can't help it, Mark. She's fine." Turning to me, he asks, "Who's your doctor?"

"Dr. Flores. She—" My mouth snaps closed with a clack of my teeth. *Fuck, fuck, fuck.* "I forgot to call her."

"That's all right." The friendly nurse claps me on the shoulder. "I don't think we'll have time to wait for her to get here now, but our on-duty OB is great, and your girl doesn't look like she's going to need much help."

"We're having twins," I blurt. That seems like pretty fucking important information.

He's unfazed by it. "That's great. Congratulations, man!"

The elevator dings, and the doors slide open as Gwen screams. That gets, well, pretty much everyone's attention, and a moment later we've been whisked into a room. There's some discussion about moving her into a proper bed and getting her into a hospital gown, but in the end, there isn't time.

Someone removes her pants and someone else puts her foot in my hand. One of the nurses has her other leg, and she nods across the bed at me. *It's go time.*

Bracing my other arm on the pillow near her head, I kiss her forehead then lean back to ask, "Are you ready to meet the twins?"

She nods and immediately follows it with a shake. "They weren't supposed to be here until after the election."

I can't help it, I laugh, and for a fraction of a second it seems like she does too. One of the nurses tells her to push on three and starts the count out loud. In the space between two and three, Gwen whispers, "I love you," and squeezes her eyes closed tight.

What I thought was pushing in the elevator turns out to be nothing compared to the mighty sustained effort Gwen gives it now. I encourage her as best I can, telling her I love her and she's doing an amazing job, and I mean every word of it, even when I tell her she's more beautiful right this very minute than she was the night we met. I wish there was something else I could do to help, but to be honest, she doesn't really need it. Now that the big moment's arrived, she's no longer cussing or screaming or writhing. She's all business, focusing everything she has on bringing our babies into the world, and at eleven thirty-seven, eighteen minutes after our arrival at the main entrance, the first of our twins greets us with a wail.

Someone shouts that it's a boy. Gwen chokes on a half laugh, half sob and weakly dubs him Oliver Alexander. Unable to find the words, I nod my agreement, but I haven't seen him yet; I can hardly see her, my eyes are so bleary with tears. *Jesus, when did I start crying?* But there's little time to worry about that, or even for celebration, because Oliver's sibling is in a rush to join him, and at eleven forty-five, Zachary Joseph arrives with an outraged howl that prompts one of the doctors to joke that he must've wanted to be first.

CHAPTER 20

GWEN

NEVER IN MY life have I ever needed a nap as much as I do right now. The problem is, despite my total exhaustion and considerable discomfort, I can't stop staring at my new babies. I'd blame it on a hormone high if Mac weren't suffering from a similar affliction. Weary lines wrinkle the corners of his eyes, but he's sitting at my bedside, slunk down in his chair, enthralled by a sleeping Zach, who's tucked against his chest. Glancing down, I study Oliver, who's happily nursing. His eyelids are heavy, and it seems as if he too will be sound asleep once his belly's full.

I can't get over how much they both look like Tristan when he was a newborn, with thick black hair and pudgy cheeks. I forgot how good babies smell, though, and drop my nose to the top of Ollie's head for another hit.

"Are you smelling him?" His tone suggests I'm doing something weird, but that's his inexperience talking. He hasn't been around newborns enough to know how wonderful they smell or that the very best naps of his life will be the ones he'll take with a baby on his chest. I mean, it's my duty to educate him about these things, isn't it?

"Yes, and it's incredible. You should try it."

One eyebrow arches with his skepticism but he raises his arms, holding Zach close to his face, and takes a whiff. Both eyebrows climb up his forehead, and his eyes widen. "Oh, yeah, okay, that's…" Another deep inhale, like he's double-checking to be sure he didn't imagine it the first time, and then, "That's amazing."

"I told you so." It isn't gloating so much as relishing this moment, watching Mac snuggle one of our twins and discover the parts of fatherhood he missed with Tristan. It's a magical moment, and so different from Tristan's birth. That was special too, of course, and the only thing that could make this moment better is if Tris were already here, but I was so scared and worried when he was born, I almost don't know what to do with all my unrestrained happiness now. There's so much of it I can't hold it all in.

Today couldn't have been more perfect. Well, all right, I could've done without the almost-not-making-it-to-the-hospital-in-time part, but even that wasn't as scary as it could've been because of Mac. He was rock solid, always seeming to know what I needed him to do or say. He was exactly what I needed. Exactly what I'll always need.

"The things you said today…" He looks up from the baby to meet my eyes, and my voice cracks a little. "You meant them?"

"The stuff at the townhouse? Every word." Nestling Zach into the crook of his arm, he rubs his jaw with his other hand, and I could swear his ears are turning red. "After that? Probably, but things are a little hazy, so you might need to remind me."

I know how he feels, but I remember every syllable he uttered. Concentrating on what he was saying gave me something to focus on, to distract myself from what my body was doing. But Oliver's finished nursing, so I take a few minutes to reposition him and pull the front of my nightgown back into place.

Once we got settled, Mac found Olivia—and my bag—so I was able to wear my own clothes and skip the awful hospital gown altogether. She returned with him for a quick introduction to the twins but has otherwise made herself scarce, giving us time alone with our new sons. Plural. It's strange to think we have three of them now. Still buttoning my nightgown, I watch Mac from the corner of my eye to gauge his reaction to my next question. "Did you mean the part about maybe having another baby someday?"

His head flies up and he wheezes, "I said that?"

It's impossible not to laugh. "You did, but it's okay if you didn't mean it. I'm feeling pretty done at the moment. It surprised me to hear you say it, that's all."

"Well, I don't remember that, but I think…" He shrugs and sinks lower into his chair, relaxing again. "I don't hate the idea? It's way too soon to say I want more when these two haven't even come home with us yet. Maybe a few sleepless nights with them will convince me to get that vasectomy after all. But I don't feel the same way about it I did a year ago, when I was dead set on never having kids." He glances down at Zach, tracing one round cheek with his finger. As curious as I was about what he'd say, this is like watching Mac poke around in his own brain, figuring it all out for himself, and I've got a front-row seat while he does. It's fascinating, especially when he says, "In hindsight, I don't think it was ever really about having kids. It was about being a father, or not knowing how to be one, I guess. But that's one of the reasons Daddy has a therapist now, isn't it, Zachary?" He bends close, rubbing the baby's nose with the tip of his, and it's a good thing he isn't paying any attention to me, because I've been reduced to nothing but a pile of love and goo. "Anyway, maybe one day we'll decide we want to try for a girl. Or maybe we'll want to see what it's like to do all this on purpose for once. And maybe we won't. We'll figure it out together, right?"

It's almost as if the last week never happened. He's once again all in with me and our family. Maybe I'm naive and foolish for believing it'll last, that when life gets hard, he won't bolt again. To be honest, I'm the one who took off the first time, and it makes it easier to understand where he was coming from and forgive him now. And it isn't only that. He came back, not just with promises of love and marriage —which we also need to talk about—but with more awareness of his issues and real, tangible steps to fix them. I still can't quite believe it. "You were serious about that? The therapist, I mean?"

"Yes. And I'll have you know I found him and scheduled the appointment myself. I didn't even have Cece do it for me." His grin, wide and open and a little bit silly, reminds me of Tris when he first learned to tie his shoes.

"I'm proud of you. It must've been hard." I don't mean making the appointment, or I guess maybe I do mean that, but even more so realizing it was something he needed.

He seems to understand that, because his smile dims and his brow furrows like he's choosing his words carefully. "I didn't get what you and Alex were trying to tell me about…" His Adam's apple bobs in his throat. "You know, the stuff with Jess. But I kind of spilled my guts in the car this morning, and Olivia said what Jess did was…"

Rape. He can't bring himself to say the word even now, and so I make it easier for him with a quiet, "I know." I don't want to say it, either, and couldn't before. I'm betting Alex felt the same. In our own ways, we were both too close to the situation, with our own pain and baggage complicating it. But Olivia—loud, outspoken, fearless Olivia —she'd said what we couldn't.

"You won't be surprised to hear I argued with her about it. But she asked how I'd feel if some boy at school did that to her and, I mean, she kind of had me there. I'm still not comfortable with some of the words she used, and I don't feel the way I think I'm supposed to feel, if that makes any sense, but Alex had suggested a therapist the other day, and that all made me realize he was right. Because I do love you and I want to spend the rest of my life with you, but I've got a boatload of issues and I want to be the kind of partner you deserve. That means fixing my shit, right?"

God, I love him so much. My eyes are stinging, and my throat is tight with emotions. To lighten the moment, I make a joke, except it might only be partly a joke. "You aren't the only one with issues. I could finance a new yacht for some lucky therapist with all of mine."

Mac gets up to come sit on the bed next to me. He stretches one leg out next to mine and drapes an arm around my shoulders, Zach still cradled in his other elbow. Grinning down at me, he says, "I'm game. We'll get Willa to watch the kids while we go to our separate therapists, and meet up afterward for dinner and kinky sex before we have to pick them up."

Laughing through tears, I wipe my eyes and lay my head against his chest. It's so good to have him close again, to hear the steady, reassuring thud of his heartbeat. "I love you so much."

"I know, baby. I love you too." He drops a kiss on top of my head before adding, "And I was serious about the other stuff too. Like quitting drinking and getting married and—"

"Do you really want to get married? Or are you saying that because you think it's what I want?"

"No, I really want to, I think. I'm committed to you and our family and our future. I want your forever, and I want you to feel safe and secure in that. I don't want you to worry that next time things get rough, I'll take off again. I'm in this for the long haul, and that's what marriage is, right?"

I can't lie, that gives me a warm and fuzzy feeling that starts in my chest and spreads through me until even the tips of my fingers and toes tingle with it. But I'm still reluctant and confused, because I don't know why I feel that way. "I guess."

He hesitates. "Do...do you not want to get married?"

"Would you be mad?" Silence. And then his chest starts to vibrate and his chin digs into the top of my head. *He's laughing.* I jab my elbow between his ribs. "What's so funny?"

But he doesn't answer my question and he's still chuckling to himself when he asks one of his own. "Why not?"

"It feels like we've been reacting to something all year. Seeing each other again. Telling you about Tristan. Getting pregnant and everything that's come with that. And your family and the campaign...it's been a lot, and I don't want to get married as one more reaction to the wild year we've had. I don't care if we ever get married. As long as we're together, that's all that matters to me. Maybe after we've had some time to just be and settle into our life a bit, I'll change my mind, but I don't need that to know you're committed, Mac. That's why I didn't give up on you this last week. I knew you'd come back, and you did."

He takes the news well, better than I probably would've if our roles were reversed, and nods in acceptance. "Okay, we won't get married. For now. I can't promise I won't ask again, though."

That makes me laugh. "You didn't ask this time. You barged into the nursery and declared we were getting married, maybe even today."

"I'll get better at it. I have a feeling I'm going to get a lot of practice."

"You still haven't told me what you were laughing about a minute ago."

"It's just, you know, now I'm the one who wants to get married and maybe have another baby, and you're the one who doesn't want either. Considering that's totally opposite of how things have always been, it's pretty funny when you think about it."

It *is* funny, and that's exactly how Alex and Tristan find us, crammed in my hospital bed together, the twins nestled between us, laughing like loons.

～

MAC

"I've got him, Dad."

Tristan wouldn't be happy to know I find his exasperation with me adorable but unmoving. Although he's sitting very still and doing an excellent job supporting Zach's head, he's stuck with my hovering. Gwen, on the other hand, is blissfully unconcerned with what's happening on this side of the room.

As soon as Alex and Tris arrived, she passed Oliver to my brother, who'd never admit it but definitely got a little misty-eyed when he learned his new nephew's name. Since then, she's been recounting our morning for him. The poor guy can't even get a word in, except I'm not sure he's even noticed, he's that enamored with the twins.

She's reached the point in the story where her water breaks when Olivia returns and comes to stand next to me by Tristan's chair. She watches her sister retell the story with great flair and more energy than a woman who delivered twins less than five hours ago ought to have, and after a minute she gives me a sidelong smile and says, "Well, you did say we'd all have a story to tell."

"Eh, yeah, but it could've been better. We did make it to the hospital."

"Yeah." She sighs with faux disappointment but perks up to add, "Maybe next time."

Across the room, Alex is beginning to get a little squeamish. Gwen is describing in excruciating detail exactly what her contractions felt like, and it seems the baby magic is no longer sufficient to keep him docile. His eyes find mine and he blurts, "Dad called this morning."

I have to give him credit, that might've been the only thing he could've said to stop Gwen from finishing her story. It hasn't silenced her, though, because she's the one who asks, "What did he want?"

There's a part of me that hates that Dad has managed to intrude on this moment, even by reference, but I too would like an answer to Gwen's question. The only reason I can think of for him to reach out now is to tell us how he'd like to handle the business. Still, a part of me is uneasy, waiting for more of his dirty tricks.

"He wants us to buy him out." He frowns down at Oliver. "Have you talked to Mom today?"

"Not really. I texted her after the twins were born, and she sent back about three hundred emojis and said she'd be up in a bit to visit. Why?"

His frown deepens, his gaze shifting from the baby back to me. "Dad said something weird about needing the money and I got the impression from her the other day that her family money's still keeping them afloat. You don't think things are worse than she let on, do you?"

"I doubt it. Maybe she's cut him off or decided to leave him. I'm sure she'll let us know when she's ready." Am I bad person for hoping they'll divorce? Maybe in most cases, but I'm not so sure in this one. I guess that's one more thing I can talk to my therapist about.

Alex shrugs and lets that part of the discussion drop. "Anyway, the reason I brought it up is because we need to think about our next steps. It's going to take a pretty big chunk of change to—"

Olivia interrupts, glaring at him and throwing her arms wide, like she's ready to rumble. "Oh, my God, Alex. Could you maybe give him twenty-four hours with his new sons before you start haranguing him about work? I mean, I know parental leave sucks in this country, but come on!"

Christ, I love that kid. But I don't mind a little shop talk—at least, not for a few minutes. There's one more thing I haven't had a chance to talk to Gwen about yet and it involves Alex too, so now's as good a time as any. Laying one hand on her arm, I say, "It's okay, Liv." And it's almost as if he senses I could use a little help, because Zach starts fussing in Tristan's lap. Olivia diverts her attention to helping the older brother manage the younger brother, and I turn back to Gwen and Alex. "I've been doing a lot of thinking the last few days, and I think closing the agency will be the easiest way to handle it all. If we liquidate the assets—the biggest of which is the building—we can use the money to pay Dad off and get him out of our life for good without too much impact on our personal lives. Well, I mean, except that we'll all be unemployed."

"But we can start over, right? A clean break with Dad and a fresh start. It'll be tight for a while, especially if we try to keep the entire staff. But we can do it, right?" I can see the confidence in his eyes wavering. He's looking at me for hope, for direction. Because I'm his big brother and I've always had answers, even when I wouldn't tell him what they were. I don't anymore, and it's...kind of awful.

I don't want anyone to lose their job because of me, but I also don't want to rebuild the business from scratch. A lot of our clients would stick with us, so I guess it wouldn't be completely from scratch, but overhead would be a lot higher with having to get new office space, and we'd be doing it without the benefit of Dad's equity. It's doable, probably, but it'd be a lot of work, and I don't want to give that much of myself to anything but Gwen and the kids—not for a while, anyway. But I also have a family to support, one that's almost doubled in size today. I'm luckier than most in that our financial situation is pretty okay. The added cushion cashing out my share of the MacKenzie Agency would provide would be a big help too. But nothing has changed since Kim offered me the Press Secretary gig. The idea of being unemployed, no matter how secure we are, is terrifying when I have all these mouths to feed. It adds up to a harsh reality—there's no way to balance all the competing demands, not without compromising somewhere.

"I think…" I hesitate, wondering how best to break the bad news, because it'll have consequences for him too. But in the end, it seems like the only way to do it is to rip the Band-Aid off. "I don't think I want to start over again, Alex."

He's crestfallen, his disappointment palpable. If he intends to start over, it just got a lot harder, and he'll almost certainly have to let some of the staff go. He can't carry such a big operation on his own until the business takes off. But he only broods for a minute, his expression thoughtful when he turns to Gwen. "What about you? Are you planning to be a stay-at-home mom now?"

We've talked about this before, so I'm not surprised when she shakes her head. "I don't want to work every waking moment like I did when Tristan was little, but I don't think I'm cut out to spend all day at home with these hooligans."

Tristan's been telling Olivia about the twins—he's an expert on their likes and dislikes already—but the word "hooligan" snags his attention. He objects, both on his and the twins' behalf, and everyone laughs, but as soon as Olivia has distracted him again, Gwen turns to me.

She's been working over the problem, because she asks, "Could you still give him the money you get from closing the agency? Like an investor, I guess, instead of a partner?"

"Or you could be my partner," Alex suggests, staring down at her with the beginnings of a smile. As soon as the words have left his mouth, I can see it.

Gwen doesn't yet, because she laughs and waves one hand at him. "I'm flattered, Alex, but A, I don't have the experience you guys do, and B, I don't have any money. I bring literally nothing to the table here."

Alex isn't swayed, and he crosses both arms over his chest to stare down at her. "Don't undersell yourself, Gwen. You're a hard worker, which is the most important thing with a new business, and you're smart, with the right education. There's no reason you can't do this. And you're shacking up with the best in the business, and you and I both know he won't be able to resist offering advice whether we want it or not."

That gets her to laugh, but her uncertainty is written all over her face when our eyes meet. Stepping closer to the bed, opposite Alex, I take her hand. "He's right. After what you did this morning, running a business will be a piece of cake. But it's fine if you don't want to do it. I'm not trying to pressure you, and neither is Alex. If this is what you want, though, I'll stake you." That surprises them both, and Gwen, not unexpectedly, sets her jaw, ready to argue. I don't give her the chance. "We're a team now, remember? Well, if this is what you want, the money I get from shutting down the agency is yours to put into a new venture with Alex."

"What will you do?" It's a restrained, quiet question, but there's a glint of excitement in her eyes, and the room feels charged with possibility.

"Maybe I'll be a stay-at-home dad for a while. And I could probably do a little consulting for you two here and there, to keep my toe in the water." But even as I couch it in "maybe" and "probably," the idea crystallizes in my mind. This is what I want, to spend my days with my kids and my nights with Gwen, and if that means she's the breadwinner for the next few years, I'm good with that, so long as she is.

Her lips spread in a slow smile, like she's starting to see it too, but Oliver erupts in a series of grunts that progress to a furious, red-faced wail. Alex's eyes widen in panic, and he passes the crying baby to Gwen. He's gentle about it but still manages to give the impression that he's afraid of losing a game of hot potato. It's hilarious, and it only gets funnier when he realizes she's unbuttoning her nightgown to nurse. I'm not sure I've ever seen anyone spin on their heel so fast without falling over. There's no time to mock him because the commotion has also woken Zach, and I take him from Olivia and Tris, bouncing him against my shoulder.

Once things have settled down again, Gwen grins at my brother's back. "Well, I'll need an office with a locking door if you're this squeamish about boobs, Alex. I wouldn't want you to walk in on me pumping and run screaming from the building."

He's never going to live this down and judging by the way his shoulders droop at her teasing, he knows it. "Is that a yes?"

Alex can't see it but she nods, her smile growing bigger. "Yeah, I'm in. But I still want my whole maternity leave."

"Of course. It'll take at least that long to wrap things up with the MacKenzie Agency, and we have to do that before we can launch..." He looks over his shoulder at me. "What should we call it?"

"The Pierce MacKenzie Agency," Gwen suggests. Dropping her gaze to Oliver, she runs one hand over the back of his head. Then her eyes find mine and she adds, "Like the kids."

My heart slams in my chest, and I'm afraid I'm gaping at her like a fish on the hook. We never talked about the twins' surname. Tristan's is Pierce, because she didn't even know mine when she had him. I assumed the twins would be the same, especially if we didn't marry. The inside of my nose tickles with the threat of tears, and an enormous lump forms in my throat. I don't understand my own reaction. The MacKenzie name is another thing I got from the asshole my mom married. Why should I care so much about my own children carrying something that was once his? I can't answer that, but it seems I do care. A lot.

"MacKenzie Pierce sounds better, don't you think?" Alex asks, oblivious to the moment unfolding behind him. "And it's alphabetical."

"Sure, Alex, that's fine." But she's still smiling at me, both brows raised in question. Too choked up to answer—seriously, what the fuck is wrong with me?—I manage a nod. She calls Tristan over, and he comes to stand next to me. Still soothing a fussy Zach, I hold him against one shoulder and lay my other hand on the back of Tris's neck, pulling him close to my side as Gwen asks, "Would you like to change your last name, Tris? So you'll have mine and your dad's name?"

Tristan tilts his head up, eyes wide with excitement. "We can do that?"

"Yeah, of course. It's your name, tiger. We can make it whatever you want." Realizing what she's said, Gwen hastily adds, "Well, within reason." It's a good call, really, or we might find ourselves filling out paperwork to rename him Steven Tristan Rogers after Captain America, or Tristan Shoto Todoroki after his favorite manga character.

And because I'm all too familiar with the stress and pressure of parental expectations, I make an addendum of my own. "If you like your name the way it is, that's okay too. You don't have to change it."

"But I could have your name." He points at me, then his mother. "And her name?"

"Yup, if that's what you want."

"I do!" His bright smile turns mischievous and he continues, mentioning his best friend from school, "Rob only has his dad's name. He'll be so jealous when he finds out I get to have both."

Weird flex, kiddo, but whatever makes you happy. And there's no pretending it doesn't make me happy too. Happy enough that I don't even care about the connection with my dad. It doesn't matter, and it was wrong to think about it in the first place. He and our ugly history have nothing to do with this moment. Tristan doesn't even know about any of that, he just wants the name because it's mine, and that's...enough. Actually, it's pretty fucking amazing. In the grand scheme of things, I might still be new at this whole father thing, and I still have a lot to learn, but I never looked at my dad the way Tris is looking at me right now, with adoration and excitement and so much love he might burst with it. And that seems like a fucking great sign I'm doing something right.

CHAPTER 21

GWEN

"Do you want me to get rid of them?" Mac whispers. He's on my bed with me, propped up against the pillows, letting me lean against his chest, and he's been so busy chatting with Alex, I didn't think he was paying any attention to me. My drooping head is probably pretty hard to miss, though.

As the evening's worn on, a crowd has gathered in my hospital room. His mother and Cece have pulled up chairs on one side of my bed, passing Zach back and forth between them. Willa and Diane are on the couch under the window, debating a trip to the cafeteria for coffee and snacks, while Tristan hangs over Oliver's crib, talking his ear off about all the things the three of them are going to do together someday. There's a lot going on, and underneath it all, the talking heads on the TV at the end of my bed are droning on and on about the election returns—still too close to call—in voices so bland and monotonous they're hypnotizing. Or maybe I'm just that exhausted. That's probably it. Despite all the noise and activity in my room, my eyes keep drifting closed whether I want them to or not.

But no, I don't want anyone to leave. This is such a contrast to my first experience with having a baby. I was so alone and scared, and now I'm surrounded by people who love me and my kids and Mac. I don't ever want this moment to end. Even if I do keep dozing off.

"Oh, look, look!" Olivia's been planted at the foot of my bed ever since someone turned the TV on, and now she's flailing one arm at the blue-and-red graphic dominating the screen. "I think they're going to call another state."

"Which one?" Mac demands, leaning forward and squinting at the screen. I'm not even bothered by how swiftly his attention's been diverted. We've worked hard for this, and I'm as invested as he is in the results.

Before Olivia can respond, the anchor appears on screen, a gray outline of Pennsylvania behind her. "We can now call the state of Pennsylvania for Representative Kimberly Dunn, and with that, ladies and gentlemen, we can also call the race. Representative Kimberly Dunn of Virginia will be the next President of the United States."

Olivia leaps off the end of the bed with a victory cry so high-pitched it makes my ears ring, and both twins let out a startled squall. The lower-pitched cheers and claps of everyone else in the room adds to the cacophony, but Alex, already gaining confidence with his youngest nephews, scoops Ollie from his crib over Tristan's protest to soothe the crying baby. Cece is doing the same for Zach, rocking him in her arms, and there's this weird moment where their eyes catch.

Did I imagine that? Alex staring at her, like he's never seen her before. And the way Cece's smile softens and she glances down at Zach, almost as if she's…shy? But no. Our Cece is the furthest thing from shy. I must've imagined it, and after the exhausting, hormone-fueled, emotional day I've had, who could blame me? I'm so full of happiness and love that my sentimental brain is trying to foist it off on anyone within reach, that's all. And speaking of love…

The room is still overflowing with the sounds of celebration, so I catch Mac's fingers with mine, tugging until I've gotten his attention. His face is split by a beaming smile that makes my heart skip several beats. *Lord, but he's handsome when he's happy.* All the time, really, but when he's happy it's on a whole other level. Like, "maybe I want to have another baby, after all" kind of level. I have to hope he never figures out just how big a sucker I am for that smile, or I might end up with a dozen kids.

"We did it." He squeezes my hand, and his impossibly brilliant smile gets even bigger. He leans in, and I know he's going to kiss me, so I tip my chin up to meet him.

I'm desperate for this brief moment of intimacy, this small piece of him that belongs to me alone. He's hesitant at first, or rather, cautious, I think. It makes me love him more that he's so thoughtful and careful of me, but this isn't what I need, and I bite his lower lip, tugging it between my teeth. Mac laughs into my mouth and cups my face in his hand, his tongue tangling with mine.

"Ew, they're making out!" Olivia's overloud voice rises above all the happy chatter taking place around us, drawing everyone's attention to my bed.

Surprisingly, it's Joan who rises to our defense. "Oh, leave them alone. It's a celebratory kiss, and we all have a lot to celebrate today, don't we? New babies, winning the election, my divorce." She adds that last point in a breezy tone, like we're all already aware of what the hell she's talking about.

Mac leans back, his eyebrows knitting together. "Did you say divorce?"

"I did." She nods and folds her hands in her lap. "I don't want to make a big deal out of this, but it's something I should've done a long time ago. It would've spared you boys a lot of grief. I'm sorry for that, and I'm going to ensure he can't spread his poison to the next generation." Well, that explains Senior's sudden decision to sell his share of the business, doesn't it? Alex and Mac share a long look, but before either of them can comment, Joan, who's more uncomfortable with discussing her soon-to-be ex-husband than she'd like us to realize, changes the subject. "Do you think Kim will ask you to be her Press Secretary again?"

"Of course she will," Cece says in a sing-song voice, Zach held tight against her chest. "Your daddy is going to be press secretary."

Mac clears his throat, his smile dimming a little. "He's not, actually." A shake of his head and then, with more authority, "I'm not."

"You don't think she'll ask again?" Joan sounds skeptical. There's been a lot of speculation in the press about who Kim might choose for her cabinet and various other administration roles. His name's been at the top of most people's list for Press Secretary, and it seems even his mom is susceptible to the D.C. rumor mill. Or maybe it's a mother's hope to see her son reach the highest peaks of his profession.

"She will," Mac admits. "But nothing's changed since the last time I told her no. Well, no, actually it has, but only in ways that make me even more unwilling to take the job."

Joan squares her shoulders, her chin raised with determination. "Is this about your father and the business? Because—"

"I won't lie to you, Mom. At first that was part of it, but now…" He shrugs, his gaze sweeping the room, searching out our kids. Tristan, who among all the commotion still managed to fall asleep with his head in Willa's lap. Oliver quietly grunting against Alex's shoulder while his uncle makes awkwardly adorable shushing sounds. And Zach, sound asleep in Cece's arms. "My priorities have changed, that's all. It's nothing to do with Dad anymore and everything to do with my kids."

I can't help but think about that first night Mac and I met in a nightclub in Ann Arbor. He was young and handsome and had a reckless, devil-may-care air about him. In other words, he was irresistible to a girl like me. But this Mac, still handsome but more mature and totally in love with our kids and committed to our family? No question, this is better, and my heart feels so full of love and joy and so, so much gratitude that we've found our way to this wonderful place, I'm afraid it might burst.

Joan seems to be having an emotional moment of her own and she smiles and nods, one hand over her heart. If she's disappointed she won't get to brag to her Bridge Club that her oldest son is Press Secretary, you'd never know. She's as proud as any mother could be.

"He's going to be a stay-at-home dad while Gwen and Alex get the new business off the ground," Olivia announces, bringing everyone up to speed. "But maybe in a few years, like if she wins a second term, you'll want to do it, Mac?" It isn't hard to notice the glimmer of hope in her eyes and guess what she's thinking. She's a political junkie and having him working in the White House would give her access. Now would've been good, but in a few years, when she's finished school or close to it? Even better. Like cartoon thought bubbles, I can almost see her daydreams of an internship or job of her own floating over her head.

"You never know." True, but he's humoring her, and everyone in the room knows it. Even Olivia. Mac glances around again, not just at our children this time but at everyone gathered to celebrate the birth of our twins and the election and a future that even a few months ago seemed impossible. The enormity of it prickles my skin with goosebumps. Mac lays an arm over my shoulders and kisses the top of my head. "All I know is, right now I have everything I need."

EPILOGUE

The Following January

MAC

I MIGHT NOT HAVE BECOME Press Secretary today, but sitting a few rows back from the podium at one minute after noon and watching the woman who was once my babysitter become President of the United States is still one of the more profound moments of my life. With Tristan and Gwen sitting on either side of me, and the rest of our family further down the row, even the bitter January wind and light rain couldn't dampen my spirits, and now, hours later in a toasty-warm hotel room, it still seems a little surreal.

It was really cold, though. Too cold for Zach and Oliver, who are safe at home with the first babysitter I've ever had to hire. It's a good thing today's been so hectic, and I haven't had a lot of time to worry about it because, much to Gwen's amusement, I'm a fucking wreck. They're almost three months old, and this isn't the first time we've left them, but it's always been with family before. Willa and my mom are both eager to watch them so we can run out to the store or get a few quiet moments to ourselves. But it's never been for this long. *Overnight. What the hell was I thinking?*

No, I know what I was thinking. I'm getting laid tonight—or that's the plan, anyway. Gwen's doctor gave her the all-clear a couple of weeks ago, but with the constant demands of two fussy infants, not to mention a slightly jealous eleven-year-old, we're both exhausted all the time. Everyone says it's hard; I expected it, but I didn't understand how brutal it would be until I was in the thick of it. Which isn't to say Gwen and I haven't found all kinds of creative—and quick—ways to make each other come, but tonight is supposed to be different.

In light of that, and because I'm an idiot who didn't consider how neurotic I'd be about leaving the boys, I made arrangements for Willa and Diane to relieve the babysitter and spend the night with the kids so Gwen and I could stay in a hotel. The same hotel where the inaugural ball is being held. I even got a suite, because why the fuck not? And opportunity for undisturbed sex aside, it was a stroke of a genius. It's provided us with a convenient location to warm up after the parade and change into our evening wear. But it'd be even better if I could stop worrying about Zach and Oliver.

Emerging from the bedroom, Gwen comes up behind me, sliding her arms around my waist and pressing her breasts to my back. "Are you ready to go downstairs?"

"Should we call Ella first? To check in on them?" Ella's the sitter and she seems responsible enough, but…you never know.

She laughs and presses her cheek between my shoulder blades, rubbing it against the fabric of my tuxedo. "We talked to her an hour ago. Everything's fine. They're fine."

Right. Ella would call us if anything went wrong. And in a couple of hours, when Willa and Diane have had enough of the party, they'll go back to our place and take over. I'll feel better then. "Okay, let's go."

She releases me, and I turn, intending to take her hand, but my dick comes to attention and I drop my arm, too stunned to remember what I was reaching for. *She's fucking gorgeous.* I've always thought she's beautiful but somehow, the longer I know her, the more of our lives we share, she becomes even more radiant.

Part of it is the dress. It's black and covered in sequins with narrow straps that crisscross over her back, a plunging V-neck, and a slit that reaches halfway up her thigh. It's both sexy and elegant and does a perfect job highlighting all of her post-baby assets.

The jewelry doesn't hurt, either. She's wearing the set I gave her for Christmas. A diamond necklace with matching earrings and bracelet. It wasn't a very practical gift, given that our lives revolve around the three little tyrants we created, and it wasn't the only one I gave her, but I've never regretted the purchase, and I certainly don't now.

But most of it is just her. The way her blue eyes sparkle with excitement and her smile turns a little shy when she realizes I'm checking her out. And then the way her shoulders lift, her breath catching, when she gives me a once-over in return, her gaze lingering on my belt buckle. *Or something like that.*

"We should go. The party's already started." I have to force the words out, and my voice sounds thick and raspy, even to my own ears.

Her eyes flash, with disappointment maybe, but she nods and turns toward the door. I follow, buttoning my jacket as we go, thankful for the extra layers of clothing to help hide the erection I'm sure to get every time I look at her. *It's going to be a long night.*

In the ballroom, the party is already in full swing, and we've arrived only moments before Kim and Arnie make their grand entrance. It's impossible not to get caught up in the excitement, and I'm talking with Kim's campaign manager—well, now I guess he's officially Chief of Staff—Brian when she joins us.

After hugging us both—and seriously, what even is my life? I just got a hug from the President of the United States and she used to change my diapers—Kim gives me a brilliant smile. "I'm so glad you came."

"I wouldn't have missed it, Madam President." It's sort of a lie. The last couple of months have had some challenging moments, and at one point I did consider skipping out on today's festivities. But after a few tough conversations with my therapist, Mateo, I decided I'd regret it if I didn't come. I worked hard for Kim's campaign, this is my celebration too, and it isn't Kim's fault things are weird between me and Jess now.

Well, okay, weird is an understatement. A few days after the twins were born, Jess texted me to say congratulations. I thanked her but told her I needed space. Even though Amy isn't my kid, I have a lot of shit about how that all happened to work through, and she followed that up by...asking if I was going to tell her mom. It didn't make me feel better about the possibility of renewing our friendship someday.

I don't really think Jess is a villain. Mostly I feel sorry for her, because I think my dad did a number on her too, and I'm not sure she's ever recovered. That doesn't excuse her, and I don't think we'll ever be close again, but I haven't told Kim. I wouldn't even know how, and I still feel so ashamed about it all that I'm not particularly interested in sharing it with anyone who doesn't need to know.

But Kim must realize something's come between us. She knows how close we once were and, unless Jess has told her otherwise, probably still believes I'm Amy's dad. If that's the case, that much at least will need to be clarified, but it's waited this long and it can wait a little longer. Even as in demand as she is tonight with everyone wanting to congratulate the new President, she still wouldn't have missed that Jess and I have been avoiding one another. And that's one thing I have to give Jess credit for. After that brief exchange of texts in November, she hasn't contacted me again, and even tonight, in the confusion and chaos of a crowded ballroom, she's doing most of the work in keeping a healthy distance between us as we circulate through the crowd.

Kim has moved on again to another group of well-wishers, and I scan the crowd, seeking Gwen. She and Cece wandered off some time ago in search of champagne, and I've lost track of her, a fact I regret as soon as I find her. On the dance floor. Dancing with Brandon Bennett.

GWEN

"Is everything all right?"

It's about to be. Mac's approaching the dance floor, his full mouth pulled down in a stern frown, and as much as I don't want to, I drag my gaze away to smile at Brandon. "Sorry, I got distracted for a second."

My dance partner assumes what I hoped he would. "It's understandable. It must be hard leaving the little ones so—"

"Sorry to interrupt." Mac taps Brandon on the shoulder, and his tone suggests he isn't at all sorry. I *knew* dancing with Brandon would get his attention, and I have to bite my lip to hold in the over-excited giggle that's bubbling in my throat. "I need to borrow her for a minute."

"Of course." Brandon releases me with a smile. "It was great seeing you again, Gwen. Maybe we can finish our dance later?"

I'm about to give him a polite but noncommittal answer when Mac takes my hand, tugging me away as he answers for me. "Absolutely."

Once clear of the dance floor, Mac slips one arm around my waist, guiding me through the crowd, and I'm giddy with anticipation. Either that or too much champagne, but I only had one glass, so I'm pretty sure that's not it. Doing my best to sound nonchalant, I ask, "What's going on?"

"I think you know." His clipped voice makes him sound angry, and I stumble on my high heels, beset by doubt. *Was this a mistake?*

"Are you mad at me?"

"No, of course not." He pulls me in front of him, his hands on my hips steering me toward the door, and his voice comes soft and close to my ear. "But I am going to give you something else to think about when you finish that dance with Bennett."

Yes, please. My anticipation blossoms into desperate need. Except once we're in the foyer, he doesn't turn to the elevators, instead guiding me toward the coat check and another unmarked door beside it.

Casual as could be, he glances around to make sure no one's watching us then opens the door, poking his head inside. Satisfied by whatever he finds, he holds it wide and ushers me in, and I wonder if this is a trick he learned during his crime spree with Alex.

If the long racks of hanging outer wear are any indication, it's overflow for coat check, and a second door connects it to the main coat room, solidifying my assumption. Mac locks them both.

"We have a room upstairs," I point out stupidly, because he knows that. He's the one who made the freaking reservation.

"Yeah, sorry, can't wait." He shrugs out of his jacket and tosses it on a nearby table that's cluttered with hats and umbrellas. Hands free again, he pulls me against his chest and skims them over my ribs and down to cup my ass. "I need you now."

"Okay." It's all I can get out before his lips are on mine.

It's a blistering kiss from the first moment we connect, his tongue sliding against mine and his hands tugging up my skirt while he backs me toward the table. My skin prickles with excitement and it's hard to breathe, hard to think, hard to do anything but feel how much I need and want him.

He's managed to work his way under my dress enough to discover I'm not wearing any underpants, and he breaks away with a heaving groan. "So fucking naughty. Tell me you haven't been without panties all day."

"Not all day," I admit, pausing to let him boost me up on the table with my dress around my waist. Then I spread my thighs and grab him by the front of his shirt, pulling him closer. "But I was hoping for a quickie before we came downstairs tonight."

"I know you were." Holding me in place with one hand on the small of my back and the other on my hip, he grinds between my legs, allowing the rough fabric of his pants and the hard bar of his erection to rub me in all the right ways. "But I wanted tonight to be perfect."

I make a show of scrutinizing the room. "And the coat check room is perfect?"

"No." He lays a line of hot, wet kisses along my collarbone, finishing with a sharp bite. "But you had to go and a wave a red fucking flag out there."

A breathy laugh escapes me, and I find his belt. "I knew you'd be jealous if I danced with him."

Mac grunts, pushing my hands out of the way so he can more efficiently get his trousers open. "Did he offer you a job?"

"Yes."

"I'll kill him." More laughter, and this time it isn't only mine. But he's pressing me back on the table, his cock nudging against my entrance, and his expression sobers. "Are you sure about this?"

"Oh my God, yes, please hurry."

He grins, both eyebrows rising with amusement, and kisses me again. It's as frantic and needy as before, but despite that, he's gentle with me, entering me with a cautious rock of his hips. It doesn't hurt exactly, but it is a little uncomfortable at first, and my breath catches in my throat. He stops immediately. "Okay?"

The discomfort is already being replaced by need, coiling taut and hungry in my core, and I tug on the hem of his shirt, urging him to continue. "So, so much better than okay."

He doesn't move, except to press his forehead to mine, and for at least a minute we stay like that, silent and breathing one another's air. He was wrong earlier, we both were. Coat check room or not, this is perfect. And then he starts to move, this time burying himself inside me, wringing a moan from both of us. "I'm sorry, baby, this'll have to be quick—and quiet—if we don't want to get caught."

"Quick is good." The words come out on a gasp, and he laughs into my hair, his breath tickling my neck.

Picking up his pace, he cups my breast, thumbing my nipple through the sequined fabric of my dress, and presses his mouth to my ear. "I wanted it to be different this time."

Maybe I'm too rattled by the amazing sex to concentrate on the conversation, but he isn't making a lot of sense right now. "What do you mean?"

He shifts over me before answering, hitching one of my legs around his waist to get a deeper, better angle, and it's almost impossible to focus on what he's saying over the insistent buzz of pleasure. "Our first times, you know? That first night at the club when we were kids. We started as a rushed, anonymous one-night stand, for fuck's sake. And then you came back, and our first time was after you told me about Tris and I was a mess. But this is sort of a first time again, and I wanted it to be special or...I don't know. Different."

His whole body shudders, and if I didn't already love him, I would now. I shove my hands under the back of his dress shirt, needing that extra bit of skin on skin and wanting to hold him closer. "It is special. Every time."

He grunts and pulls my other leg up to join the first around his waist. "You know what I meant."

"Maybe this is who we are." I roll my hips to meet his increasingly vigorous thrusts, and the table creaks under me.

"What? Hornier than two teenagers and too stupid not fuck in a coat check room?"

"Why not? And later, after the party's over, we can still go upstairs and do all the things you planned to do when you reserved the room. I don't care, Mac. As long as I have you, as long as we're together, that's all I care about."

His mouth returns to mine. There's no incongruity now, the kiss and the sex equally scorching. But it still isn't enough. I've lost my shoes somewhere along the way and I dig my heels into the backs of his thighs, desperate for more. I'm hyperaware of my senses, the sounds of the party carrying from outside this room, the rough, slightly uncomfortable rub of our fancy clothes, his tongue dancing with mine as we both dash toward release.

He forces a hand between us, his thumb strumming my clit with an expertise only he has. No one else has ever known my body so well. Known me so well. My awareness narrows until there's nothing but him, and I clench my thighs around him as wave after endless wave pleasure surges through me. Mac makes a raspy, growly sound that reverberates in my chest, sending the crests of my own orgasm even higher. He bites my lip, hard enough it stings, I think to remind me to be quiet, and grinds against me, moaning into my mouth as he finds his own climax.

Still panting for breath, he straightens and strokes his hands down my thighs, which are locked around his hips. Staring up at him, it's hard to imagine why all the other men at this party bothered to get all dressed up. None of them can come close to Mac in a tuxedo. Or, three-quarters in a tuxedo, as the case may be.

Reluctantly, I relax my legs, and he takes a step back, helping me to sit up. "Do we have to go back out there?"

He chuckles and tucks himself away, refastening his pants. "Yes. We've gotten lucky—we shouldn't push it."

"I'd apologize for ruining your grand plan by taunting you with Brandon, but I'm not sorry."

"No, you were right." He bends down to retrieve my shoes and kneels in front of the table to slip them back on my feet. "This is who we are together. Risky quickies, accidental pregnancies, sex tapes and all. And you know, I wouldn't change any of it as long as I get to share it with you."

ABOUT THE AUTHOR

Liza Gaines grew up in Michigan before moving to Virginia in 2007. She misses her family and the Great Lakes but has otherwise fallen in love with her adopted home state.

A dedicated reader, Liza often has her nose in a book. She also enjoys cooking, baking, knitting, and watching terrible science fiction movies with her husband. Their small farm in Fredericksburg, Virginia is home to an ever-expanding menagerie that currently includes three dogs, five cats, two horses, and three goats.

For the latest updates and sneak peeks:
http://www.lizagaines.com/newsletter